MILKMAN

KELVIN C. BIAS

ARCHIVE
ZERO

ARCHIVE ZERO | NEW YORK | 2016
www.archivezero.com

Published by Archive Zero, LLC

Paperback ISBN: 978-0-9975442-1-3
(E-book ISBN: 978-0-9975442-0-6)

Cover design by Robson Garcia Jr.
Formatting by Polgarus Studio

For my family

1

The reluctant high five was the first sign. The rest of the you-are-a-great-father facade fell away like small chips of paint over the course of the next three weeks, each particle representing a hazard to the tiny lungs of his newborn daughter. His wife told him he was holding the baby wrong. His wife told him he was watching the TV too loudly; the baby was trying to sleep. His dirty socks sullied the baby's designated resting place on the sofa. He was being fucking lazy. He should stand up when he burped her. These minor transgressions paled to the great redemption that awaited him. But without them there would be no failed high five.

Calder Boyd knew better. His life was an amalgam of lactation, lacrimation and acrimony. He called it "lacrimony." Never out loud. It was his unspoken invention. And sometimes silence is the best intervention. The high five was his high-water mark.

Two weeks after his daughter's birth, in a misguided attempt at solidarity, he interceded in a private moment between his wife and mother-in-law, the wayward high five in question. Little Zoe took three hours to lull to sleep. Trick was a more apt description. For two hours she half cried on her mother's lap, then alighted back to dear mother-in-law, who had been a merciful presence since the immaculate birth.

Passed back and forth in a succession of arms and laps for hours, Zoe listened to a series of lullabies, animal sounds and Chopin. In the interim the molecules of time ceased to exist. Finally, the little angel lay still. Calder's wife, Maren, earned the right to humble brag.

One minute after the successful moon landing in her bassinet, Maren, and her mother, Joy, executed a silently elegant high five. Calder held up his hand and mother-in-law, with a perturbed look, dutifully accepted. It was clear Calder hadn't earned it. When Joy left soon afterward, her month-long furlough complete, Calder bore the brunt of any pent-up anxiety. They were on their own—new parents, alone in the wild—until Maren, a freelance hairstylist, left town on a pageant job in Birmingham, Alabama, a day after her mother's departure.

At 8:07 a.m. Calder tried to reach for the TV remote, but it was wedged deep into the sofa at such an angle that the leverage he needed to dislodge it might wake Zoe resting peacefully on his lap.

At 8:08 a.m., after what felt like an hour, he looked at the digital wall clock and swore it read 8:07 a.m. He couldn't be sure. Baby brain scrambled both his depth perception and perception of time.

At 8:09 a.m. Calder fantasized he was on an

Icelandic black sand beach surrounded by a gaggle of naked Norwegian blondes. His wife was Norwegian. He remained chaste in that regard. There was rarely time, nor want enough, to linger in the illusion, his leading lady, Zoe, embedded into his visual cortex. The image of Norwegian beauties dissolved, first as each black grain swirled away from an unseen centrifugal force, and then all at once disappeared, the image torn asunder by one of Zoe's piercing screams.

Feeding time. The milkman cometh.

Calder was alone, a castaway on an uncharted South Pacific island 2,000 miles from nowhere. He was the one-man support team behind enemy lines, though there was no real enemy, only his own trepidation, clinging to him like stubborn dust that no detergent could conquer. He warmed Zoe's formula as quick as he could. Failure, in the guise of tears, which broke his heart, resulted. He got better with time. Calder cherished his moment in the sun, Daddy the role of a lifetime. The more time he spent with her, the more he understood Zoe's cries.

"Diaper change time," Calder sang to ease the bodily functions.

Zoe sensed fear, and reacted to Calder's tranquil smile of pride in kind, flashing a toothless smirk that often erupted, like lava, into an adorable jag of cooing. He sent mission-report video missives to Maren when he could, and when she missed Zoe and asked for more. Another truth was discovered in this first solo weekend. Alienation crept in the corners of the room, a living presence in equal proportion to the wafts of cool air from the pink humidifier.

The high five was also a marker etched in his brain, a signpost he could pinpoint the first inkling of the phenomenon for which he would become renowned. It started as an itch, an imperceptible mental shift that lacked overt feeling. He hadn't noticed it before the attempt at baby-rearing unanimity. Today was the third of November. Maren would return the next day. Calder had relief. The holidays approached, but they would not bear the usual definition of a White Christmas.

Calder's life didn't matter anymore. He had a daughter he adored yet he tried to search for personal meaning. He hadn't dreamed in nine months. He used to devour books. Now he barely had time to devour his food. The silhouette of his former man-about-town life shadowed him wherever he went, an old friend who didn't know when to leave, or worse, never left at all and reveled in luring him down a dark path of subversive pleasure. The time away from his boutique Chelsea ad agency jumbled his normal routine. He felt displaced. His daily rhythm was erratic. But all of this was okay. He remained secure in the knowledge that his quest for answers to life's big questions would stay an elephantine enigma. There were no more *things* in his life. Only his daughter filled his mind. He almost felt he had no wife. And this miracle of focus brought about a magnanimous change.

Three days after the high-five incident, Calder Boyd began to lactate. It was early that morning, sometime after the birds began their serenade and before Zoe woke up, when he noticed a small, damp splotch on the bed. Maren usually slept next to him, dreaming about her inability to regain her pre-pregnancy figure, but even in her job-related absence, he rushed to the bathroom so she could not discover any disobedient milk days later.

Calder did not like this version of the man in the mirror. He was not going to become a feminist icon. He stared at his flat Earth breasts and then back into the unforgiving glass as if continuing this newfound ritual would somehow make it false, a brief nightmare. But this was before his enlightenment. The denouement he knew had to come. Calder didn't understand why he had begun lactating. His mood was like a 16th century explorer on the high seas fearful of plunging over the edge of the world into the abyss.

In the meantime, the milk seeped from Calder's right nipple. The left revealed no hint of its future success. The right nipple was enough of a shock. It would have to suffice. A slow dribble made him feel he had just played a three-hour game of one-on-one with someone equally inept at dribbling and shooting—basketballs that is—one never knows these days. Calder later became upset he couldn't squirt milk into his own tongue. Minutes earlier, upon the lactating man discovery, he had locked the bathroom door despite the fact there was no one home except for Zoe and she wasn't talking. He swore she said "yes" one afternoon, but it might have been wishful thinking. Maybe his daughter would be hypnotized in a future regression and recall her father stuffing a handful of paper towels under his 25-year-old Public Enemy T-shirt, and it would be misinterpreted as some form of molestation and she would write a tell-all book.

At first, Calder thought the sweet milky substance was a pestilent zit or a plague of boils excreting pus. Graphic, yes, but his imagination was his gift. It served him well in the fast-paced ad world. Sometimes he wrote slogans in his sleep. He kept a book of titles tucked away on the shelf of his cubicle. He didn't even want to get started on that issue.

A year ago, just about the time Maren sprang the happy news onto his non-chaotic life, Calder lost his office. Not lost per se, he knew exactly where it was: down the hall on the south side of the building, Office 206-14. It was an old monument with a new tenant, some junior account manager from the business side. The agency was experimenting with a newfangled "group" office setting that, they claimed, promoted workplace creativity and solidarity—that concept again. It might have been the deep-rooted impetus for the high five. Neither was true.

The apartment buzzer broke his lactation concentration. Luckily Zoe kept sleeping soundly in the nursery annex, a bassinet attached to the bed for vigilant access. The main nursery was also known as the living room, the all-purpose Zoe activity area in their small one-bedroom apartment on the Upper East Side. Mobiles, teething toys, piles of books—arranged in no particular order—diapers, hand sanitizer, mountains of formula and plastic bottles lined every conceivable empty space in their 600 square foot domicile. Calder basked in the relative joy of having signed a two-year lease. Their previous Manhattan sojourn on the Lower East Side eight years prior had been a one-year lease, a grand mistake even if it was only a single-room studio.

Who had sent them a package? It was for Zoe or Zoe-related. Calder knew that without thinking. He didn't use Kiehl's bath soaps—Maren's favorite—or baby powder. Still groggy, he stumbled out of the bathroom, careful to avoid streaking the mirror with lactate, and pressed the button to allow the delivery.

"Hello?" Calder heard the mailman at the bottom of the stairs one floor below, but the newly christened milkman didn't register he had to sign for the package. It could not be left without his John Hancock.

Calder managed to slide on a pair of black sweatpants and his neon orange sneakers, and after checking to make sure Zoe remained asleep in her bassinet, bounded down the stairs shirtless. If Maren saw him do this, he would hear the end of it sometime in the year 3113, just after an archaeologist unearthed his fossilized head, severed from his still undiscovered skeletal remains.

The mailman, Calder imagined his name was Bill, stood at an identical six feet, and they saw eye to eye, though not in any metaphorical sense. The mailman handed Calder the package after lording over the official signature.

"Bill"—his presumptive moniker instilled—stared at Calder's chest for a good three seconds. Calder mistook it for a feeble attempt at male bonding before realizing a veneer of milk covered his chest.

"Sorry for the delay. I had a little bottle accident," Calder said. "I spilled formula all over myself. You startled me when you rang the buzzer."

"Don't pin this on me," "Bill" laughed.

"I still haven't learned how to hold the bottle at the correct angle for a wiggling world champion."

"Well, this should help," "Bill" said. "It's a breast pump, no?"

Calder was spooked. Did this mailman immediately know he was a medical oddity? Both Calder and the visitor looked perplexed.

"Didn't mean to scare you. It says so on the side of the box. I figured it has to be a breast pump. I delivered quite a few of these this past week, and of course a lot of diapers to your address. I'd swear we were in the midst of a second Baby Boom."

"Could be," Calder attempted to continue the conversation. "Bill" was his lifeline; the first fellow man he'd seen during the past two weeks. Calder saved his last weeks of annual vacation for Zoe's arrival. Maren missed Zoe terribly, but the money was good. Sweet home, Alabama. The first day alone with Zoe had been tough. The apprehension hung on his face like a visible ghost waiting to pounce. Please, Zoe, don't wake up. That mantra fell away after a six-day stint alone while Maren worked for a private, high-paying client. Now Calder was a diaper connoisseur.

The mailman hesitated for a second, as if he too did not want this human contact to end. His hair greased into a pseudo pompadour, "Bill's" two-day stubble had flecks of gray, but there was no intimation of it in his perfect brown hair. Clearly he was hiding something.

"Man versus baby," "Bill" the Mailman said. The comment resonated. Calder believed all postal carriers were perceptive, in the same sense that bartenders supposedly are. Yet, this comment stung Calder. The reason was simple. He felt a pang of guilt for not knowing his mailman's actual name. He had seen him many times in the foyer by the mailboxes, and once or twice on the sidewalk in front of the building, sorting the mail, though had never spoken to him more than a perfunctory and utterly meaningless 'hello'.

"Well, that'll be all. Good luck with the breast pump. And no more spills."

"What's your name?" Calder asked out of the established rhythm.

The mailman, almost at the front door, turned and said, "William, but everyone calls me Varick. It's my middle name. My father was British and my mother German, well a few generations ago. I bleed red, white and blue."

The United States Postal Service was going bankrupt, but no one had questioned Varick's patriotism. Calder thought it strange to mention another color of blood besides red. No excuse. He should know the man. Perhaps Calder had heard one of the other tenants in the 12-unit building greet him and simply forgotten.

"Calder, nice to finally meet you."

"I met you when you first moved in last February," Varick said.

Indeed, Calder *had* forgotten. At least he remembered he had forgotten. Or was that the same as remembering?

"I'm so sorry." Calder knew his life was hectic but had baby brain affected him this much?

"No worries. I'll say it again. Man versus baby. Though saying versus makes it a negative thing, which it isn't. You know what I mean. I have a three-year-old son who lives with my ex-girlfriend. I see him on weekends."

Indeed, Calder thought, the mailman had craved adult conversation. "I'll leave you to it," Varick said. Maybe not, Calder recalibrated. Varick vanished, off to complete his rounds.

Calder bounded back up the stairs, breast pump tucked under his left armpit, and waited for a second before his own apartment door. He took a deep breath, a private moment for himself before reentering the baby battlefield. It wasn't Man versus baby. It was Calder against himself.

Then he turned the doorknob, and true madness descended.

The door was locked.

Calder tried it again, unable to accept the horrific truth. The knob betrayed him. Panic. It started as a dull sweat, and then within 30 seconds devolved into a profuse maelstrom. Why hadn't he put on his shirt? That was his first thought; his second was why did I think of something as unimportant as that? *Zoe...Zoe!*

Zoe was alone inside the apartment. Nothing was likely to happen. But in this moment of stupidity

Calder could only imagine a succession of terrible outcomes. Think fast. Maren would be home from Birmingham in 30 minutes. This incident was something she did not have to know about. Truth be damned. A peaceful, argument-free atmosphere trumped the ugly facts.

Calder ran downstairs to the front entrance of the building and plunged bare-chested into the 30-degree air. An early cold front descended on the city and snow was in the forecast. There had been a Halloween blizzard a few years earlier. This was a blizzard of a different sort. He had been cooped up inside for so long—save for the Maren-approved grocery runs—that the cool air felt like he was trapped inside an air-conditioner.

"Varick? Varick!"

Calder swiveled his head. There was no sign of his fast friend. He looked up at the fire escape. It was a good 15 feet above street level. Agility was an old acquaintance that left him long ago for the latest, meaning youngest, tech gadget. At 39, Calder still maintained the look of a 25-year-old. In fact an ex-girlfriend once told him, angrily, that he didn't age. Good genes, his mother-in-law said, no doubt from his Norwegian side. His father was former NBA player, James "Bib" Boyd. The name stemmed from one of his infamous post-game interviews during his hyped rookie season, when he opined: "I put [my opponents] to sleep like a baby drinking warm milk. They need a bib." Calder had heard that *Sports Illustrated* quote from the late '70s so much, it was part of his genome. His mother, Pernille, an artist, and father raised him in suburban L.A. away from the spotlight and he never took a liking to basketball—blasphemy, he knew.

Nevertheless, Calder's muscles were not 25 and his father's athletic genes had long since failed him in the vertical leap department. Zoe needed a bib right now. It was feeding time. His mind raced. Calder's breaths became faster and faster as dread massed for the kill. The fire escape taunted him. There was no way he could scale the outside of the building without assistance in the form of a human platform. Terror tightened its grip. He sensed the first sting of claustrophobia even though he was outside. The nervousness was the same. The cold bit into his skin, reminding him of a Norwegian winter.

The street was devoid of any useful activity. No one in his visible spectrum could assist him in the precious present. Calder absorbed this as another blow. He didn't count the elderly lady walking her Scottish terrier. She crossed to the other side of the street the moment she noticed Calder's naked torso.

Calder thought he heard Zoe crying. He had an active imagination, but he was certain. Dread won in a knockout, and his pace and blood quickened.

Varick couldn't have gotten far. Calder checked the buildings on either side to no avail. His lips felt numb. His blood seemed to stop its natural progression through his veins. His thought process was stunted. His hands pressed deeper into his scalp. Then, he saw Varick emerge from the brownstone two doors to his left. Only a mere 10 feet kept him from spotting him on his own. What other things had he missed in his life by not going an extra 10 feet?

"Let's be honest," Varick said. "You missed me didn't you? You're making me blush. You gotta at least take a girl out for a drink before you go crazy over her."

Varick then noticed the urgency in Calder's eyes and his lack of proper clothing. The mailman immediately changed tact.

"What happened?"

"No time. Lift me up just a little on the parapet so I can reach the fire escape."

Varick looked up and back at Calder.

A red brick facade enveloped the main entrance to the building. Rows of bright purple, green and white ornamental cabbage lined its base on each side, a nice touch planted by one of Calder's unknown neighbors. He had seen the man planting them one evening earlier that fall and mistook him for a thief. The man startled Calder but he was otherwise harmless. In the aftermath, the man avoided Calder in the hallway.

The brick facade's sharp corners had cut both Calder and Varick more than once. All the tenants hated them, circulating a petition to have them removed even though Calder had never met any of them. Nonetheless, they were still standing, and posed a formidable opponent. The vicious masonry rose approximately five feet, protecting the building and giving the appearance that a pharaoh was buried inside.

"I locked myself out and my one-month old daughter is asleep in her bassinet," Calder blurted. "I need to get inside my apartment. Help me, please. "

"Say no more."

Varick deposited his mail rucksack—Calder had no idea what to call it—to the left side of the bricks. Calder appreciated Varick's lack of hesitation, his innate instinct gave him the entire picture of Calder's thin-ice marriage and the mailman didn't even have to ask. Divorced men had that look, infinite knowledge passing between them in a telepathic "I know" sort of way. Maren was Calder's second marriage; he had first married very young and it lasted less than a year, a starter marriage that didn't seem to exist. Calder considered Maren his first, only and, regardless of outcome, last marriage.

Stooping his bulky, 230-pound frame, Varick cupped his hands a few inches from the ground. Calder stepped in and his charge catapulted him into the air. Calder's knuckles scraped the edge at a horrific angle, a chunk of flesh gouged out in a breath. Thirty seconds passed before blood spewed from the wound. He lifted it toward his mouth to lick it, a technique he mastered in childhood. Drops of blood streaked his chest, mixing with the breast milk to create a pink waterfall from Calder's right nipple. He quickly wiped it clean.

If Calder could get atop the brick facade, he should be able to pull himself up to the fire escape. What he would do when he got there was another problem he'd have to solve, and quickly.

The mailman intervened: "Let me do this. It'll be easier."

Varick contorted his arms and pulled himself up

the right section of the facade, defying gravity like the brick parapet was only two feet off the ground—not six—as Calder had recalibrated. He found he often did that. Readjusting his imaginative thoughts to conform to an unpleasant reality. Had marriage done that to him?

Don't be fucking lazy.

Maren's words rang in his ear. Calder knew the harsh comments would bubble like magma if she were here witnessing this scene. He had to make sure she didn't. His friend Gerald—a happily single friend Maren was no longer enthusiastic that Calder hung out with—had warned him. This kind of thing can be avoided, he said like a psychic who lacked credibility yet was 100 percent accurate. Gerald offered to hold an extra set of keys in case of emergency. There was no greater emergency.

Calder watched, helpless, as Varick did his dirty work. Varick was on the fire escape in a blink and the next two minutes escaped Calder's perception. Time stretched and became like malleable putty in his scrambled brain.

"Is the window open?" Calder called up.

"No."

Before Calder could stop him, Varick forced the window open, breaking the interior latch in the process.

"Come on up. She's a real beauty man," Varick craned his neck out of the stripped window frame.

Calder, shivering and his teeth beginning to chatter, remembered he didn't have his keys. Without discriminating, he pressed every apartment buzzer in the six-story building. Surely 5D would answer. 5D was always home and always gossiping about what she saw and heard on the street.

5D buzzed Calder up. Two minutes later, Varick cradled Zoe in his arms.

"Your wife has emasculated you, man," Varick proffered as Zoe began to coo. "It's painfully apparent. Your joy is missing. At least I think you are aware of it. The first step."

The first step to what? Adultery? Divorce? Alimony? Child support payments? Financial ruin? Calder could hear the song of the Rockefeller Center subway station homeless prophet: "It's cheaper to keep her...it's cheaper to keep her."

Varick transformed into an empowerment life coach in a matter of seconds. His chest expanded, his eyes formed a singularity and pumped energy into the stale air.

"Marriage is a construct of the powers that be to keep society under control," he began. "Single people breed chaos and chaos is the enemy of control. That's what they want you to believe. Marriage is for poor people who need two incomes to survive on this God forsaken island. There is more sex, money and most of all freedom if you stay single."

Neither of them heard the rattling of keys in the door, the opening of said door and the light footsteps of the house's true center of power.

"Stay single? We're way past that dear. Calder, who is this man and why is he holding Zoe?" Maren dug her left index finger into the crook of her right arm, her tell that she was, in fact, quite upset.

"This is my friend, Varick. He delivered this."

Calder thrust the breast pump box into Maren's hands. Sensing he should make his escape, Varick interjected gracefully.

"Here's my card."

Calder looked at the card in his right hand, not realizing his bare breasts were fully engorged. He put on his shirt before Maren noticed any leaking breast milk. It was a picture of Cupid's arrow being wiped out in one fatal swoop by a Teutonic-looking man wielding a battle-axe. A black hawk with diabolical red eyes sat on the man's shoulder.

"A friend?" Maren asked, not expecting an answer.

"Indeed," Varick filled the awkward silence. His words making it clear no such thing was true.

"He's great with children," Calder added, keeping their secret intact.

"Did you wash your hands?"

It's cheaper to keep her...

2

There were few things in the world comparable to the blue of Maren's eyes. The bottomless azure irises permeated everything in their line of sight, felling men, women and children alike. They drew Calder in from the moment he first met her, and had him trapped ever since. He loved being trapped in her web. The walks on the beach, the trips to the Caribbean, making love underneath the wooden façade of a rest stop barbecue pit, they were fleeting memories. Not enough new happy ones replaced them, so Calder dwelled on the beginning, the time when nothing could be wrong.

The first day he had spoken to Maren was snowy and the precipitation made her eyes no less dazzling. They were ice skating at Rockefeller Center as part of a charity event put on by a mutual friend who had since moved away and lost touch. It was a typical New York City introduction, a path to the city's middle rung of movers and shakers. Though nobody wanted to admit it, Calder, on his game after being a man about town for the previous two years, couldn't shake the feeling he had met his future wife, or the Future-Ex-Mrs.-Boyd as Gerald often joked—every utterance one time too many. They discussed the three taboos—politics, they both abhorred the electoral college, sex, yes please, and lots of it, and religion, spiritual people but without a need to ruin it by bringing God, or guilt into the equation. They both wanted children. They talked for hours without realizing the rink was closing in five minutes.

Butterscotch sealed the deal. "Do you like butterscotch?" Maren asked, the non sequitur unprompted. A massive irregularly formed snowflake landed on her left cheek and stayed there like a friendly ladybug for five minutes. "I love it," Calder answered unnecessarily, the ear-to-ear grin on his face was easy to read.

This moment blurred in Calder's memory. Sitting alone with Zoe and feeding her formula because his nipples became too sore, the memory exhibited the first signs of fading. The edges of the rink were black and only the golden Prometheus stood out. Calder lingered in this winter tapestry a little while longer. It was a touchstone when arguments became too heated or quiet resentment trickled into his daily thoughts insidiously or when she was out of town working, like she was again—for a big video gig in Nashville—taking full advantage of Calder's paternity leave he had tacked on to his final week of vacation. Maren bemoaned there were no direct flights from any of New York's three airports.

Airports. Calder remembered something Maren said on her way out the door. Her friend, Astrid, a somewhat known Swedish TV personality, and her tag along wild child running mate, Essy Frisk, a free-spirited performance artist—and erstwhile adult film star, who knew no boundaries—were heading to the city. They would arrive today or tomorrow and be in town for a few months. They represented connections to Maren's wilder, carefree past, the days when she could do whatever she wanted and get every man to bend to her will. Calder caught her in a lull, when she had done all she could and wanted to settle down.

Timing is everything.

He wondered how their arrival would affect her, meaning him, but the moment passed. Calder stared around the living room, *the* room. A knickknack Rockefeller Center ice-skating ticket hung framed on the wall, the sole accouterment and a testament to the couple's coupling. His breast milk in the bottle matched the color of the Rockefeller Center ice that night. He realized he hadn't heated Zoe's bottle properly and a few stubborn ice crystals held out in the upper reaches. They disappeared in an instant when Calder shook the bottle. He plopped it back in the pan and like Goldilocks the milk was just right. Calder returned to the Rockefeller rink, his happy Rock of Gibraltar remembrance.

Maren and Calder had been the last two people to leave the ice. The way their eyes remained locked and their legs on the verge of intertwining, they could have been the last two people on Earth. A young girl, no more than 17, approached them, her voice barely audible over the silent snowfall.

"We're closing now."

Her boss was lenient, but employees had to go home. Cries of get a room would not have been out of place. Calder and his catch—or maybe his seducer—skated to the exit door, hand in hand, a spontaneous clutching of gloved fingers devoid of any awkwardness.

The young girl tried to be patient, watching the two lovebirds flutter around each other on the benches while they changed out of their ice skates. It was clear that the two passed her limit, despite her high threshold for public displays of affection.

"Where can we get butterscotch on a snowy Wednesday night?"

"I'll make some," she answered. "You're coming home with me."

"I am?" Calder smiled and neither one of them had a defense.

***

Calder moonlighted as an usher on Broadway. It didn't interfere with his main gig at the ad agency, and at first, the extra cash was helpful in funding his independent films. With Zoe's arrival, he really needed the money. Her passport alone was $140. She was a two-month-old baby, for god sakes. *$140*. And then before receiving his gift, formula and other baby expenses bent his meager salary. Meager in the sense that it was significantly less than his wife's, which she pointed out on numerous occasions.

"You choose a failing show about magicians over your family," Maren objected. "I don't see that extra cash anyway."

There's always something.

Calder felt unable to ever get ahead or save. Maren could pocket in two days what Calder took home in two weeks if it was a high-profile fashion shoot or hairstyling for a celebrity. They did not share a joint checking account. Calder paid rent and the family plan cell phone bill as well as medical bills and groceries. This is why she didn't see that extra cash, to make no mention of his outstanding school loans. Maren paid for cable and electricity and saved money so they might one day purchase a condo in the city. At least this was the agreement in theory, and in theory it should work well enough. But theory eroded under the deluge of reality.

Calder often found he was short on the Wednesday morning before his bi-weekly agency paycheck. A man was supposed to provide for his family. These were niggling problems, nothing that tipped the iceberg, but there were problems lurking in the unseen depths. If they weren't careful, the *Titanic* awaited, or worse, nuclear fallout.

Calder wondered if hiding his newfound lactation skills from Maren was a good idea. He figured she might take advantage of the situation. He was certain he would be bound to the house like a prisoner, at least in his own mind. *The cold deluge of reality.*

For the first week, Calder fed Zoe in private when Maren went out for groceries or other errands. The second and third weeks and well into the month of December he did it late at night while Maren slept, or in the morning before she awoke. He used a bottle when the threat of discovery was high. The deception would wear thin, he presumed, but he kept that future a comfortable distance over the horizon, the curvature-of-the-Earth hindsight being 20/20.

Dec. 13

7:57-8:07 a.m. bottle-fed Zoe 55 ml. of pumped breast milk. She pushed the bottle out. Changed her diaper (pee). 8:15-8:19 a.m. She drank 10 ml more; pooped while drinking. Changed her diaper (poo). Some poop leaked out the back. Changed her clothes. Put lotion all over her body. Changed the changing table towel. 8:43-8:48 a.m. Bottle-fed her the remaining 60 ml of formula. ***125 ml total over 50 minutes.

Sometimes Calder was too exhausted to breastfeed, and on those long nights, and also to mask his charade and maintain the upper hand, Calder reverted to formula. Lactamil. Infalac. LactaSim. They all purported to be the best for a newborn. They all also seemed to contain some facsimile of a pediatrician organization's seal of approval. It all seemed bogus.

Zoe's first Christmas and New Year's were special. With the advent of Zoe, Maren and Calder both became picture fiends. Snapping every "first" ad nauseum, no matter how seemingly insignificant. Nothing was minor in their eyes. On Christmas Eve, Calder placed two golden Oreo cookies on a plate near the four-foot high artificial tree with a note that read: "To Santa, From Zoe." Of course, Calder took infinite photos of that.

For Christmas, he bought Maren the latest smartphone and also finally got around to getting her anniversary present, nearly two months late. It was a pair of shoes and a gift card to some high-society spa in midtown. New Year's was much less eventful. Zoe was asleep by 9 p.m. and Maren and Calder were in bed on the verge of sleep when the fireworks and exultations below their second floor window began. They didn't bother to watch the Times Square ridiculousness. That was a place to be avoided at all costs. Why people wanted to be crammed together, forced like lemmings in a funnel to walk 20 blocks out of the way to get in, or at the end, go out, was beyond him—especially at the stroke of midnight. Never again, Calder vowed. The first few days of January were routine. He maintained his feeding and diaper change log with meticulous dates and times.

Jan. 6

12:31-12:45 p.m. Bottle-fed Zoe 50 ml of formula (she kept pushing it out with her tongue). Changed diaper (pee). Burped her. Put her down on the sofa at 12:48 p.m. Read two books then retried the rest of the 125 ml bottle. 1:06-1:18 p.m. She drank the remaining 75 ml (125 ml total this bifurcated feeding).

Bifurcated. Nobody but an aspiring filmmaker and novelist used such vocabulary in a feeding log.

Calder thought himself exceptional—more so with his secret milk powers.

Pride cometh before the fall.

Early the next morning, Maren nearly spotted Calder using the breast pump. His breast had been engorged and he had to do something—the pain was unbearable. His nipples were cracked, and he swore, bloody. Maren awakened at 5:45 a.m. to use the bathroom. Calder, on night duty, quickly hid the pump under Zoe's blanket. There was a wayward bottle, and the suction cup was visible, but Maren didn't notice it in the dim, pre-dawn light. She lumbered to and from the bathroom like a zombie.

Jan. 7

5:55-6:06 a.m. Bottle fed Zoe 75 ml of formula. She didn't take the bottle well. She appears to have gotten used to the male breast. Makes no difference to her. Changed her diaper (big, stinky, brown mustard-colored poo). Burped her and put her back down in her bassinet at 6:19 a.m.

Calder had to give his nipples a break sometime. But soon, he would have to go see a medical professional. This presented a major problem.

There's always something.

Going to see his doctor would take equal parts candor and subterfuge. He could tell a half-truth and inform his wife he was going to see Dr. West for a routine physical for their new insurance policy, which was in fact required. Or he could not say anything and slip away on his lunch break. He opted for the latter approach and scheduled his appointment for 1 p.m. on Wednesday, the second week of January.

A blizzard struck the city that day.

The usual 10-minute subway ride to midtown took much longer, nearly 30 minutes. Calder slipped on a patch of snow-covered ice making his way down the stairs to the subterranean motorway. An elderly woman bent over him, and asked if he was okay.

"More embarrassed than anything," Calder answered. The woman peered into Calder's face. She reached out and wiped her withered hands across his mocha cheeks.

"Your skin is glowing," she commented. "If I didn't know any better, I'd say you were pregnant."

"Thank you ma'am. I am a new father."

"I knew it. I can just tell."

And with that, the old woman was gone. She had sensed his lie and his gift all in one touch of the cheek. Maren, he could be sure, had her doubts. As Calder waited for the train, he noticed his right shoe was untied. He stooped to lace it, lest he slip again by his own making. When he stood up, he laughed. The subway movie poster he stood in front of blared some interesting philosophical graffiti written with a magic marker. Five simple words ran across the left side beneath the lead actress: *Pussy is stronger than God*.

Maybe the phrase needed some clarification but Calder made a note of it in his smartphone. He could spin a great campaign with the provocative statement. He ruminated about the possibilities all the rest of the journey to Dr. West's office on West 50th Street. At the Rockefeller Center station, the homeless guy wasn't singing his common refrain: "It's cheaper to keep her." The folly of the man's song always brought a smile to Calder's face.

Upon rising above ground, the snow crunched under his feet. He arrived 10 minutes late. Though there were no clocks at Dr. West's office, but Calder's smartphone relayed this data. There wasn't much else there either. Dr. West was not Calder's regular doctor. He was an oncologist. Calder told his primary care physician, Dr. Megan Hopper, that he thought he had a lump in his breast and asked for a referral. After he had said this, the silence on the other end of the phone lasted five long seconds. When she spoke, her voice splintered but Calder assured her that it was probably nothing. It was nothing, but he just wanted to get it checked out to make sure.

"A wise move," Dr. Hopper said.

"Please don't tell my wife."

"Understood."

Though Calder and Maren didn't share the same primary care physician, he felt it was necessary to make the distinction. Delineate a border, i.e. a wall of deception. Anyway, Maren thought she was a quack—no one was as good as a Norwegian doctor— hence the reason for the differing "health care providers."

Dr. West's office sat on the 15th floor of a granite skyscraper on 50th Street in Rockefeller Center. He had just moved there and the walls lacked any usual doctor decor. There was simply one painting hanging on the wall in the waiting room: Rene Magritte's "The Seducer." In the painting—a surrealist masterpiece—a double-masted sailboat floats on choppy ocean waves surrounded by cotton-puff cumulus in the pale blue background; however, the ship itself is composed of the indigo waves. They blended together as one, leaving only the outline of the ship against the cloudy blue sky.

Calder loved Magritte. The ad creative often utilized the influence in his award- winning *Why Be The Same?* campaign for a popular line of men's and women's underwear. The ad featured a man and a woman in undergarments going about their normal ferry-to-train-to-subway commute while everyone else around them, men and women, wore a black suit with a black bowler hat perched atop their head. It was pilfered from Magritte's painting "Golconda" and also utilized in the 1999 remake of *The Thomas Crown Affair*.

Calder took the painting as a good omen but quickly forgot about it. The rest of the suite consisted of blank white walls and a paltry magazine rack that consisted of a lone issue of *Sports Illustrated*. Calder picked it up and immediately put it back down when he saw that it was three years old. He wished it had been the swimsuit issue.

A relevant brunette receptionist/assistant—it appeared some of the regular staff didn't make the move—led him to an empty examination room.

"The doctor will be with you shortly," she said and smiled. The brunette handed Calder a blue medical gown and instructed him to undress to his underwear. She left after reiterating the doctor would be in soon, a clear indication it would be a while.

As he waited, Calder's eyes wandered out the window. One floor below, there was a small landing with access to a roof garden. The withered branches of an oak tree stretched toward the wintry sky. About 200 feet below, the subway rattled through. The building's subterranean passageways served a clean compliment to the grittiness of the city's prime underground mover.

Pussy is stronger than God.

A few minutes turned into 15, and Calder felt like he was back on his baby-inflected perception of existence. To pass time during his *Waiting for Godot* doctor's visit—quietly fearful of a horrific cancer diagnosis, though he was certain he was lactating and the visit was pointless—Calder wondered who the subway mantra writer might be. Whoever it was might have pushed him out of a job. The economy steamed along, but that was never a good prospect. It was likely some high school kid at an all-boys Catholic school who got laid for the first time, finishing prematurely in the process. No, too literal. Calder reexamined, returning to his favorite pastime.

What if it had been a woman? A furtive scribble at 3:30 a.m. after a night of drinking by a young professional who had spurned the advances of a lascivious male and gone home and masturbated. Calder's mind slid into depravity. Maybe he had masturbated one time too many himself, and he projected the same condition onto imaginary other people who may or may not have etched a dogmatic screed on a movie poster. Nevertheless, the digression prompted Calder to lift his pants and exam his penis. It hadn't been put to proper use since Zoe's conception.

"Is it still there?" Dr. West interjected. Deep in imaginative ad writing thought, Calder didn't notice him enter. This was becoming a dangerous habit.

Dr. West clasped Calder's hand in a vise-like power grip—definitely an alpha move. He flipped open the chart, which meant the medical history Calder had filled out centuries before in the waiting room.

"What brings you here today?"

"I'm lactating," Calder answered, brushing aside context and pretext equally.

"So certain?"

"I've been secretly breastfeeding my newborn daughter for the past two months. How is this possible?"

"Let me examine you first before you jump to any conclusions."

"You're not hearing me. I. Am. Lactating. Spontaneous lactation. There have been a few documented cases. I read about it in a medical journal, or online somewhere. I can't remember. Let me put to you this way. My wife is sleeping with the milkman."

Calder's joke fell flat. His misguided attempt to slogan-ize what was happening to him did not have the intended effect. Calder, to his discredit, didn't know what effect he had wanted. Ad-speak hijacked his tongue.

Dr. West proceeded with his examination without any further conversation. He immediately fell into a strictly business attitude, wearing the awkwardness of the situation like a badge of honor. The moment Dr. West placed his blue-gloved hands on Calder's breast a splurge of foamy cream spilled all over the examining table's paper roll.

"I don't feel any lumps, but let's get you an MRI to be sure."

"How about a biopsy? I can squeeze some of my milk into a glass and you can see for yourself."

Dr. West frowned.

An hour later, Calder sat at his desk secure in the notion that he was indeed lactating. He wasn't concerned with any other results. He must maintain his secrecy from Maren, and because he was so focused on Zoe, anything contrary was not forefront in his mind. On the subway ride home, Calder kept his head on a swivel seeking another subway poet who might vandalize a poster or a tiled underground wall. There were the usual crude dicks and hairy vaginas scrawled on the walls, and he saw another slogan, *War is for suckas*—the 'k' purposefully written backwards like a small child—but Calder found nothing with the profound panache of "Pussy is stronger than God."

Pussy, for lack of a better word, was what Calder desperately needed. More specifically, he needed to seduce his wife. It mattered not if Maren had the best body, and his wasn't meatloaf, if neither of them regularly experienced each other's flesh. In Calder's opinion, the pleasures of the flesh were integral to any marriage. It was a two-way street, both parties responsible for the sexual enmity that existed between them before and after Zoe's arrival.

The reasons for the malaise were myriad, yet neither party could articulate them and anytime the subject was broached it precipitated an argument. After one ungodly row, each claimed the other wasn't sexual enough. Calder contended he was shot down so many times that he stopped trying. He suspected she was having an affair. If there was an affair they had an unwritten agreement—a haphazard discussion years earlier before the wedding—that neither would mention it. Look the other way for the sake of their continued coupling. This seemed doomed from the start. Oddly, this pseudo-pact brought them closer together—before the fighting— and they had unrepentant nights of sexual bliss, contorting into positions they hadn't dared since the night they met.

But this too shall pass, Calder thought. They entered another drought. A friend recommended a therapist. Maren and Calder could always agree on that. They loathed shrinks, therapists, psychoanalysts, psychiatrists, psychologists or whatever they called themselves, regardless of their varying meanings. Calder longed to have sex with his wife: his sanity was at stake. And, he suspected, Maren's. He had to figure out how to breach the abyss. He didn't want to complain directly to her for the sake of harmony. That's why he hadn't pressed the issue.

Zoe was a perfect child. Her smile at 5:15 in the morning after a clandestine feeding provided Calder with enough happiness to power the entire city. Power companies should determine a way to harness the infinite joy spread by newborn babies. Zoe's coos were tantamount to manna, a direct link to the heavens.

Calder revisited the theological subway slogan. What was stronger than God? Pussy couldn't be that powerful. In the bustle of the city, Calder had lost faith in religion, the cause of so many wars throughout history. When he was young—and even every now and then when he returned home to L.A.— he was an altar boy. Calder's mother knew he didn't have the attention span to sit through an hour-long service unless he was an active participant. He loved to put extra incense in the thurible and smoke out the worshippers when he twirled it down the aisle during the Christmas processional. This was a minor transgression compared to humanity's long list of horrific things done in the name of God. Calder viewed jihadism as a fundamentalist threat no matter the denomination or faith. While his faith in formal religion had wavered, he never gave up on love. Love was supreme. *War is for suckas.*

Maren's flesh-colored skin complimented Calder's golden brown skin in a veneer that resembled sunlight. When they made love, their intertwined bodies looked like dawn rays shimmering across undulating sand dunes. The word skin itself originated in Scandinavia, from the Old Norse word "skinn." Their union epitomized perfection in the moment of conception.

Maren announced one fall day the previous year that they were getting pregnant, meaning Calder's sex renaissance would commence. For three months, Calder and Maren deepened their love in their quest to create life. It was also the most sex they had had in the previous seven years. Maren traveled three or four times a month, oftentimes to exotic or untold locales from Albania to Zanzibar. So Calder got it while he could.

Be careful what you wish for.

During those magnificent months, the age-old slogan wafted into Calder's thoughts and set up residence. He was on a schedule now. He had to be ready. Calder convinced Maren, or tried to convince her, that multiple lovemaking sessions, a scatter shooting, cover all your bases, approach, was the way to do it. Sometimes she obliged, humorously with a sarcastic comment such as, "Does it still work?" Once Calder had been too tired. He wasn't really. He just said it to see the look on his wife's face, a failed attempt at winning back power. "You're lying," she said. She sniffed him out. Back then, they watched movies online sitting in bed between sessions of baby making. Today, he watched movies in sections. It took him two weeks to get though Kurosawa's *Ikiru*. The title meant "To Live" in Japanese.

To live, it was the answer to the meaning of life.

Just before he bounded into his apartment building—after his doctor's visit and finishing up at the office—Calder took notice of a 50-something homeless man slumped in the Lotus position atop a steam grate. His head drooped forward to the snow-covered pavement, the back of his head tilted to the dark sky, exposing his pale leathery skin to the lingering flurries. We're all covered in *skinn* Calder mused.

Calder had never seen him before. There was the shopping cart lady with Tourette's who coughed, hacked and screamed on most mornings and the woman in the knit stocking cap who floated in and around the Korean deli on the corner. He never gave them money but would offer a donut or part of his morning croissant if he passed them on his way to the 77th Street subway station. Calder noticed the withered man because a cardboard sign, bent in half and resting on the sidewalk, expressed his mantra: *The one who helps you up is the one who knows what it's like to fall down.*

Calder went into the deli, bought an apple and placed it in the man's hand. No words were exchanged. But the man echoed gratitude through his eyes. Calder wondered about his own financial standing. Incessant calls from the credit card company or school loans. He could never get ahead.

"This is Citi Card calling about your account...."

"Your school loan is 60 days past due, please submit payment to avoid delinquency...."

Later that night, with Zoe resting peacefully, Calder mentioned the homeless man to Maren in passing just before going to bed. He wondered how many tragic steps removed the average person in Manhattan was away from homelessness.

"I don't want to be married to someone who

compares themselves to a homeless person," Maren scalded Calder's soul.

"I'm not. I'm simply pointing out life is a series of events and decisions that if you aren't careful can leave you on the streets."

"You didn't give him any money did you? They are drug addicts."

She'd asked a rhetorical question, but the lack of empathy was surprising. They were blessed with jobs and a beautiful child. Calder let the issue lie. His tongue had caused problems before, leading down a rabbit hole of innuendo and animosity. An uncomfortable silence knifed between them. Calder draped his right hand over his wife's naked hips. The silence was silenced.

Maren's tears were invisible in the dim light trying to pierce through tiny lattices in the bargain basement window shade. The fingers of the full moon bent down from the darkness and managed to illuminate her nude body. She moved her arm around her husband's fist and clenched it. They melted into each other like Russian dolls, each touch, each curve, waiting to reveal something hidden deeper. Emotions had no physical form in the near darkness. Calder had no idea how much Maren needed this too. Caught up in his own follies, he misinterpreted her coldness for a lack of desire.

Slowly, Calder slid his hand down the curve of her buttocks, up toward the spinal indentation on her back—a road map to bliss—and massaged her left breast. He was almost crying himself, but for selfish reasons, nothing tantamount to the stress they both harbored. Even in making love they were anchored on a strange coast with no inhabitants and no indigenous plants or wild animals to replenish their internal cargo hold. It had been so long that Maren's body felt foreign to him. "We can't wake her up," Maren said, releasing an ecstatic sigh as her husband entered her.

They shimmered quietly. No explanation was necessary. It was quite clear who "her" was. Zoe slept in a body-contorting slumber no more than a foot from the edge of their large bed, nestled in a just-big-enough bedroom. The small wisps of air from her tiny lungs made a perfect rhythm paralleling her parents' melodic prostrations.

Calder tried to leverage his body to apply undulating pressure for Maren while simultaneously not making noise. Maren started to move beneath him with more thrust. She moved her arms to Calder's chest, pushing tighter the closer she was to orgasm.

In the midst of ecstasy, a suffocating fear overwhelmed Calder. Maren's hands squeezed his engorged breasts. He felt a sharp pain but could not scream. She noticed a weird sensation. It wasn't sweat. It felt sticky in her fingertips.

When she climaxed, it ended Calder's charade. She squeezed his nipples so hard that a spray of lactated milk squirted into her eye.

"What the fuck?"

So much for romance. *It's always something.* Though some things, like this, were much bigger than others, and eventually, the something becomes an even bigger problem leading toward the disintegration into nothing. Calder did not respond.

"What the hell?" Maren rephrased her earlier plea. The same tone, and she expected an answer now. Maren always wanted things to be done on her schedule.

Calder jumped out of bed, and bumped Zoe's bassinet in his haste to hide his oddity. Zoe's cries echoed through the fleeting moonlight, his beeline to the bathroom thwarted.

"Stop right there. Are you seeing someone else? You're sweating bullets."

Maren's silhouette haunted him. She sat up on the bed, and realized immediately it wasn't sweat. She hopped up and flicked on the nightstand lamp. The soupy milk flowed between her breasts and it was evident it wasn't ejaculate. Maren dipped her right index finger into the milieu and tasted it. The jig flat lined. "Breast milk?" She uttered incredulously.

"How long has this been going on? Don't bend the truth."

The one who helps you up is the one who knows what it's like to fall down.

3

Calder stood in Central Park at 6:13 a.m. the next morning amidst an infinite field of white. Only two things pierced the first major snowstorm's chokehold on the horizon. His black overcoat and dark branches reaching for an unseen sun combined to give the appearance of a silent black and white film. There was no one else. The temperature hovered at 20 degrees, gnawing at his reason.

Six pumped bottles of father's milk lined the right side of the refrigerator back at the apartment. They earned him a reprieve. He had to escape. The absurdity of the situation rendered all non-baby things in his life suddenly less meaningful. Maren's mélange of confusion and anger left Calder in a state of interrupted equilibrium. He couldn't sleep and slithered out of the bedroom and into the snow for some solitude. He'd wandered a little further than he'd planned. He was going to go to work early but took a slight detour not unlike the one his mind and body accomplished to flip nature on its head.

Instead of hopping on the 6 train and transferring

to the N/Q/R line, Calder walked past the subway entrance at Lexington and 77th Street. The blizzard conditions abated but the snow still fell in a steady stream like Times Square-confetti on New Year's Eve. He took a few cell phone photos of the pristine snow before like-minded winter lovers claimed their private kingdoms to sled or fall backward into the powder before it froze, sweeping their arms top to bottom in parallel semicircles. Everybody made angels. Why not make a snow elephant or a snow giraffe?

Now, here in this whiteness, a stranger approached. At first he thought it was a park worker or a jogger but it was neither. A similarly dressed man sat down on the obscured bench next to Calder. He was slightly younger, definitely in his 30s, and his brown hair slid down the side of his face in orderly rows, framing his glasses like static cling.

It was odd. Calder, so distraught, didn't think to move or really think anything extraordinary was about to happen.

"Calder Boyd?"

He didn't answer.

"My name is Thomas Spooner, a city reporter for the independent *New York Sentinel*. You didn't answer any of my calls yesterday."

"I'm not interested."

"Is it true? Can you verify things a source close to you has confirmed?"

"I don't mean to be rude but I have to get back to my family."

"The story will run tomorrow whether or not you

talk to me. I think it's smarter if you do. This could open a few doors."

Calder took his cue, unaware of his lack of curiosity. There were only two suspects, Varick and Dr. West. He bet on the latter, owing it to Dr. West wasn't his usual doctor and perhaps the person tasked with cleaning up the milk mess, a milk maid if you will, had spilled the beans. He chuckled to himself while listening to the crunch of his boots in the snowdrifts. If Calder hadn't been in this section of the park before, he might have gotten lost. Thomas Spooner's pleas faded into the snow.

The day at the agency seemed unending. Calder briefly proofread some low-level ad copy for a web banner that had to go out that afternoon, but he spent a good hour trolling the web, lamenting the Doomsday Clock had been pushed forward two minutes—three minutes to midnight. The ergonomic-inflected space around his cubicle did not lend itself well to creating a fortress. Late last year, they remodeled the paint to a passive lime green. He didn't dislike it—it reminded him of the pastel green motif in Zoe's "nursery". Maren had picked the color so it wasn't a subconscious bleed form the work world taken home. The sleek obsidian floor tiles contrasted nicely with the idyllic interior, and the powers that be had been kind enough to let him keep his old chair. He slid across the black gloss to and fro in his tiny domain, soothing his focus on the lecture from Maren that he knew awaited.

He ate lunch alone, tuna on rye with a sliver of avocado, at a bistro around the corner. He didn't have any close colleagues at the firm—his best friend left eight years ago—and hadn't availed himself to making any others. Perhaps this contributed to his lack of a promotion in his 10-year run, the term job squatting was apropos. Apathy, it was as much a substance that could be abused as drugs or alcohol. However, the benefits were great, and his failed artistic pursuits kept him afloat mentally.

Calder retired to the men's room more frequently because the lactation was becoming a problem. Hell, it had been a problem. He had to bring an extra shirt or two to work to mask the milk stains. They could be confused for something else. Calder momentarily pondered why milk and semen were the same color. There were a few close calls, but he didn't think any of his colleagues knew anything. He left work 30 minutes before five, if any one noticed, though he had arrived well before anyone else after his Central Park sojourn. He didn't give a damn. He was a new father and could milk that fact for a few more months. Today, it was a conceit.

Despite the fact that he loved his daughter and still loved his wife—did he really have to convince himself—Calder delayed his voyage home. The snow had finally stopped. Patches of ice lurked beneath the fresh coat piled high on the margins of the filthy sidewalks and ratty curbs. The streets would shine for a few hours, and then the snow would blacken. He was excited to see his family, even if he went to the Met for 15 minutes before it closed. Calder went to the back and stared at a massive Clyfford Still abstract mural until the guard shooed him out. The alone time relaxed him, balm for the sleep-deprived. That night, if he thought about Still's red and blue swath of colors, he might be able to slide into dreamland.

He didn't even remember speaking to Maren. When he unlocked the door, the sound initiated Zoe's radar and she cried for his milk. There was no argument. Maren and Calder were both exhausted.

"Are you all right?" she asked and that was it. They were the only words spoken between them. He only looked at her and nodded.

Calder fed Zoe with his right breast, and that's the last thing he could recall. Waking up at 6 a.m. and walking in Central Park during a snowstorm might have had something to do with it. Maren's own on-duty malaise never subsided with a newborn. She retired to the bedroom while Calder's legs heaved in horrific jerks on Sofa Island. If she wasn't married to him, Maren might have urged Calder to see a specialist. But she was, and knew he wouldn't. Calder regressed. He babbled in his sleep. He could fall asleep in any position. The insomnia had left the building. He was the baby on board.

Calder remembered sitting down on Sofa Island. The TV was on, another reality show, but after that, it was a void. He passed out almost the same second he sat down, Maren later told him. He woke in the early morning darkness with Zoe sucking on his left nipple. It too had finally arrived. The sound emulated a squeaky wheel on a child's toy. Again, there was no memory of the interceding time. Calder awoke 30 minutes later from Maren's pleas. Drool dribbled down his lip and all over his white T-shirt. Baby on board indeed. Zoe cried incessantly and he hadn't sprung up from the couch fast enough because he had slipped back into a coma.

"Why didn't you feed her?" Maren's disembodied voice filtered through the wooden door into the pale dawn light of the living room.

It was a minor injustice that singularly meant little but a series of which collectively burgeoned resentment. The lack of a previous argument revealed the remaining rancor. Calder wondered why she often jumped to the wrong assumption. Being a new mother is not easy, he knew that, but the new paradigm didn't need to be exacerbated. Of course he fed her. What did she think he was doing at 6:54 a.m. on his sofa island?

Calder remained silent, with a hangdog grin.

Sleeping on the sofa night after night—a routine solidified in their first month without Joy's help—gave Calder a modicum of private time, a welcome luxury. Sometimes he would sit in the darkness and listen to the cadence of her breathing, a soothing metronome that welled his soul with equal parts pride, joy, concern and love. No, love is supreme. It had pushed the others aside like a heavyweight champion's left hook.

Other nights were restless, insomnia taking up residency. On those eternal nights, he was a forensic sleepologist, trying to ascertain how many hours he had slept by scouring the time stamps on his overnight note taking and emails. Calder took to the habit of trying to remember what position he was in when he awoke at whatever hour of the night and day, in the hopes of finding the Holy Grail of defeating his insomnia. His mind constantly churned, weaving his numerous ideas into a creamy butter. Or better yet, distilled into a fine liqueur. Yet he was unable to hold a conversation with Sofa Island's other sometime denizen, Zoe. Calder understood what Maren had said about feeling lonely when she was home alone with the baby, isolated from the rest of the world.

Come to Sofa Island.

The sofa locale also buttressed the growing divide between Calder and his wife. He had to try harder to connect: a touch on the neck, a stolen kiss in the shower—a joint session that was a rarity—and holding her hand while watching TV. He hated her programs but grin and be happy worked well. Eventually he began to accept the spate of mind-numbing "reality" programming. He also tried to sleep in the same bed with Maren as much as he could without disturbing her, his insomnia as much a reason for his nocturnal visits to Sofa Island as the lurking resentment.

If not going to bed mad were a commandment, then he and Maren were hell bound. Calder didn't believe in hell. It didn't make sense to him logically. If souls continued infinitely, how could someone be damned eternally for something they did in their finite human lifetime? Calder conceded that, just maybe, someone could be damned for a time equal to the length of their physical human existence, but not eternity, so maybe 80 years, 100 if you happened to be born in the early 21st century like Zoe. He deduced only small personal hells existed. Whether he accepted it or not, Calder was responsible for his own. His thoughts continued their spiral. The average lifespan of a black man in the United States was 72. That wasn't even a billionth of a millisecond in the grand scheme of time. And who said time started when it did? What happened before the Big Bang? Lots of arguing, that's what. There was a time make-up sex dangled on the visible horizon. There was none now. He was a self-serving fool.

On some bed respite nights, Calder defied logic. He blatantly used his smartphone to check email and play word games, or when an ad idea struck him, knowing damn well that his wife couldn't sleep with the glaring glow illuminating their bodies like a lighthouse. He did it because he could. Maren needed his breast milk because Zoe needed his breast milk.

"Do you have to do it tonight? Can it wait until tomorrow?"

Calder complied, but that's not how inspiration worked. He wrote down his ideas immediately or they might be lost forever. He had lost untold ideas before he started keeping a dream journal on the nightstand, if it could be considered that given its minuscule proportions.

It was the next day or the day after that—Maren rarely used the actual days of the week—when she told Calder when and where she was working. He needed advance notice to take the days off from work but Calder believed she just assumed he would no matter what, given his lactation proficiency. He could trade days and work during the weekend if he wanted to shuffle days. His Greek boss, the agency founder Marcus Mathos, was lenient since he had two young kids of his own, boys. Calder had unwittingly become friends with Mathos, trading feeding and diaper-changing war stories at the proverbial water cooler. How far did the longest poop blowout shoot? What was the most diapers Zoe went through in a day? These were earth-shattering topics of conversation. Mathos asked his litany of poop-related questions, to him, a pursuit worthy of a championship pedigree.

The friendship frayed on a late afternoon when Mathos mentioned future play dates, and with 100 percent seriousness, that Zoe would marry one of his boys one day. Knowing Maren was fiercely protective, as any mother should be, Calder politely tried to change the subject. Mathos pressed.

"Come on, man. Imagine us drinking ouzo on Santorini, watching the sunset."

Calder walked away without any explanation. He grabbed his book and left. It was five minutes to five.

"Boyd. Boyd, where are you going?"

"Wait. I'll walk out with you," Mathos continued.

Calder sprinted out the door. A cloud of red felt tip markers fell from his pencil holder onto the floor. He did not look back.

War is for suckas.

He and Mathos didn't talk again for two weeks. Calder lied and said it was a family emergency.

***

Jan. 13

4:16-4:30 a.m. Bottle fed Zoe 85 ml of pumped breast milk. Changed her diaper (pee). Burped her. Mixed the leftover into a new bottle of pumped milk. My nipples are super raw.

7:31-7:56 a.m. Zoe was very fussy and crying. Held her. Warmed refrigerated breast milk as quick as I could. Bottle fed Zoe 90 ml. She fell asleep while drinking. Changed her diaper (pee). Put lotion on her legs and moisturizer on her face and knees, which were very dry. She was awake for about 15 minutes then passed out on the bed at 8:15 a.m.

10:02 a.m. Changed Zoe's diaper (big poo, darker brown than usual). Put lotion on her legs and moisturizer on her face.

11:15-11:29 a.m. Bottle fed Zoe 115 ml of formula. Put her to sleep in the stroller at 11:33 a.m. 11:48 a.m. Put moisturizer on her cheeks.

Calder's pas de deux with Mathos was on a Wednesday, an ordinary day with no ominous overtones. January 14. Calder remembered the date because a "blizzard of epic proportions" bore down on the city. That's what *they* said, the eponymous "they."

Mathos deferred to the mayor and the governor's

incessant pleadings. Snow again. It was the winter of Calder's content. He loved snow. Growing up in suburban L.A., after his father ended his career with the Lakers in the early '80s, he never witnessed snowstorms. A freak hailstorm in Huntington Beach one Christmas morning was the closest he'd ever come to a White Christmas—his own lactation predicament notwithstanding.

Twenty-five degrees and snowing. The inclement weather overtook the city that never slept. Standing outside the closed door of his old office—the junior account manager was on his honeymoon in Jamaica—Calder watched the flakes flutter past his window to the outside world, peering through the frosted glass like a child on the closed facade of a candy store. His cubicle did not afford views of the "storm of the century." Winter Storm Magnus, the media proclaimed. Such a Norse name. Mayor So-and-So pontificated about the necessity of road closures and only calling 911 in a real emergency, and 311 for lesser evils. When did they start naming winter storms anyway? And who? Prognosticators, pundits and people who penciled in "pussy is stronger than God" on subway platform posters, Calder surmised. A nexus of frenzy descended over the city, more so than actual snow. *Spin, spin, spin.*

Don't believe the hype.

Calder wished he'd invented the slogan. Public Enemy beat him to it. An armchair weatherman, Calder knew the brunt of the storm would impact Boston, Cape Cod and far eastern Long Island. Ever since Mayor What's-His-Name underplayed a brutal

28-inch dumping a few years earlier, the city was on high alert, overplaying every potential chance at winter chaos. Calder welcomed a legitimate reason to leave the agency early.

The entire city had the same idea. Calder jockeyed for position on the subway, careful not to let anyone score a direct hit on his cracked nipples. He wanted to apply nipple cream right then and there, but couldn't reveal his prolactin-producing powers in public. Calder nearly toppled over after the motorman came to an abrupt halt just before Grand Central Station.

Please be patient, train traffic ahead.

Grumbling ensued. Through the musty car's haze of dismay, Calder felt strange stares. Nothing obvious, but more a barely perceptible gaze as if he were a zoo animal. He surreptitiously opened his winter coat to ensure nothing leaked. He looked down to the grimy subway car's floor. No pool of milk existed.

As he trudged up Third Avenue toward the family domicile, heavier snow fell, coating the ground like a child heaping too much sugar on his cereal. Calder had no sense of the gloom bearing down, not only on the city, but him as well. A grand surprise awaited.

He opened the door to paradise. His wife was in a playful mood. She had no choice.

Laugh clown, laugh.

How do you know she's the one? She laughs with you, not against you.

Tears of a clown?

No slogan fit the impending moment.

Maren stood naked from head to toe in the middle of the room, holding an open newspaper to hide her breasts. The pages ruffled and made a slight wafting sound as the air from the slightly opened window shot through their modest abode. Both of their nipples were firm, Calder surmised.

"Attention, attention! Read all about it!"

Maren possessed a wicked sense of humor. Sarcasm heaped upon sarcasm, not unlike the falling snow.

She thrust the *New York Sentinel* into Calder's hands.

"Look at the magazine. Not my tits."

"But I'm your husband."

"So they say."

Then she read the first few lines of columnist Thomas Spooner's cover story.

"Calder Boyd does not have a cold. He lactates. In the winter of our discontent, the sexual revolution has a new twist. While women have made immeasurable leaps in the workplace, so has this ordinary family man on the domestic front. According to sources close to the family, Mr. Boyd, it seems, has the ability to produce father's milk."

Maren paused. "Shall I continue?"

"No."

She continued. "The proper medical term is galactorrhea. There have been several cases in medical history but it is a rare phenomenon. Mr. Boyd declined to be interviewed for this story despite repeated attempts to reach him. In any regard, the milkman cometh, and the emasculation of man is complete."

The front page cartoon featured a grotesque looking baby suckling at an overly satirical version of Calder. *The Sentinel* was the city's weekly independent rag, and Spooner, a glorified hack who could barely spell his name but who beamed the sarcasm that draped the metropolis on a regular basis.

"Take off your clothes," Maren ordered.

Calder's surprise rendered him immobile.

"Just do it," Maren attacked her husband. Calder felt a level of ribaldry unseen since their pre-argument lovemaking session a week earlier.

"I want to make love to my husband before the rest of the world does," she explained.

Calder happily obliged. He sensed an ulterior motive. Indeed, pussy may be stronger than God.

4

The stench of cigarette smoke wafted upward from the rust-colored sofa into Calder's defeated nostrils. He stifled a sneeze, not wanting to interrupt the mailman slash motivational speaker—or woman hater in some circles—as he spewed his philosophy of dominating manhood as it pertained to attaining and taming the human female species.

"You must remain mysterious at all costs," Varick's baritone intonation lulled one man to sleep and kept Calder awake.

"You must answer her questions with an enigma. But not too vague. You don't want her to lose interest. Use humor to charm. For example, if a woman asks what you do, say: I make money. You all make money. She will fill in the rest with whatever preconceived and deep-seated desires she wants you to fulfill. Fulfill her needs. Don't talk about yourself. Listen."

Calder didn't know exactly why he skipped a night of ushering and the $50 after taxes it brought to his wallet, to spend time with a gaggle of, what in

Calder's modest assessment, were a ragtag bunch of losers. He refused to commit wholeheartedly to that description because he was right alongside them. Maybe he hoped he could learn something to improve his marriage. However, Calder did not view himself as a loser. To use Varick's introductory term, call us the unenlightened, Calder mused. That sounded much more socially acceptable.

Ten other male "students" filled the room, ranging in age from a 19-year-old NYU student who wanted to seduce more women, to a 65-year-old Vietnam veteran who admittedly hadn't had much success with the fairer sex, and seven other non-descript slobs—the tenth was a heavyset slumbering man who squeezed Calder off the edge of the sofa. During the first 10 minutes of the seminar, if it could be called such a thing, Varick had participants introduce themselves and state their objectives and what they had learned in the previous four workshops. Then he turned to his newest charge.

"We have a celebrity in our midst," Varick said at the top of the hour. "This course is practical for the married man as well as the single man. Women have taken our manhood. And we must reclaim it. We are all equal under the sun."

Varick, his hair slicked back with a large goop of hair gel, paid the dozing man no attention. What did the glorified mailman care? He already had the man's "tuition"; each person would receive a "diploma" at the end of this fifth and final session with the guru of male self-improvement. The mailman with an exit plan was too busy preaching his stump spiel like a politician in an early primary state to care if one of the men slept through the proceedings.

Calder scanned Varick's spacious apartment. It had the decor of a man perennially trapped in the year 1977. Shag carpeting and a semicircle of folding chairs in front of a gaudy brown plush sofa formed a kind of proscenium stage for Varick to address his pupils, who paid $100 a pop to be here. There was a Power Point presentation on a white pull down screen in one corner of the living room. The faces of the main "types" of women—in Varick's estimation—flashed on and off in a constant loop. An hour into the seminar, Varick fell into an easy rhythm. He even woke the sleeping giant. The eyes of the fat man latched to the lothario like epoxy.

"You must be a sexual threat from the moment you first meet a woman. That is, someone she wants to have sex with. A sex partner. Or else you will be relegated to friend zone status. You do not want to be her friend. You want to be her lover, her sexual guru, the Alpha male she secretly wants to tell her what to do—in the bedroom and in her life. When you first encounter her, treat her like you've already slept with her. Exude confidence."

The planned two-hour seminar looped like a Mobius strip with no beginning and no end. Calder felt as if he'd been in this large but dingy apartment for a week.

Varick continued: "Stick together. Other men are not the enemy. You can use their failures as a drawing board to your own success. Trade information. Learn from her colleagues and former suitors. Information is the key to success. A pillar in the pyramid of seduction."

Calder forgave the mixed metaphor. Varick was rhapsodizing.

Do not let women divide and conquer.

Over the final hour, Varick skipped through a batch of key words and phrases.

Confidence breeds success.

Master the art of the female ejaculation (see enclosed brochure).

Pheromone release is an aphrodisiac.

Be a sensitive jerk.

Do not always be available.

Mix compliments with an occasional humorous put down.

Tantric sex.

Do not give up easily.

Command respect by saying no.

Be a man.

Nice guys finish last.

This last missive stung Calder. Where had he gone wrong in his marriage? When exactly had he lost her respect? He fell into a trance as Varick disseminated information in chunks of indigestible, but lurid, sexism.

Strangely, Calder saw twisted logic in *some* of what Varick preached. Yet, its divisive us vs. them tone seemed laughable. Did this stuff really work? He was sitting on a sofa surrounded by a roomful of desperate men somewhere in Queens. Varick couldn't be serious.

Mercifully, the session ended and Varick thanked the men for their participation. Each man recited the parting mantra, "be a man," as Varick dispensed their diplomas, a piece of embossed papyrus with their names and completion date written in Old English lettering.

"What did you think, man?"

Calder dreaded being pinned down. He felt indebted to the mailman for helping him get out of his predicament two months earlier. Perhaps Calder came to add fuel to the notion that the mailman was indeed a friend, lest Maren investigate the reasons for a strange man holding Zoe any further. That was a viable concern; if she knew where her husband was right now, she would not be happy.

Calder did not know how to answer the man. Luckily, Varick was full of himself and continued talking.

"I'm perfecting my technique and I need to find a more professional locale to host the course, but I'm on my way. I don't want to be delivering mail when I turn 40."

"Sounds like you have it all figured out."

"These techniques apply to married men as well. Treat your wife like you are trying to seduce her every night."

For all his bluster, Varick's pearl burrowed into his star student. He reached into a nearby ottoman and thrust a blank diploma into Calder's hands.

"Be whoever you want to be," he said.

Calder escaped Varick's man camp and hopped on the 7 train. He had a 40-minute ride back home. As long as he was back by 11:15 p.m.—his usual return on a late shift show at the theater—he would be okay.

That night, Calder decided to ooze mystery. Every question Maren had he answered with an enigma. And every time, his humor failed miserably, and Maren asked, "What's wrong with you?"

Her preconceived notions of who he was worked against him. He would change that.

5

Jan. 15

4:31-4:41 a.m. Bottle fed Zoe 125 ml of stored breast milk. Changed her diaper (pee). Put lotion on her legs and torso and moisturizer on her face. Burped her (big burp at 4:57 a.m.). Put her back to sleep at 5:04 a.m. Exhausted. At least Maren is sleeping peacefully.

When Calder left his apartment the next morning, a clandestine photographer snapped his photo and ran away. Or he tried to. The snow was knee deep, and it was still coming down. This was not a good omen, snow days being significant markers for Calder. Cars looked like massive art installations of frosted cornflakes.

Zoe's eye was slightly puffy and, according to Maren, had been discharging a small amount of a mucous-like substance all the previous day. So Calder, tasked with taking their daughter to the doctor, was caught baby handed, the money shot for the budding celebrity.

Calder believed the paparazzo vacated the scene of the crime, and that the coast was clear, only to discover him across Third Avenue focusing his zoom lens. The photographer stalked his prey across the street like the perilous bird on Varick's card and would strike at the most inopportune moment. Good for the photographer. Bad for Calder. He raised his right hand in a halfhearted attempt to shield his face. Calder had selected a pediatrician right around the corner from their apartment—a wise move in a particularly cold and snowy winter—but in this instance, he wished he had selected one across town, allowing him to escape the paparazzo's gaze by hopping into a cab.

While pushing the stroller around a snow bank, Calder ignored his cell phone. It vibrated non-stop all morning. A producer from CNN, all three major networks' New York affiliates and a producer for *60 Minutes* all jockeyed for an on-camera interview.

Dr. Mehta diagnosed Zoe as having a blocked tear duct and prescribed erythromycin. While at the pharmacy, a 40-something woman smiled at him. Had she read the *Sentinel* piece? The weekly catered to the left crowd. She looked the bohemian part with her ruffled long brown tresses that would not have been out of place at Woodstock and a retro, psychedelic print down jacket that would serve her well at Burning Man. Maybe the bohemian was just being friendly.

"How old is she?"

The woman had not been smiling at Calder. Zoe was her catch. Calder still didn't exist. He answered politely and congratulated her on her soon-to-be bundle of joy and otherwise made a hasty retreat, all the while continuing to scan the store in case another paparazzo lurked on the feminine hygiene aisle.

This random encounter, not unlike the old woman entering the subway who had seen right through his lactation ruse, might be his last day of anonymity. The 10th circle of personal hell is a small circle. And then it happened. Calder came close to the gates.

The unholiest of shrieks terrified the 10 brave souls in the store. Two seconds earlier, Muzak-infused calm dominated the aisles of household items and over-the-counter medicine. Zoe had been peaceful, and asleep Calder thought. One second, it was dreamland, rapid eye movement and spasmodic smiles in her slumber; the next, a piercing scream startled the bohemian woman. For the next two minutes, it seemed everyone in the pharmacy and then the store's general population eyed Calder crookedly. Blizzard be damned.

In the small tacky green chair section of the pharmacy's waiting area, Calder felt inadequate. He had just fed Zoe an hour earlier. It couldn't be that, could it?

"Somebody needs to feed that baby," a woman of a certain age pointed out to no one in particular. Then she repeated it. Calder didn't know if she was talking to him or to her imaginary friend as she did not make direct eye contact and there was no one within 10 feet of her. Had she been a new mother long ago? Maybe she had sage wisdom to impart.

Doubtful.

The pharmacist spoke to her like one would to a child. "Mrs. King, I already filled your prescription. No more refills." Then he continued with the present customer.

Zoe's screams became biblical. Two women from the next aisle peeked around household cleaners to see what the hell was the matter, or in the sense that they jumped to such a conclusion, to make sure Calder was not abusing his child.

"Don't worry. It gets worse," the bohemian woman said, then disappeared in a cloud of stonewashed jeans and bra-less defiance of the elements.

Zoe's cries sounded as if she was about to be sacrificed to a Mayan deity. She cried so much her breathing stopped momentarily. The rattle, cradling her, lullabies, her plush vibrating ladybug toy, none of them worked. The 10-member peanut gallery glared at Calder. Some of them shook their head, recalling some incident in their own history they didn't want to relive.

There was only one solution.

Calder sat in the chair furthest in the corner, trying to make himself scarce. He didn't have a shawl or any other form of defense. He was about to breastfeed in public. *Quelle horreur!* The level of disgust unmistakable in one woman's glint surprised him. Her chin creased open like she was about to swallow Zoe whole to end the disturbance in one fatal swoop. Nothing proved a greater enmity than his public display of his special new power.

This was a place of business. That business was

getting their happy pills baby free and unobstructed. They had conquered the elements for a reason.

As Calder took off layers of clothes—he had not expected Zoe to raise the dead with her cries—the pharmacist gave a judgmental sideways glance. It took a few tries for Zoe to get a proper latch, but in one of Calder's favorite moments each nursing, Zoe's screams vanished the instant his nipple filled her mouth, as if his daughter had stepped into a vacuum.

The pharmacy and adjacent aisles became eerily quiet. Calder, focused intently on Zoe, did not notice the wall of curious onlookers, peeking over each other jockeying for position: an old man with a service dog, the bohemian woman, who had mysteriously returned; a teenager with pimples all over his face and green hoodie totally underdressed for winter; a little girl clutching a doll and her young mother and about ten other women ranging in age from 18 to 54 who looked on with particular interest—at least one with a hint of lust in her eye. The population in the store had somehow doubled. Perhaps they were all clandestine paparazzi.

When Calder looked over, many in the throng looked away, feigning interest in toilet bowl plungers. One woman kept her smartphone trained on the scene, her hand not wavering in the slightest. The little girl dropped her doll but would have won a starting contest with anyone foolish enough to challenge her. Not all of these people were here when he came into the Duane Reade. He was convinced of that and soon of the fact that he was a spectacle. Calder felt obliged to address the throng.

"I guess there's one thing even New Yorkers haven't seen," he said. "Do you mind? I'm sharing a private moment with my daughter."

Nobody moved. More smartphones emerged. Calder ignored them until from the corner of his eye, he noticed a series of flashes. He looked over and inadvertently gave the same stalking paparazzo from earlier the best money shot of his miserable life. A spray of milk shot into Zoe's face as Calder tried to cover both of their faces with his pseudo-free right hand. He nearly dropped Zoe. Two minutes later, it was over. The exasperated manager arrived on scene and dispersed the crowd.

Everyone in New York City is going to hell.

The unfamiliar homeless man camped outside the pharmacy said as much. Calder slipped a vastly overpriced two-dollar banana he had purchased at Upper East Side rates into the man's hands. It was a welcome distraction from the throng of gawkers he had just experienced.

"Thank you, brother," the man said.

He used the word in the brotherly sort of way, signifying a human connection, not in the black man sense. Calder didn't view himself as black or white. He was a human being. He chafed at the oft-asked question from strangers and their well intentions.

What are you?

Calder's typical response, which confused most people, was: "My dad is a human being and my mom is a human being so I guess that makes me a human being." Sometimes the asker might realize their gumption and apologize. Other times, they put Calder at fault.

"Smart ass," one woman accosted him.

It was almost always a woman who asked him. They usually were admiring his handsome skin tone or light brown-to-blondish curls atop his symmetrical head if he had grown it long. Calder had shaved his head last year and the Buddhist monk look made deciphering his ethnicity even harder. But we were all humans and we were all going to hell. For a finite period, naturally. Identity is elusive. Be elusive, Calder thought. Another possible ad slogan. At home, on the snowy sidewalk, and everywhere else he went, his identity was solidified.

Father.

***

Back at home, Zoe cooed and kept her gaze locked on her father. Calder treasured these moments. He interpreted them as a telepathic display of love. His trips to Fairway for groceries, or to the doctor's office, or to the pharmacy had become his sanctuaries. Nothing could disturb him there. Calder would brush the masses to the side like shoveled snow, ignoring them until they melted away. He was performing his beloved duties without any demands. He walked freely. Proud. He stood up and wasn't being fucking lazy. He maneuvered down the street, stroller in hand, with a new sense of purpose. There were no faults, so long as his milk was coming in strong.

Adding to her already hectic schedule, Maren became his de facto press agent. She organized calls and who to contact first. She lined up the *Today* show, *Good Morning America* and *The Andrea Peabody Show*, the nation's hottest daytime talk show. But there was one outlet Calder had to make a special concession for, Maren's childhood friend, Astrid, the host of a local Swedish talk show. In the beginning, Maren relished the celebrity more than Calder, who found it odd. A Swedish TV crew would have the European exclusive. It was a way Maren could help out her old friend, who was now in New York meeting with producers about opportunities in the U.S. Calder objected until he saw Astrid's picture. He hadn't met her before. Astrid had been covering the stateless war in the Middle East on their wedding day.

With the media circling, Calder's privacy all but disappeared. He, the lone cactus washed away in a flash flood, had to find a way to milk this—pun intended—to his advantage. The phenomena had numerous unexpected consequences. First, Maren needed him now more than ever. Sure, she could prepare formula, but her inability to lactate wore on her. Through no controllable fault of her own, a power shift had taken place. He had become the Lord of East 81st Street.

The snow became a distant memory to both baby and daddy, each falling into unconsciousness in a gentle nod of their head—Calder on Sofa Island and Zoe in her bassinet no more than two feet away. Calder reminded Zoe it was time to feed, gently waking her from a four-hour midday slumber. Zoe was such a good baby—rarely crying, to her detriment; discovering the reason proved an adventure. Her desires were simple. Unlike Calder's food, sex and solace, hers were food, sweet father's milk, and no other.

Maren was working. A low-paying job that Calder started to believe was an excuse to get her away from home for a few short hours. Was this the ulterior motive he suspected the night before? Maren felt a slight sense of ease with Calder's gift and seemed to already take advantage of being able to leave Zoe alone with her dad for long stretches. In fact, Maren packed Zoe's go bag that morning, leaving a pouch next to the row of Zoe's books in case of a catastrophic diaper leak. Calder hoped she trusted him.

Calder ignored several more phone calls, media inquires for certain. When he checked the mailbox— he took great pains to leave the apartment door unlocked and wear a full set of clothes—it was empty except for a snowy landscape postcard of the Swedish ice hotel. Maren's friend Astrid had dropped it in the mail a few weeks before, an eerie coincidence dovetailing with her arrival.

The rest of the day passed without incident, meaning nothing bad happened. Zoe still had 10 fingers and 10 toes. Maren returned home to a mountain of Zoe's toys and books on and around Sofa Island. Calder was reprimanded for not cleaning up the mess.

Adult conversion. Calder waded into it on pins and needles, given his tendency to put his foot in his mouth and the great possibility Maren would be drained too.

"Why didn't you answer your phone? I've been trying to reach you all day."

So it began. The rest of the evening deteriorated from there. The Lord of East 81st Street's reign had been short.

Little things added up. The lack of privacy, the use of sex as a weapon or a commodity to be doled out at her prerogative, and most importantly, a lack of sleep. Exhaustion exacerbated arguments over what he thought were silly subjects. Maren had always insulated a temper, a scalding cauldron Calder learned to ignore by cultivating a sense of preternatural calm.

Ignorance is bliss. The meaning of this mantra surely lies in marriage, Calder chuckled, careful not to make it noticeable. He coughed or sniffled to mask the intent. Conflict Avoidance 101. He laughed to himself frequently, a habit many of his close friends commented on, a pattern they recommended he break.

The simmering anger, peppered by harsh comments, came and went. Calder often bore the brunt of Maren's ire because of stupid things he said or did. He had already abdicated the throne. His parapet breached. That night, every small inconvenience seemed a tectonic shift in mood. The layout of their small apartment blocked a clear path to the toilet. The small entry hallway was an obstacle course consisting of the coat rack, a red metal drawer and a wall-mounted shoe rack that took up infinity. And this simple interior design problem begat problems for both of them.

For example, when both of them leapt from the sofa at the exact same moment to use the facilities, Calder was cut off at the pass and angered as he could barely control his bowel—or vowel—movements. He opened his mouth, spoke a coterie of vowels and assorted consonants, and otherwise threw sand into the oil.

"Don't go right now. I gotta go. I can't hold it," he explained.

Who was the baby and who was the parent? Zoe just let it rip. There was never a negotiation for her to use the facilities.

"If you were that urgent, why didn't you go earlier?" Maren retorted while her forehead contorted. She was beyond tired.

The ridiculous timing precipitated another argument, the two-day peace that had been proffered in their current spate of sexual bliss long broken. When she ended her bathroom session earlier than planned, Calder was typing a new slogan idea in his smartphone. She viewed this as being ignored. Insert clever slogan here, he thought.

"You're so dramatic," she needled him further. "I thought you were going to poop in your pants. Are you going to go now? Calder?"

Calder didn't answer. Zoe slept peacefully. Maren stewed.

"Calder? Calder! Don't make me upset."

Calder thought she was already upset and no words would soothe her combination of resentment and fatigue. She had every right to be mad, but Calder felt he wasn't offered the same courtesy. She could be tired, but he couldn't.

Be a man.

He was trying. Breast milk tended to recalibrate any man's point of view, especially when it spewed from his own nipples and had the ability to shoot wildly into his own mouth like a grotesque party trick or titillating—pun intended—carnival act. Calder turned to her and had no expression. He slowly got up and did what needed to be done in the bathroom. He liked to call it the loo, for shits and giggles, knowing full well he was being ridiculous. Maren had a playful side also, but it had been pushed aside and often buried under the necessities of raising a newborn. Calder longed for the smile, the laughs that they used to privately share. They still had sarcastic bouts of good fun; however, the frequency was much less. Both of them doted on Zoe, and showered her with smiles, love and laughter. Zoe always brought her parents' personal dynamic back to the center, away from their dual extremist tendencies, happy or mad, with little middle ground.

Just before midnight, Maren kissed Calder, a spontaneous kiss without explanation, as if it was needed. Calder could get some more marriage mileage out of it. Tender moments often got lost in the Zoe shuffle. Calder volunteered for night duty. Parenting was the apt term. He was being a parent. They were parents now. The notion popped into consciousness in crystal clarity out of the blue sometimes. Wow. He was a dad. Something he aspired to but wasn't sure if it would ever happen. Now that it had, Calder had an instant source of contentment no matter what else was going on in his life. A mountain peak had been conquered. Maren's kiss was a peak too.

Peaks and valleys.

Go climb a mountain.

The next day, a new storm arose.

On his daily subway commute, the bane of Calder's existence was on display for the entire world to see. Calder counted no less than five people in his car reading the *New York Post*.

MILKMAN

In massive block letters, the moniker would never fade. Calder would have to wear it like a favorite suit whether he liked it or not. The photo of him breastfeeding Zoe in the pharmacy was front-page news. The world awaited, and later that day, a siren would call.

He scanned the subway car, making sure nobody noticed him. He got off one station early and walked the rest of the way to the agency. They were working on the final art for a large pizza chain's Super Bowl subway banner ads. In the city, like much of the country, pizza sales skyrocketed during the big game. The chain Big Pizza was touting a two for the price of one promotion on ads throughout the 656 revenue track miles of the New York subway system. Who paid for this stuff? Calder did not want to know. It provided a job and he was proficient, if mostly invisible until today.

His main concern was whether or not the border of the ads should be red or blue. They tested both. Marketing tests, anathema to creativity, were the scourge of the Earth. Calder buried his head in his desk as soon as he got there. He tried too, anyway, which proved rather difficult.

Mathos had already made his mark.

Calder's cubicle looked like a paper mâché sculpture of a milk bottle. Ten to fifteen copies—it was hard to count—of the morning's MILKMAN *Post* littered his desk while the crude milk bottle rose in a twisted floral-like arrangement from the center. Two wadded-up *Posts* rubber-banded together formed the stalk. Mathos led a mocking chorus of cackles as a group of onlookers, including the new junior executive tenant of Calder's old office—a man who looked young enough to pass for a high school student. This was the first time Calder had actually seen him up close. He tried to avoid him as much as he could, not wanting to wallow in the indignity of losing his office to someone so young.

"For he's a jolly good fellow, for he's a jolly good fellow...for he's a jolly good fellow, and nobody can deny," Mathos belted out the popular ditty to the curious onlookers. No one joined him.

Calder would begin to label everyone, friend or foe, as a curious onlooker. He was the latest attraction at the Central Park Zoo. Thankfully, Calder's other colleagues were merciful enough not to participate. Mathos being the boss, there was little anyone could do. The stench of imminent layoffs draped the office. Two weeks earlier, an emergency staff meeting had been called and the word layoff had been discussed. It was possible a larger conglomerate would even absorb the firm. Everyone was on edge except for Calder. He maintained calm because there were two or three other people who had less seniority than him, and that's usually how these things went. He'd already made it through two downsizings since the financial collapse.

Mathos' impromptu town hall meeting at Calder's expense soon dissipated, leaving only the instigator.

"All this time, and you were holding out on me," he began. "I mean this is wild. Your home life must be a mess. I feel for you, buddy."

His home life was a mess, but not for the reason Mathos or any one of the city's 11 million people who had probably seen the *Post's* latest "gotcha" front-page headline.

"Yeah, it's a living hell. But don't quote me on that. I'll know who the source is."

"A little paranoid, I see. A little paranoia never hurt anyone."

You're not being paranoid if they really are out to get you.

Calder played along with his boss's game, telling him what he wanted to hear about a media blitz Thomas Spooner had initiated. Wow. Mathos said it 10 times within two minutes.

"Can I see?"

This is where Calder drew the line. He had reached his limit, his *gendo* point in Japanese. He often scoured old DVD racks for obscure—to most of the American public anyway—Japanese films. It was one of his secret hobbies. A small guilty pleasure that got him out of his own head, and helped him in these type of situations. He imagined a samurai chopping

Mathos head off. They were a salve, the films of Akira Kurosawa and Nagisa Oshima in particular. Takashi Miike was a provocative genius as well. Sometimes he got ad ideas from them. Subversive missives hidden in the copy that only a true cinephile might catch.

The meaning of life is to live.

Calder often thought of Kurosawa's 1952 post World War II film *Ikiru* now that he was in his current media milkman predicament. The film was a personal favorite. A Tokyo bureaucrat realizes he only has six months to live and finally begins to do something with his life. To live, that's what the title meant and that's what Calder had to do. But at what cost to his marriage? Living was what everyone had to do. Maren was no different. Compromise interceded all things.

Happy wife, happy life.

Who made that up? It gave short shrift to the husband. The sexual revolution was over. Women won, and rightfully so, something that only a fool would argue. Calder was no fool, though occasionally a laughing-to-himself clown.

"Calder? Hey man, where did you go? You fell into a trance there."

"Sorry, I was thinking about a new ad campaign for the latest Calvin Klein cologne for men. I can mock something up if you like."

"I've been meaning tell you. We're taking you off that account."

"Why?"

"A conflict of interest."

"What?"

"We've been approached by a major breast pump manufacturer to design an ad campaign around you. They didn't approach you first?"

Calder was speechless. He looked at his cell phone. Thirteen new messages.

"I guess they've been trying to reach you. They want our agency to handle your account. Well, they are signing with us to ensure your cooperation."

"How much are we talking here?"

"Mid six figures to start."

It's cheaper to keep her...

Calder played it close to the vest. He told Mathos he'd get back to him. Maybe they would up the price. He'd been at the ad game long enough to know a hot commodity when he saw it, even if he was said commodity. He would be extra vigilant against blind spots.

He had a lunch date with Astrid Persson awaiting him and hunkered down to ignore everyone suddenly stopping by the cubicle of the latest celebrity. Calder wondered how many minutes of fame remained. Surely he utilized all 15 already. Calder sprung for a cab—despite his ongoing war against their shady meter-gouging practices—because he didn't want to ruin his shoes. Maren purchased his eye-catching pair of brown leather loafers, and they must be treated with respect. He had to push back a little; he was losing his identity. While stuck in traffic on Park Avenue, he reached into his wallet and pulled out Varick's card. The symbol of the bird of prey made sense now. He was soaring, taking his pick of what the land offered. Calder quickly returned the card to its rightful place, hidden out of sight.

Astrid Persson existed in her own world, if she existed at all in Calder's eyes. When Maren jokingly said, "be careful," when he offered to meet her at her hotel for his "interview," he knew she was an antidote to *lacrimony*.

Meeting Astrid was a blessing and a curse. Easy on the eyes, she possessed a single-minded focus, a burning look that said she got whatever she wanted. Her talk show was big in Sweden and syndicated across Scandinavia. Calder had a vague idea of what she looked like from an old university photo Maren thrust before his face as a frame of reference.

Blonde.

What else is new?

There's nothing new under the sun except our products.

She was stereotypically Swedish with blonde locks and blue eyes regaling Calder's line of vision in all their glory. He allowed his mind to wallow in crude thoughts. Every now and then they were necessary, a small defiance he afforded himself to keep what little grip remained of his manhood—at least his furious self-image of what he once had been—like a window looking toward his past incarnation. He giggled out loud before controlling his garish tic.

Astrid didn't walk through the lobby of the St. Regis Hotel so much as glide. She covered the 20 feet between the elevator doors opening and Calder in one fluid motion. Calder, expecting a stunning beauty, was still taken aback by her physical elegance. She belonged on the moon as not to cause unneeded commotion here on Earth. Several businessmen in Italian suits and loafers turned their heads as she passed. Their fixed eyes exposed their lust. Calder was the only man in the room who appeared nonchalant about her presence. This was his first mistake. There would be many others in her regard.

"Calder?"

She knew damn well it was him, but played innocent, displaying a girlish quality that held on tight like a Venus flytrap. Calder was the fly preparing to meet his doom.

"Calder? Is that you? You look so different than your photo."

"Like a new father I hope."

"You fit the part perfectly. The public clamors for a new hero."

She stood six feet two in heels, slightly taller than Calder, and her shimmering blue cocktail dress—at noon no less—radiated seduction. But then, she didn't need the dress for that. Her mischievous eyes and red heels were more than enough. The dress bordered on overkill. She never missed her target. Calder had done his research. She could be tough, but her intelligence made her even more desirable. Seeing her, Calder understood the reason for Maren's admonition to be careful.

"You're gonna be a star. You are already a star," she said, clutching a copy of the *Post*. "And you're much better-looking in person."

"Likewise."

No, he fell into her trap. She didn't need any more compliments. They were a foregone conclusion. Smart, sexy, serious. She gripped all three qualities in equal measure and was determined to get what she wanted: an interview with the Milkman. Calder soon discovered that Astrid was in New York to meet with rival network executives about hosting her own morning show to compete with *The Andrea Peabody Show*. This was another one of Maren's not-so-secret intentions. She was giving Astrid a leg up on the competition, as if there were any. Scoring an interview with Calder, even if it were for the European market, would be a coup.

"I don't know why you didn't want to come upstairs. The room service is bar none the best in the city. The tea is divine."

She was one of those people, Calder thought, fighting the urge to roll his eyes, and chuckle at the same time. Superlatives were her trademark. Something was always "the best," "superior," "second to none." The list was endless.

Then she gave him a hug, the type of embrace reserved for close friends even though this was the first time he had met her. Her beauty gave people the wrong idea no matter how innocuous a conversation or gesture might be.

Calder truly was doomed. Her neck smelled of lavender and vanilla, a perfect blend of some new perfume—one of the freebies she was constantly being sent. Astrid, hesitant to walk in heels in the snow, even curbside to hail a cab, made a command decision to stay and grab lunch at the hotel's in-house eatery/bar. Calder gallantly held out his arm as she sat at a table in a darkened nook of the hotel's King Cole Bar. They reveled in their quiet anonymity. No one would bother them at the St. Regis. The waiter politely placed lunch menus in front of them with a master's touch that neither of them noticed. The Swedish beauty laid out the particulars of her interview before the waiter returned.

She was direct and to the point, Calder appreciated that. No questions would be off limits, she warned, before ordering a midday mimosa. Calder had chamomile tea.

"Such an adventurer," she half-joked.

"Can't. Breastfeeding, remember."

Astrid's focus, worn on her face like a Halloween mask, reminded Calder of his own trance state when he was hatching creative ad ideas or inspiration struck him for a short film or novel idea. His short films had been accepted into a few middling festivals but were more art projects than useful steppingstones to directing commercials. Of course, none of his novels were completed; he'd attempted four, but just the first few chapters. His longtime dream to be a stay-at-home dad and get paid to write novels was stalled in first gear. And with his time even more limited since Zoe's arrival, Calder found time to write only in the wee hours after he had put her back down to sleep following her night feedings. Hunting and pecking with one finger on the darkness was no way to write *War and Peace*, a good title for the state of his marriage—many marriages, he suspected.

Maren swore he had attention deficit disorder. Privately, Calder believed he did have ADD. When Maren got on his nerves, he tuned her out and paid attention to something else—Words With Friends, a book or magazine or an obscure Japanese film.

Never out loud.

Calder kept his thoughts about Astrid within his own head. She knew the affect she had on men, feeding into their hype of what their supposed fantasies of Swedish women should be. As a result, most men failed to win her over. At 36, she was unmarried with no children, something of an anomaly in her small hometown just outside of Stockholm.

She had known Maren since they were 12. They met by happenstance at a Scandinavian girls' summer retreat in Finse. Most of the campers were Norwegian, but there were also a few Swedes and Danes. Maren, a precocious bootlegger, had spilled wine all over Astrid's dress at an unauthorized lodge party late one night. The next afternoon they walked the blue ice of the Hardangerjøkulen glacier, becoming fast friends and then pen pals who saw each other every summer for the next 10 years.

Astrid, despite her outward veneer of complete control, was a very forgiving person. It served her well in her interview process, possessing the ability to get her subjects to open up about topics they never would otherwise. Calder, aware of her abilities, still fell prey. He studied her face, and noticed for the first time a small scar just underneath her lower lip. It made her more human, a mere mortal like the rest of us. Calder smiled; Astrid, taking it as a mild flirtation, smiled back.

"How does it feel to be a trending topic on social media? I hear the hashtag #Milkman is picking up steam. You should get out in front of this thing. Monetize your gift. I hear the vultures are circling. Don't be left out."

"I'm working on it."

"Do tell."

"I thought that's what an interview is for."

"The purpose of this lunch date is to get to know each other better. So we're not reacquainting ourselves for the first time on camera."

"I see. I can wait. I have nothing to hide at this point. It's all out there plain as day."

Calder gestured to the table across the room. An old man was ensconced in his copy of the *Post*. Did people who read the *Post* really stay at the St. Regis? It catered to the lower brow tabloid sensationalism New Yorkers had come to expect.

JACKO ON HIS BACKO

That was Calder's personal favorite *Post* missive of all time, plastered across the top when Michael Jackson collapsed while rehearsing at the Beacon Theater on Broadway on the Upper West Side. Such insensitivity. Such bravado. The city ate it up.

ADD. Attention deficit disorder.

Calder brought his mind back to the present moment. He had wandered for a split second and Astrid, nor anyone else, had no idea. Maren would have sensed his digression though.

Astrid spoke almost non-stop for an hour, delving

into topics Calder had long since forgotten: high school girlfriends, college parties, his upbringing, race—Calder's humanistic tendencies would play better if he talked about racial identity, Astrid said— his favorite schoolteacher and why, eating habits, inspirations, his first crush, etc.

She also asked him about his father. Calder nearly cried, then told her he wouldn't discuss his famous dad until cameras were rolling—it would play better and humanize him more, Calder said.

They ended the meeting on good terms, having worked out the specifics and general tenor of the interview. Tonight, back at her room, they would tape, and a few hours later, it would be on Swedish TV sets and in hotel and cable outlets across Europe, and on the SwedeSet website and all social media platforms of course. Social media, the new king, was an unpleasant must for Calder. He hated social media. The inanities people posted turned Calder completely against it and he was convinced a global privacy backlash was coming. Nonetheless, Astrid longed to be first. Calder and Maren, who later claimed it was solely her idea, were doing Astrid a grand favor. Maren scheduled the *Today* show and *Good Morning America* interviews on subsequent mornings. *60 Minutes* could wait.

When they parted, Calder and Astrid shared an awkward embrace. The smell of her perfume lingered in his cab ride back to the agency. Calder hoped he hadn't unwittingly illuminated areas of his life he wanted, or needed, to keep private. Hell, he was on the front page of the *Post*—obviously a slow news day—and who was he kidding?

Little things.

That night at 4:44 a.m. and with Zoe in a deep slumber, Maren asked him to open the window of their bedroom because the runaway radiator transformed the air in the room into the tropics. However, the window was barred, and more troubling, the 18-degree temperature—it has been below freezing for five straight days—froze the sill. At the weird angle, Calder could not get any leverage and subsequently failed to open the window. It was a microcosm of his marriage. Despite his newfound fame, there would always be something he would fail at mastering. Maren said it was okay, but the trace of disappointment in her voice betrayed her true feelings, as did her body language. She rolled back over and instantly went back to sleep. She had no time for such nonsense. Grin and bear it. Calder felt a tinge of sadness that he hadn't been able to complete a simple task and please his wife. Producing prolactin was his saving grace, and as he fell asleep that night he thought of his father. He wished he could call and talk to him now.

"Did you change her diaper?"

His father's words echoed. He hoped they weren't true.

Dream killer.

Jan. 16

4:47-4:58 a.m. Bottle fed Zoe 113 ml of formula, a good approximation. Changed her diaper (pee). Put lotion on her legs and torso and more moisturizer on her face (on Maren's orders). Put her back to sleep in her new crib at 5:11 a.m. Used the vibration control button and she fell right back asleep. We may have found the Holy Grail.

Despite Calder's burgeoning isolation, he knew parenting was not a solitary journey. They had been mentally ready, if not unprepared, for the changes in lifestyle. In the parenting regard, Calder and Maren were in complete solidarity. The word gained traction when Zoe's future was in the discussion. No video games. No cell phone until she was at least 13, if not older. No watching TV unless it was an educational program. No sleepovers until she was 9 or 10. No snobby private daycares or nursery schools that required an "interview" for admittance. No using the word "no" while she was learning to speak. Neither of them wanted her first word to be "no." Yes was a better word, if used properly.

Positive reinforcement, encouragement of her natural interests, reading, educational field trips to all the Manhattan art museums and the Museum of Natural History, picnics and ice skating in Central Park. These are the philosophies and activities from which they wanted Zoe to be inspired. They wanted to maximize blue-sky days and minimize stubbed toes and other boo boos, parenting or otherwise. But foremost in Calder's mind was his child's health and wellbeing. Protecting Zoe at all costs was daddy's main job like the President's goal of keeping Americans safe. He couldn't help but stare at Zoe while she slept in her crib every night. His eyes peering over the railing must be an unusual view for her, a daddy sunrise consisting of two beaming gray eyes.

The ayes and eyes have it.

6

Thirteen months before Zoe was born, James "Bib" Boyd died of sepsis in a suburban L.A. hospital. He would never meet her in this lifetime, however, Calder liked to think Zoe met him in the womb when her consciousness was forming and she could be in the gateway of the spirit world along with him.

Calder remembered the phone call. The unease, brimming on deep sadness, underscored his mother's voice.

"Your father is sick."

Pernille Boyd—nee Jespersen—was a Stoic in the truest sense. She rarely revealed her emotions. Yet, on that early September morning, in the waning days of summer, her voice revealed everything.

Calder hopped on the first plane he could get. Why hadn't his mother warned him sooner that his father might not recover? He realized later that imminent death is a tough truth to accept. You bargain with God, whether you believe in her or not. Calder always had been a contrarian. God, logically, had to be androgynous at best. Women give birth to new life—at least among the human species.

James Boyd had been admitted two days earlier with what they thought was pneumonia or the flu. In summer? Maybe Calder should have already been on the plane, like he usually was when his mother told him dad wasn't getting any better. Dad had been hospitalized twice for two minor strokes earlier in the year and Calder had flown out immediately. But this unexpected time, though the signs of decline were evident, he had been in Washington, D.C., wearing an official black T-shirt emblazoned "marshal," complete with an image of Dr. Martin Luther King. Interlocked with other T-shirt wearing marshal volunteers, Calder was leading an MLK March down Connecticut Avenue toward the National Mall. He slipped out of the parade without telling anyone a thing and rushed back to New York on the first train that afternoon.

Calder was too proud to accept money from his wife. A last-minute direct flight to LAX from JFK cost more than $1,500, while one with a solitary stop in Phoenix cost just over $600. The direct flight would face him at his father's bedside by noon while the one-stop connecting flight he would get to there by 4:30 p.m. if traffic was light. Approaching rush hour in L.A.? This was unlikely at best. Maren insisted she pay, but Calder was too stubborn and proud to have to be in debt to her. It always made him feel inferior, less responsible as a working adult. Calder was too much in shock to see his fallacious thinking. He heard Maren in his ear, the never-ending dirge that Calder hadn't saved any money while he was single and living in a $510 a month sublet single room apartment, with a tiny sink and bathroom. Partying too much and now she—and by extension Zoe—was paying the price.

Ten minutes before his flight landed in Phoenix, Calder broke down. What an idiot, he thought through the sad lacrimation. He prayed his father would hold on long enough for him to both recognize and speak with his eldest son one last time. Tears stained his gray dress shirt. The male flight attendant looked at him with compassionate eyes.

"Are you okay, sir?"

"My father is about to die." The attendant moved away, unable to find the appropriate words. Calder didn't blame him. He blamed himself.

Why hadn't he taken the earlier flight? How much was the last day of his father's life worth? As the plane began its final approach to Sky Harbor airport, Calder started down at Sun Devil Stadium. He'd seen Public Enemy perform "By The Time I Get To Arizona" on tour with U2 while in college over 20 years earlier. By the time Calder got to Arizona, his father could be dead.

While waiting an hour for his connection to L.A., Calder dreaded seeing any texts or messages on his cell phone. He ignored them, and he was too afraid to call his mother and let him know he had safely arrived in Phoenix.

Calder prayed then, he prayed a lot, and even after Zoe's birth continued to do so. In fact, he prayed for Zoe's health everyday. His father, who rarely went to church, had once told him praying never hurt anyone. Calder remembered telling his father that he thought prayer should be for others and not for one's self, that praying was an act of desperation for believers and unbelievers alike. "Do you really believe that?" His father said, and then implored Calder gently to pray for himself too. "God will answer you."

Though he didn't know it, by the time Calder got to Arizona, his father was still alive. By the time he landed in L.A., rented a car, beat the rush hour traffic and arrived at the hospital, his father was still alive. God had answered his first selfish prayer.

It was 5:15 p.m. when he arrived at the hospital. Upon entering the intensive care wing, Calder saw his Uncle Bob and Aunt Billie, Uncle Davis and Aunt Karen and several of his neighbors. He talked with them briefly—his mind in a disbelieving funk— somehow finding the wherewithal, he thought, to thank them for being there, waiting with his mother. His younger brother was still in route and wouldn't arrive until late that night. Calder had to wait an additional 10 minutes to be at his father's side because he was in the middle of dialysis. The dutiful son could only see his father from about 15 feet away. Not wanting to disturb the privacy of the surrounding critical patients, Calder returned to the waiting area.

When Calder finally grasped his father's hand, he was still partially coherent but deteriorating fast. Tubes everywhere crisscrossed his large torso like a lariat. The silence was what Calder remembered most about his father's last day with his family. The small room—dissected by the adjustable hospital bed and the comings and goings of doctors—suffocated Calder. It seemed as if even the doctors were waiting for his father to die. Helpless. That was the word it felt like. Helpless to help his father. Calder hated this condition, a state of waiting for life to pass you by and death to stop by for a check up. In hindsight, Calder wished he had said more to his father. He told them that he and Maren were starting to try to have a baby. Calder thought a tiny smile creased his father's lips when he said that but there was no certainty.

Calder's mother remained in the waiting area, he surmised to allow her son some private final moments with his father. Calder didn't know she had been at the hospital for five days running until a few days later. Perhaps she didn't want Calder there because it was too demoralizing, seeing your father at his weakest and most vulnerable as your last living memory. Pernille and James had enjoyed a long life together, raising three boys into great young men.

James "Bib" Boyd always regretted the *Sports Illustrated* quote. On the court, he was a fierce competitor but his on court persona was not the sole legacy of a father to a son, nor was it a nickname. He had warned his son on numerous occasions about the "perils of the media." He had a semi-private death room and the doctors tried there best to explain the situation but nobody was at ease. The medical staff tried to make Calder's father comfortable but nothing could be done. He would pass away at 1:11 a.m. Triple ones for a man who was a first-class husband, father and human being, "the type of man they write folk songs about," his eldest sibling, Calder's aunt Denise, would later say at the memorial service.

Calder slept little that night, his mind numb thinking of all the amazing memories, large and small, public and private, which he had shared with his father. He knew he would eulogize his father one day. He just thought he had a little more time.

Time is of the essence.

Calder's youngest brother, Brice, flew in from Orlando and had just made it to the hospital to whisper last words into their father's ear. Calder hoped dad had been cogent enough to hear them. His last few hours he was unconscious, fighting the infection that ravaged his body. Dad had been waiting for all of his sons to arrive, and once they did, he could allow his spirit to leave. After a briefing from the doctors in which exploratory surgery was vetoed, the family had kept vigil over their father in his final hours.

When Maren stepped off the plane the next morning, he was already gone. They embraced near baggage claim as the tears flowed completely unaware of anyone else in the terminal. Calder's dad had been a fixture at the airport, picking up his eldest son, waiting curbside or at the bottom of the last elevator beyond which you could not return to the gate area. Calder wanted to tell her in person.

"Why didn't you tell me?"

"That's not the kind of news to deliver over the phone, I wanted you to have a peaceful flight. There's nothing you could have done."

Calder embraced his wife for a long time, the fluid running down their cheeks like a tributary of the Grand Canyon, fast and sharp. Brice's family would arrive later that morning, so they accompanied him to the car rental place. Brice's wife knew their father had passed, but not his two kids, Zander, the elder, 9, and Emma, 7. Alan had been at the hospital all the previous two days and was exhausted. He returned to his Buena Park hotel to get some urgent rest. The brothers did not say much to each other the next morning at their old family house. Their father's jovial smile and blueberry muffins would not be making an appearance today, and not one of them felt like whipping up a batch.

Dad was always there. He stressed the importance of education over athletics, seeing participation in sports as an important character-building undertaking but more a means to a college scholarship and not the stacked odds of making it as a pro. Bib Boyd's career began in the cocaine and haymaker-throwing era of the NBA a year after the ABA merger. His rookie year was so brilliant, no one could have predicted the trajectory the rest of his career would take.

1977.

The Yankees downed the Dodgers in the World Series and again the following year. That had been young Calder's first major sports disappointment. The second came in 1981 when the Houston Rockets shocked the defending champion L.A. Lakers in a three-game miniseries. But by far, his worst sports moment came in the spring of 1983 when his father broke his ankle and then shocked the sports world by retiring that summer.

Go out on your own terms.

Quit while you're ahead.

Go fly a kite.

Any of the three slogans would have been appropriate. Everyone used slogans whether they wanted to admit to it or not. Calder made them his business and readily admitted that. In death, he applied them to his father's life. They were a means to both ease his mind of the overwhelming sadness and to help him write his father's eulogy.

The problem with Bib Boyd's proclamation, which came in an interview with a small Norwegian paper while he was visiting his wife Pernille's family in Bergen, was that no one believed him. They thought it was one of his brash interview comments. It took a full three days before the Associated Press picked up the story. This was before the instant global tool known as social media. But Bib Boyd was serious. He'd already won a championship as a key role player, and he had interests outside the game. He opened three separate businesses: dry cleaning, pest control and most importantly college preparation classes.

Reading is fundamental.

A mind is a terrible thing to waste.

The eldest Boyd brother, also the most famous, catered to the needs of minorities, primarily to the black community in South-Central where his businesses were located. He was keenly aware of his status as a role model long before Charles Barkley shattered that concept with his groundbreaking ad "I Am Not A Role Model." Calder wished he had thought of an iconic campaign. The commercial had sparked his interest in advertising while he was in college at USC, but it was his father's burden of being a role model that guided Calder most of all.

Being "Dad" was Bib Boyd's greatest legacy. He was always there for his three boys. And this was the main factor causing his retirement. He simply wanted to spend more time with his family. Calder later learned the move had saved his hemorrhaging marriage, which had lost all form and would have been represented as a black shapeless blob by Matisse. He was there for every practice, every track meet—Calder had been something of a high hurdler for a quick minute—every confusing chemistry assignment, every girlfriend woe, and tantamount, every graduation.

Education was something engrained in Bib's mind by his own father, Thatcher Raymond Boyd, one of the few black students at the University of Michigan in the late 1930s. He received his Ph.D. in mathematics and went on to a distinguished career as a writer, educator, scholar and later statesman—he served as U.S. ambassador to Benin in the early 1980s.

Calder had been in his father's life classroom since birth and now the star teacher was gone, the windows to his classroom shuttered. Negative. Calder realized his dad was always with him; in thought, word and deed, he truly was his father's son. Calder ensured this theme was the through line of his eulogy.

Later that morning, about eight hours after his father's silent passing, Reverend Morrison came to the house with his wife and asked each of the boys what memory they had of their father. Calder was initially stumped, but as the eldest, he went last, which gave him time to think. He wanted to find the perfect words for his father, somehow having to be at his best in a moment of deep sorrow. He felt he had to find a deep well to properly honor his father, as if he was on a stage before thousands of people like his father in a crowded basketball arena.

Eleven minutes past one o'clock in the morning, it was an indelible time stamp, a lantern in the dark sadness in Calder's mind. He had witnessed his father's final heave in eerie silence and then shed tears collectively as he embraced his mother and brothers in the hospital room. The room seemed detached from the rest of the universe, floating freely in a protected void. He might be stuck in this moment forever. Not because he wanted to, but because he held onto the sadness as a testament to how much he loved his father. So Calder used that sentiment as he listened to his brother's memories and searched his own, sitting around the dining room table where dad had poked fun, laughed and given each of his sons "The Look"—a sign they were doing something wrong—and where he reigned. Each of the sons had a different experience with their father but all of them were loved equally and loved him deeply in return.

Mom was in no condition to have to worry about a funeral. Calder asked her that afternoon and she said she didn't want a funeral. She wanted a memorial service, but not right away. After pondering this for a few minutes, Calder told her they should at least have a private family and friends gathering at the house. A funeral, with all the NBA well wishers and many others who loved his father, would be an undertaking. That was not Bib Boyd's private style. A big sendoff, which he never had in the NBA, would be expected. Uncle Davis, who could have been a minister if he wanted to, told the family, if that's what their mother wanted to do then that's what they should do. It was hard enough dealing with his father's absence, so Calder did not fault his mother. He completely understood. Though he felt they should do something in the immediate aftermath. Sunday would be best. Mom agreed.

The day his father died had been a Friday. Not a good Friday, but a long one. Each hour seemed like an eternity in much the same way it would in the early weeks of being a father. Gradually, over the course of the subsequent days and weeks, Calder could sanitize his sadness, make it less a tangible tightness in his chest—the result of holding it all in—and more intellectual. Friday night was no different than any other. The perennial 77-degrees-and-sunny weather—with an offshore breeze—of the day gave way to a slight rise in temperature as the warm Santa Ana winds swept into the L.A. Basin at night. Blowing southward from the Mojave Desert north of the metropolitan sprawl, the winds cleaned the city much like a rare September thunderstorm.

The Santa Ana gusts reminded Calder of home,

the nights his father camped out in the backyard with his three boys, of when their mother would join them under the stars barely visible above the city lights, of the time dad built a clubhouse in their backyard for all the neighborhood kids, and when fall gave way to cooler winter nights, his father had taught Calder how to make s'mores.

Alone with his thoughts at 3:13 a.m. Saturday, Calder wrestled with squeezing every memory. For the second night in a row a jag of diligent tears washed away the microscopic dust and shame from his face, the shame of not living up to the standard his father had set. This belief always haunted Calder, whether he knew it or not; most often not, he supposed. Did supposition mean he consciously knew? His thoughts carried him to melancholic places.

Wait, Calder thought, that is not what his father taught him. He had taught him, among many other things, about the classical philosophers, and it was the bedrock of his father's Stoicism that had gotten him through the racial indignities he had suffered growing up in rural Georgia during the turbulent 1960s. The words of the last of the Five Good Emperors, Marcus Aurelius, would serve Calder well that second night of quiet contemplation trying to squeeze every perfect memory into the eulogy he would deliver three months later.

The soul becomes dyed with the color of its thoughts.

Living as a human on Earth, Calder never understood the seeming need of most people to categorize things. Calder was neither black nor white. His parents raised him blind to color. The content of character, to paraphrase MLK, was what they wanted Calder to cultivate. There were no other black people in the family's La Habra Hills neighborhood. When they first got married in 1975—Pernille had been a foreign exchange student at USC—James Boyd and his new bride with milky skin moved to an apartment across the street from the L.A. Memorial Coliseum, not far from the epicenter of the 1965 Watts riots. They were young and felt caught up in the cultural freedoms of L.A. Nobody cared who married who in L.A. For the most part. Secretly, Pernille would tell her son as an adult, many people thought they were just a passing fling, a curiosity that looked great together—their combined skin tones forming a golden glow whenever they walked hand in hand—but would not last.

When James graduated from USC and was drafted by the Lakers, he took Pernille to a tiny wedding chapel on the Las Vegas strip. They had initially met in an art history class. It was one of the "electives" recommended to the basketball players to keep their grades up. The elder Boyd railed against this type of thinking, and only took the class because he had a keen interest in art. Magritte was his favorite, but the class introduced him to the French symbolists. Alphonse Osbert's "Vision," which they had seen on their honeymoon in Paris at the Musee D'Orsay, was a shared favorite. The angelic woman surrounded by a halo of light and flanked on her left by a lone sheep reminded Calder's father of his wife. He had his glowing significant other. And Calder believed this was the origin of his father's on-court brashness. It was a defense mechanism against the whispered cries of you're an Uncle Tom, why couldn't you find a strong black woman, who do you think you are, that followed his father in some circles, NBA and otherwise.

Love will set you free.

Some opponents needled his father incessantly about his blonde wife and on some road trips—Milwaukee and Atlanta were particularly tough—Bib Boyd would counter their unenlightened views by saying, "she's just light-skinned." He and his wife got a kick out of that. They found solace in the Hollywood community and doing charity work in the black community. But his father hated labels. Everyone was a human being. The color of your thoughts was much more important.

Calder adored the photo of their wedding night that hung in the hallway of the family home, his father, handsome in a black suit and tie and his mother in white, looking like Grace Kelly, together about to conquer the world and any negative energy. He awoke again at 4:22 a.m. and on the way to the bathroom stopped and stared at the photo. The happiness jumped from the wall and into Calder's soul, he felt his father's hand and the sadness lifted, transformed into a loving appreciation and thankfulness for the time in this plane of existence he had shared with his father.

A few minutes later, Calder slipped back into bed

alongside Maren. She looked serene in the sliver of light running across her face from the neighbor's lighthouse-challenging porch light on the opposite side of the street. While Maren slept like an astronaut in suspended animation on a deep space mission, Calder could not fall back to sleep. For 10 minutes, he stared hopelessly at the ceiling, grappling with his body to win out over his mind.

Mind over matter.

The battle was no contest. Calder's thoughts filled the power vacuum. The photo of his parents gave him a modicum of peace and wiped clean the thickest layer of sadness. Calder watched Maren as she snored. They were sleeping in the front guest bedroom, which had been his room as a child. The sky blue wooden letters of his name kept their constant vigil, running vertically down the wall opposite their present-day, queen-sized bed where Calder's boyhood bed, and later his brothers' bunk bed, once stood. In the predawn darkness, the letters looked gray. Yet, even so, Calder knew the last letter hung lopsided. His mother took great pains to leave vestiges of his old room intact even after all these years. "I want you to feel like you always have a place to call home," she said.

The window was to the left of the C-A-L-D-E-R display, his bed dutifully erected by his father and feng shui-ed by his mother to maximize the morning sunlight. Dawn was a couple hours away and Calder knew the sun would bathe the room in gentle light even if the curtains were drawn. His mother always knew how to illuminate things to foster greatness.

Other memories—not just of his father and mother—flooded into his skull, swirling thoughts and childhood fears metastasized into adult problems. Calder remembered a pre-dawn argument he had with Maren in this very bed, early in their marriage when they almost split. Thankfully, his parents were away at their beach house in Cambria. However, they might never had argued so grotesquely had their been other people in the house. Calder had put his wife in a smothering bear hug to prevent his anger from escalating any further after Maren had slapped him when he angrily asked how it was possible to have a kid when they didn't have sex. He then left the house and slept at a hotel. The recollection stained his brain like a Rembrandt, with all its dank qualities brought to light. He let it pass, and instead of lingering, scanned the room for something else to focus on, hoping it induced rest.

He peered through the darkness at the sliding white closet doors and the cabinets above them. They still stood silent guard over Calder and his imagination as they had long ago. He could make out shadowy figures in the closet that were coming to get him, and the top right cabinet above the closet remained fidgety, not shutting properly on its hinge to give the appearance of a ghostly hand. Calder bred his imagination here, alone in the dark before his brothers arrived.

He recalled the Great Spanking Incident of 1981, when in his grand genius, he had stuffed a soccer shin guard down his pants to avoid the pain of his mother's hand. He had cursed at her or some other spank-worthy transgression—he couldn't remember—and went into his room to await his fate. The impending doom had been averted when his mother burst into laughter seeing what her son had done to prevent pain. She admired his cleverness.

"Calder? Are you awake?" Maren interjected into his childhood trope.

For a moment, Calder feigned he was asleep, wanting to stay with his jovial boyhood past. But he knew it would have to remain in the murky shadows. He was a grown man with adult concerns, and a wife with adult concerns of her own.

Maren grabbed his hand and squeezed tightly. The pressure released the tension elsewhere in his body and just as he dozed off to sleep he heard her whisper words in his ear: "Let's have a baby."

Calder smiled, like he often involuntarily did in his sleep, though this time he was fully conscious.

"Yes, I think we should."

He draped his right hand over his wife's torso and kissed her.

"I can't sleep," he said.

"Neither can I."

Both of them lay together in silence for a full minute. Each of them hoping they would fall asleep naturally but not wanting to be the one to disturb the descending of unconsciousness if it occurred at that particular instant. Calder moved his arm decisively over Maren's bare breasts, an instinctual move to let her know he was both awake and despite the great absence preoccupying his mind, was willing to give it a try.

"We could try right now, though it seems weird given the circumstances," Maren said, taking the cue that it was okay to speak because sleep was not imminent.

Sex was a good sleep inducer, but it also served as a mind eraser. Calder was about to enter his wife when another voice pierced the darkness.

"Calder? Calder? Are you awake?"

It was his mother. She could not sleep either.

Ten minutes later, the entire family was sitting around the dining room table laughing and crying and prodding and reminiscing about dad. Nobody could sleep, and nobody had to be alone with his or her thoughts either. Pernille made tea—Calder noted it as a sure fire sleep inducer—and the energy exuded in the dawn family festivity brewed an indelible, happy blink in the long count of time. All of them would sleep deeper than they ever had later that morning and well into Saturday afternoon.

Matter finally won a round.

The rest of Saturday passed in a blur, though apparently Calder had called all of his father's siblings, three brothers and one sister. Or maybe he had called them Friday. He couldn't recall such details in the wake of the family's loss.

Friday night's impromptu family cope-fest gave way to Sunday's gathering, an even greater outpouring of love, laughter and commiseration. Secretly, the Sunday wake-but-don't-call-it-wake seemed anticlimactic. The wee hours tea party laughs, jokes, remembrances and cries would stay with Calder much longer. Despite Aunt Billie's gracious help organizing the event, Calder felt on-duty all day Sunday. He made it a point to talk to everyone who came to offer condolences. The koi pond and the putting green in the expansive backyard were magnets for the children. In one of the few private moments that afternoon, Maren and Calder sat on a redwood patio chair and watched his cousins and their kids feed the fish bread crumbs, and as the toddlers tried to hit the ball into the cup with kiddie-size putters. It was endearing. Maren smiled and their decision was solidified.

Uncle Davis and Aunt Gwen brought a bucket of fried chicken from Roscoe's Chicken and Waffles, the tastiest food Calder had eaten in a while. The extended family knew exactly what was needed. In the sorrow, the Bib Boyd branch of the family had forgotten to eat. Everyone asked if there was anything they could do. The day was sunny as hell, and Calder's father would have enjoyed that. Calder imagined a game of pool out in the garage, all of his brothers laughing and drinking beer—those that drank anyway—knocking the cue ball around while trading stories about how many men their sister dated at the same time.

When the laughter and joy of fond memories ended, and the sun vanished somewhere over the Pacific, some 20 miles away, and the guests were gone and after Aunt Billie choreographed the cleaning and trash removal, the silence returned. The ghost of laughter was vanquished, replaced by the tenor of solemnity. Before Uncle Davis left, he pulled Calder, Alan and Brice aside and told them their father wanted them to do things, meaning to accomplish great things, follow their dreams, pursue life's pursuits with zest and reach the zenith of happiness. The boys and their uncle, who looked eerily similar to his father with the same chocolate complexion and white afro, stood in the driveway beneath a luminous full moon as they had after numerous family gatherings—usually at youngest brother Dedrick and Aunt Billie's house in San Dimas. Uncle Davis, three years older, confessed he thought he would be the first of their family to go.

Denise, the oldest, Davis, James, Charles and Dedrick, the youngest, escaped to Southern California —Pasadena to be specific—with their father, Thatcher, and mother, Norma, after a second cross had been burned in their single brick house outside of Macon, two years after James' birth. This was in 1955 when the reprisals of the Supreme Court's Brown vs. the Board of Education decision a year earlier had become unbearable. The second wave of blacks moved to L.A. in the 1940s. Thatcher tried to hold out in the South as long as he could but there were more opportunities on the Pacific. Calder's father rarely spoke of this. His mother knew a little more, but Thatcher and Norma passed well before Calder arrived on the scene. He wished he had met his paternal grandparents, the breadth of wisdom and struggle inspired him even so.

Alan and Brice retired back to the house, having young kids of their own to tend to—Calder was the oldest but the only one without children. They worked in reverse order. But he was both the first—if you counted his failed early marriage—and the last one to get married. Calder listened to his oldest uncle for almost an hour, stories of past marathon domino games and family history that never got old. Uncle Davis was a veritable encyclopedia of family lore. They talked perhaps because they thought James would rise up from the trimmed Bermuda grass resurrected before their eyes on the front yard or maybe descend from the heavens above, reborn. But it had to end sometime and Aunt Gwen asked Uncle Davis if he was ready to go. She worried about him driving on the freeway at night.

Uncle Davis and Aunt Gwen got into their Lexus and before they headed back toward L.A. proper—they lived not far from LAX off the 405—Calder's uncle uttered a final uplifting truth. He rolled down the window and handed Calder a brimming envelope. There was no money inside but the paper was worn and under great stress.

"It's a letter your father wrote to you on the night you were born," Uncle Davis said. "He wanted you to read it when you had your first child. He made me keep a copy just in case. I guess it's just in case time."

And with that the Lexus escaped into the night.

7

Amnesia was the key to a healthy marriage. If there were no memories, there would be no angst, or viral bouts of anger or isolation based on remembrances or grudges. Each half of the couple would constantly be new to the other and would have less reason to argue, their brain spending the greater part of its time manufacturing a portrait of their significant other.

It was also a key coping mechanism for the fact Calder was a lactating male. Worrying if Zoe received enough nutrients, or was eating too much, weighed at him constantly like an errant insect bite that migrated all over his body but would never heal. He didn't have a support group. He couldn't show up at the 92nd Street Y and sit in a room surrounded by other men and commiserate, a middleman moderating the middling complaints.

Yeah, my nipples are chafed too.

What's the best solution to a clogged duct?

How does your wife feel about a key mommy role bring pre-empted by a man?

This last hypothetical question wasn't a problem in his marriage. Or so Calder believed. Maren started going out of the house more and more as her husband's responsibilities grew. Sometimes she wasn't home when Calder returned home from work. His day at the office had been strangely quiet after Mathos' mention of lucrative ad opportunities utilizing Calder's newfound notoriety. He hadn't been assigned any new clients in a week, but had been kept busy meeting deadlines on several smaller projects—an indie film one-sheet, a subway ad for an infamously comical skin specialist, brainstorming new logos ideas for a small bank about to go under but defiantly refusing to admit it and another web banner campaign.

When he arrived home to prepare for his exclusive interview with Astrid, nobody was home. A large spilled milk stain on Sofa Island remained as possible evidence that Maren was feeling iced out. She left the door to the apartment unlocked, the toilet filled with a strand of tissue paper she forgot to flush and one of Zoe's drawers overstuffed and at its breaking point. She was notorious for breaking drawers, each one a victim of too many clothes, too many shoes or too many things that should have been thrown away long ago, especially since they had moved into an apartment three times smaller than their previous slumlord-owned, yet rent-controlled apartment in Greenpoint—the northernmost crag of Brooklyn just over the Pulaski Bridge from Queens.

Maren had trusted her husband to find a new apartment, and allowed him to see the apartments and make the decision at his discretion. And now, while they lived in a primo location, they were in a perpetual state of tripping over each other. Some of their marital strife could be pinpointed to this decision. Maren often expressed her anger at having to downsize her considerable shoe holdings. Calder finally got around to installing a wall-mounted shoe rack but it had collapsed under the weight of countless shoes Maren never wore though couldn't part with. In actuality, Calder had installed it improperly.

Maren's text vibrated in Calder's left front pocket. *Since u haven't gone shopping, we're at Fairway.*

Calder sprung into action. He didn't know how much time he would have before Hurricane Maren— his unspoken pet name—would return and ask him to do something that would delay his departure. He was squeezing in an early shift at the Kenilworth Theater, working in the grand lobby at *Illusions of Grandeur*, the new magic review musical, before meeting Astrid at her room in the St. Regis for the interview. He got $56.53 per show regardless of whether he was there just for the walk-in or had to stay for the whole show. Calder picked up the very flexible second job after the ugly argument about money they had had at his parents' house five years ago.

Tonight he only had to be at the theater until about 8:15 p.m. Then he would walk up 10 blocks and two avenues over to the St. Regis. Maren seemed to like the job at first but during pregnancy, and even more since Zoe's world premiere into existence, it caused a meandering rift.

Calder took a quick shower and changed into the very trim black Zara suit, brown belt and brown shoes Maren had bought him. He splashed on a dash of cologne. Did he think he was going to get laid? Maren would see right through it. He quickly splashed water over his neck to rid himself of the scent.

When Maren returned the first words out of her mouth were: "You have no idea what it's like to be left alone with a fussy baby do you? It's easy for you to run off to work every day. You should be the one at home since my breast milk isn't coming in. Fresh breast milk is much better than frozen, reheated milk, no? Where are you going now?"

"Illusions of Grandeur."

You didn't tell me you were going. I told you to take tonight off for the interview."

"I'm going there afterward. I'm early tonight."

Maren took Zoe out of her carrier and gently laid her down on the sofa. Calder was ensconced in the restroom, already running late, and they were having a back and forth chat through the bathroom door.

"You're making my friend wait way later for a lousy fifty bucks?"

Fifty-six, Calder thought.

Zoe opened the door.

"Can you watch Zoe for a second? I gotta pee."

"I gotta go!"

Any languishing good will Calder built up was surely gone now. He barged past Maren and picked up Zoe. Calder eyed the cable box clock. He would be sent home unpaid if he didn't make it by 7:10 p.m. sharp. As soon as Maren exited the bathroom, Calder handed Zoe back to her.

Bobbing Zoe in her arms, Maren whispered—loud enough for Calder to hear—into her daughter's ear.

"You're daddy's grumpy because he's going to work on Broadway for a lousy $50 instead of spending time at home with his family. He's selfish."

Maren was right. He was grumpy. He was grumpy because he would never use Little Zoe as a sounding board for their adult problems. He never complained to Zoe.

Your mom expects daddy to do more stuff around the house but belittles him so much that he's being lazy that he doesn't feel particularly happy to oblige her. Her abrasiveness can be grating, Zoe. Calder's internal rebuttal passed without external expression.

Selfish?

The interview with Astrid had been Maren's idea.

"Can you please take out the trash. You were supposed to do it this morning."

"I have to go now."

Before the argument broke out, Calder kissed Zoe's forehead and escaped.

***

The illusions passed uneventfully and Calder rushed through Times Square at a brisk pace. There were four Cookie Monster characters within 30 feet of each other, two Woodys and four Spidermen. One Minnie Mouse had her head off and was taking a drag on a cigarette in the nook outside the theater.

He arrived two minutes late for his scheduled interview. The camera and lights were already set up. A tech assistant attached a wireless microphone to Calder's jacket. There was no need to hide the black wires because they were camouflaged against his black attire. Astrid was a totally different person. Dressed in a formal business suit that did not accentuate her shapely torso and long legs, she dove right into the questioning.

"Is your wife cheating on you?"

Calder was taken aback.

"She makes more money than you and is the personification of the career woman, your situation is becoming increasingly common as women become the breadwinners," Astrid rifled through he setup. "But your situation is unique. You can lactate. How does all of this make you feel?"

Astrid stared long and hard at Calder. This was going to be a long 15 minutes. He didn't remember anything he said to Astrid. If there was any hint of sexual attraction in their lunch meeting, it vanished during the actual on-camera interview. Calder recognized it for the trap that it was. He had let his guard down even though she had essentially warned him not to. Her questions were hard and direct, peppered with words like "honesty," "deception" and "deprivation"—nothing of the sort of what tree would you be. It was like he had been blindsided by the fluffer on a porn set.

Afterward, however, Astrid slipped right back into vixen mode, trying to utilize her beauty—in Calder's opinion—and inviting him to lunch in a few days for a follow-up print interview. She also mentioned something about art. But he was reeling from his inability to fathom what had just transpired. From time to time, Astrid wrote freelance articles for in-flight magazines and occasionally the *New York Times Magazine*. He said he would get back to her about any follow-up interviews. He treaded lightly. Beauty and the devil were one and the same.

Why couldn't he remember his basic answers? He recalled telling her how he and Maren had met, but little else. Calder's adult ADD was nothing clinically diagnosed—though even he thought he suffered from it, or mild Asperger's—but reared itself in crude notions every now and then. Who knows what nonsense he might have loose lipped about the internal workings of his marriage. Calder's working theory was that everyone in New York City suffered from Asperger's in some way, shape or form, what with all the stimulation, sexual, electronic and hydroponic.

Nobody was going to see Astrid's interview anyway. Nobody in America that is. It was embargoed until *The Andrea Peabody Show* aired its taped interview tomorrow at 3 p.m. on the East Coast. Calder deduced he had one more night of freedom. SwedeSet wasn't going to air until the wee hours on a few pirated stations at 3 a.m. Eastern time. If he said anything to embarrass himself, who cared? Europeans were more lenient and open-minded, lacking the Puritanical impulses of the U.S., their younger sibling nation. Recalibration would soon follow. Affairs? Everyone had them. The Ten

Commandments were merely guidelines.

There is no hell but the one created in the mind, Calder had forgotten his own personal slogan.

Maren emerged from their bedroom like a specter. Calder didn't notice her svelte figure against the deeper darkness further into the room, the void where they had once shared a bed and occasionally made love. He loved her. The moonlight emanating through the living room blinds highlighted her hips as she walked toward him in addition to crystallizing his wayward thoughts.

Zoe was propped up in his arms on a nursing pillow, suctioning milk from her father's left nipple. The sucking sound resonated throughout the apartment in tiny waves that seemed never-ending.

"Great job," Maren said, placing her hand on Calder's knee in the dim shadows. She sat next to him on Sofa Island.

Calder knew she was talking about taking care of Zoe, not his Swedish TV interview. It was in her intonation, lacking any trace of sarcasm. The compliment washed over him like a Gatorade bath in the middle of the Sahara. It was nice to hear; he also couldn't remember the last time she had dazzled him unexpectedly this way.

Like a robot, Maren reached beneath the TV console and dazzled Calder with the new screen saver on the shared "family" computer. She made a few clicks and keystrokes. They were soon looking at a "leaked" version of Astrid's interview earlier that night. Embargo my ass. Astrid was the prime suspect.

"Was it as bad as I now know for certain it was?"

"Worse," Maren answered. "See for yourself."

Go big or don't come at all.

"You're a great father you know."

"You're a great... "

Maren placed the laptop on the edge of Sofa Island, and put her fingers over his lips. Calder kissed them on instinct, an electrical signal wired deep inside his cerebral cortex. Maren did not move her fingers away. Nor did she spoil the fantasy blooming in Calder's head by saying he had no chance. The ambience—the early morning quiet, the sound of the radiator hissing and the white noise of the minimal traffic outside their window on Third Avenue—reminded him of the night Zoe was born. The quietude that rainy early morning when they went to the hospital created an aura of solitude as if he and Maren were the only two souls on the planet.

Tonight, while Zoe slept, they both felt like the only person on a planet. Just not Earth. Mars. The cold and remoteness of their relationship lay bare. Their personal isolation was the real problem. Each of them clung to a paradigm of singlehood and freedom that no longer existed. Sacrifices had to be drafted, executed and adhered to. Calder did not know how to guide his space probe to a safe landing on any surface. And in the vacuum of space between them, he felt obligated to fill it with words when a mere touch, "skinn-ship" as Maren called it using the Norse word.

"I just want you to listen."

"Okay. We never really talked about it."

Maren ignored Calder's foray into colder planetary waters. The "it" remained submerged, yet visible and lurking close to the surface. Any rays of forgiving light did not refract *it* into a million smaller strands that could disappear and be forgotten. Outside, Calder noticed the musical cadence of freezing rain as it began to bombard the windowpanes.

"You're not listening. Listen, like we did on that black sand beach in Iceland, with the waves crashing as we waded into the moonlit surf."

The memory stirred another instinctual move. Calder intertwined Maren's right leg between his. He gripped her right hand tightly with his right hand as he shifted Zoe to the nook of his left arm. He had to make an effort, Sisyphean or not.

"I don't care what you said tonight. Or what you'll say tomorrow," Maren said. "As long as it's the truth." Her tone was that of a judge commuting a sentence.

"How do you know what I said or did? Or what I will say tomorrow?"

Maren clicked her laptop a few times and a grainy video clip of Calder's interview with Astrid opened in another browser. She fast-forwarded through the approximately six-minute clip to the 4:42 mark.

"Wait, I want to hear what I said. Those lights really had an effect on me."

"Stop making excuses. You know what you said. Or at least what you did. Own it," Maren said as she returned her hands to Calder's knee. "Shrewd move. Brilliant. Tomorrow you're going to be an Internet sensation, a meme, a viral video or whatever you want to call it. Well played, sir. Well played."

"I wasn't acting."

"Turn the sound up," she said.

The pirated image had been shot with a smartphone. One of the two tech guys in Astrid's St. Regis room was not going to be employed past tomorrow. He had posted it online and then linked it to his own audio and music website, trying to drive traffic to his site.

Sell, sell, sell. Buy, buy, buy.

They might have been Swedish, and wallowing in their universal health care, but they had capitalism down cold.

Pun intended.

The video was taken during the last five minutes of the segment when Astrid first asked about the state of his marriage to her friend, and then segued into asking Calder directly why he had stayed with his wife knowing damn well that she had had an affair. Mr. X, she called him. The shaky video, shot surreptitiously using a strategically place mirror, framed Calder in the center of the aspect ratio, sitting in a regal leather-backed chair while Astrid crossed and uncrossed her legs, the ones that popped out of the bottom of her business suit.

"Why did you stay?" Calder started to remember now. The reason he had forgotten soon revealed itself. Calder's head bobbed a few times, unnoticeable the initial time but then like he was bobbing for apples. On the fourth bob, Calder's head slowly drooped upward and froze. He was fast asleep.

The two techs and Astrid nearly ruined the shot by each excitedly making the universal sign for continuing to roll by twirling their index fingers and by extension their hands in the air repeatedly. The longer he dozed off the better. This was a sure fire viral hit.

As the last 18 seconds of the clip wound down, the Swedish techie zoomed in and in a fortuitous instant caught from a single tear oozing from Calder's right eye, and streaming down his cheekbone.

"You're going to be a star."

How do you like them apples?

Neither Maren, nor Calder spoke for nearly a full minute. Calder rose from Sofa Island, placed Zoe in her mobile crib nearby, and then opened the blinds. Ice half an inch thick covered the window, blurring the light entering the room from the streetlamp. Calder didn't need to wait until Groundhog Day to have Punxsutawney Phil tell him how much longer winter was going to last. It was going to be brutal and he would revel in it. He stared blankly through the ice into the wintry void. They embodied the last couple on Earth at the dawn of a new Ice Age. How did the poem go? Surely the world would end in ice. Sorry Dante. There's some work to do.

A short time later, though time was relative—it stretched and turned inward on itself in a continued Mobius effect like it at had when Calder was a newbie father tending to Zoe—he returned to Sofa Island. A few more silent moments expired. The near darkness enveloped them like an old friend. Maren finally turned to her husband in the darkness, simultaneously grabbing his right knee as if there were no tomorrow.

"Do you think we can survive?"

Calder didn't answer his wife immediately. He drowned in his synapses, trying to make connections and take control of his hectic life.

What would Marcus Aurelius do?

Sleep might be tops on the list. Tomorrow, Calder still had three morning interviews lined up before heading to the agency. First, the *Today* show, then he would whisk away in a car to *Good Morning America*, near the Kenilworth Theater in Times Square, and lastly from 9 to 10 a.m., he would be ensconced on a soundstage for America's most famous daytime talk show, *The Andrea Peabody Show*.

"How many views has this video had?"

Maren peered into her browser, the light from the computer illuminated their faces making them resemble ghosts.

"25,000, and that's just in two hours. It's already on YouTube, so it'll be 50,000 easy by the start of the workday tomorrow when people truly wake up after their morning joe and spend their first hour on the clock wasting their company's time by trading salacious emails."

Calder laughed. It was a meaty laugh, stentorian in nature, a combination of release and genuine amusement.

"25,000 and counting..." Calder trailed off.

Milkman.

Finally possessing a nickname of his own, Calder wished he could talk to his father right now more than ever. They had had a particularly close relationship, each of the sons did, but theirs was a peculiar bond—in the sense that its grandiosity couldn't be defined.

They often spent long hours on the phone talking about sports, which served as conduit to expounding on a list of wide-ranging topics: chemistry, time travel, bull riding—dad rooted for the bull—existence, sand castles, evolution, politics, the vagaries of religion, National Parks, and of course, the Lakers. Every Sunday, like clockwork, they would also talk about how they did in the weekly NFL office pool. Invariably, they discussed their inability to correctly pick a Cincinnati Bengals game.

His father rarely dispensed advice. He would offer indirect guidance, weighing the pros and cons, and let his son come to his own conclusion. James Boyd had impeccable logic, and Calder's nephew Zander, Brice's son, referred to him as an "alien teacher," a special human who could teach even an advanced civilization a thing or two.

In the absence of being able to speak to the man with the prescient "Bib" nickname—almost foretelling his son's future lactation gift—Calder fell back on old conversations. And one in particular prowled in the forefront of his memory.

In the midst of the grueling and ugly argument with his wife, Calder recorded the immediate aftermath of Maren's response to her husband's comment about how the hell was she going to get pregnant if they weren't having sex—an open-fisted punch-slap—and sent the audio clip to his father's cell phone in case their were any future legal proceedings.

About six months after the incident, when his son's relationship with his wife had improved and deepened, and they had erased the transgression from their daily thinking, dad defused the entire episode by succinctly asking: "Do I need to keep this?"

The answer was clearly no.

With the public disclosure of infidelity looming, the old argument resurfaced like a revenant claiming old territory. But his father's words again kept the specter on the bench.

"Calder, we never thought we'd have to worry about you. You know right from wrong. You know what to do."

Dad was right. He was always right.

Root for the bull.

Mom was right there too. He would call her tomorrow. She was a wise sage who complimented Calder's father every step of the way for nearly 50 years.

Maren, accustomed to these long internal soliloquies, rubbed her fingers across Calder's cheeks. "I need to get some sleep."

"What about me?"

"The more haggard and sleepless you look in your interviews tomorrow, the more America will empathize with you. Fuck Sweden. This video can work in your favor. Tell the make-up artist not to put on too much makeup. In fact, refuse makeup. Trust me on this."

Maren closed the laptop and the dimness reclaimed their faces. Calder smiled. Maren had broken his trust before, but she was dead right. He remembered a glimpse of why he has fallen in love with her. Her hand gracefully slid away from his knee and disappeared into the void. She retired to the bedroom with the door all but completely shut.

Calder kissed Zoe's forehead, softer than a butterfly, and then returned to Sofa Island, the bedroom door still slightly ajar. Though he had to wake up in two hours, per the norm, Calder could not fall back asleep easily. His insomnia was not a condition; it was a permanent appendage. He rose from Sofa Island and reclaimed the laptop. Calder popped open a browser and watched the stealthy interview video over and over until it lulled him to sleep. Before he went to sleep, Zoe stirred. She was thirsty and father and his half a million-dollar breasts went into action. He finished hurriedly, wary a spontaneous dozing off might injure Zoe. He placed her back in her crib protectorate. Calder set the video on loop and he heard Astrid's voice of astonishment in the waning bob fest over and over. He never noticed his own reenactment. Life imitating life, Calder thought, before unconsciousness cradled him.

Calder dozed on Sofa Island with the scent of Astrid's perfume wafting into his dreams. Two hours later, Zoe made sure he stayed honest, piercing the peace with her cries after a nightmare.

"Why don't you feed her?"

Maren's bedroom quarterbacking lent a police

procedural tone to the quietude, sucking a small part out of Calder's joy of being a lactating human, male father.

He was already on the case, thank you.

8

Jan. 18

4:27-4:37 a.m. Bottle fed Zoe 125 ml of pumped breast milk. Changed her diaper (pee). Put lotion on her legs and moisturizer on her cheeks (her face looks much better with only a little redness). Put her back to bed in her crib at 4:54 a.m. She fell back asleep at about 5 a.m. At 5:05 a.m. the pitter patter of large snowflakes kept me awake. The third dusting this week. Only 2 inches this time the weatherman says. Stayed up and stared at the ceiling....listening to

His thoughts abruptly ended. Calder looked at his smartphone feeding notes later that morning, when he awoke, and laughed, knowing he had dozed off without finishing his thought: listening to the sound of falling snow.

The Lincoln town car driver honked the horn one more time. Miraculously, Zoe remained placid. The snow, making the window impossible to see through, changed over to ice sometime after 5 a.m. That morning, a one-inch layer of ice coated the city. The worst icing event in over 50 years, the weatherman said. Weather. What a racket. It was the only job where you can be wrong most of the time and still keep it. Nevertheless the winter scene was beautiful. The trees glistened with an apocalyptic sheen. And then it began to snow. Again.

Calder knew a momentous day was in store.

When he left their apartment, Zoe was crying—the honking town car won—and Maren had a tough time calming her. A quick latching session ended the drama. Smartly, Calder was ready to leave an hour early to allow for this type of contingency. A contagious smile creased both of Calder's ladies' faces, creating an atmosphere of content twinkle. Calder felt confident heading to his string of morning interviews. The falling snow conveyed peace as it touched his cheeks. He might have been the only one in the city enjoying it, most of the madding crowd had already grown weary of the snow and it wasn't even February, typically the city's snowiest month.

The *Today* show interview passed without incident. They questioned, but honored, Calder's request for no makeup. He asked the Japanese make-up artist if she would still be paid. She would, she assured him. To a certain degree, the set's ring of hot lights masked the circles under his eyes, though not his overall lethargy.

A producer wanted Maren and Zoe to appear with Calder, but Maren nixed that idea. Her husband agreed on this point. It was too soon for their little girl to be made an object of the tabloid and mainstream press. Not to mention the dangers of carrying a newborn into the Antarctic ice shelf strangling the city.

The *Today* co-hosts jovial groupthink won the day and they didn't dwell on the racier details, only asking a sideways question on the context of it not being easy to raise a child no matter what the status of the interpersonal bond between mother and father. Throughout the four-minute segment, Calder rubbed his eyes often, another of Maren's suggestions to emphasize and deepen empathy for the embattled dad. The host put her hand on his knee and moved in when she asked about his father and his influence on being a parent of his own. Calder did not tell her about the letter. Some things should be kept private. Maybe his relationship with his wife was one of them. Though he did not recalibrate, it was the right thing to do. He'd kept so many things inside. Getting them off his chest lightened his mood and he could feel the hurt fall away like peeled layers of an onion.

By 8 a.m.—given the viral sleeping and crying video—he'd been a feature in the first hour and was on his way across town to the set of *Good Morning America*. It too passed by quickly. They focused more on the medical aspects of his condition, talking about his pituitary gland function and the overproduction of prolactin. The host recommended he get checked out for a possible tumor. It was then that Calder remembered Dr. West's insistence on an

MRI. Nothing abnormal had shown up, or had it? Calder assured the hosts that he felt fine and that he had declined numerous offers to participate in any medical testing to study his condition. Several universities' had already left messages on his work voicemail imploring him. He also discussed the logistics of his growing infamy, how he couldn't receive new messages because his voicemail was full.

Generally speaking, it went well. Between the two morning shows, he had picked up 500,000 new social media followers. Later that day, he shut down his photo sharing accounts. He wanted to protect his family—to speak nothing of himself—not wanting to give anyone so inclined the ability to track his whereabouts. The paparazzi would lose interest naturally in a week or so he hoped. Maybe some Hollywood star would overdose, and they would shift their prying lenses elsewhere.

Where Astrid Persson was an outsider viewed with scorn, Andrea Peabody was America's Sweetheart. A billion-dollar media empire built from scratch, a loyal audience beamed into 15 million households each weekday and an adoring public, she had it all. Growing up on Chicago's South Side, Andrea—she went by one name—rose to prominence from being the daughter of a local liquor store owner gunned down in an all-too-common flurry of street violence to the CEO of a global media empire, sometime actress and political kingmaker. Standing no taller than five feet with dark chocolate skin and her trademark black-rimmed glasses—a whole cottage industry in and of themselves—her questions paled in comparison to Astrid's. Astrid was the rising villain in the whole affair du lactation. Andrea, her name writ large above the most famous couch in the U.S., if not the world, Calder had the urge to jump up and down on it when he first saw it.

Andrea's questions were tough and probing, but presented with empathy, a skill Astrid faked at the St. Regis and bludgeoned on air.

Andrea: How has this newfound skill affected your wife?

Calder: First, my wife has been very supportive. *(Maren's mouth dropped agape and a tear ran down her face, she later told him)* **I think anytime a child comes into the home there is nothing but joy. The first few weeks are tough on a new mom but luckily her mother flew in from Norway and helped us through the first month. Then my mom came for a week, so having them around was a huge help.**

Andrea: How do you feel?

Calder: A woman on my way to the subway, a total stranger, said I was beaming and had that glow of new fatherhood. I guess that's how I feel.

Andrea: What has been the biggest adjustment in your life other than Zoe?

Calder: The feeling that I'm always being watched. That people are going to follow me home. I take circuitous routes and sometimes get off the subway one or two

stations early and walk the rest of the way home.

Andrea: Given your circumstances, would you feel you had the green light to sleep with another woman?

Calder: (laughs) Or a man.

Andrea: Or a man, yes.

Be brief. Be brief and move on.

Calder: While I love women, I love my wife very much.

Why did he have to say it publicly if it was true? Who was he trying to convince? Himself?

Andrea: What are your views on marriage? You seem like a "til death do us part" kind of guy.

Calder: I'm a firm believer that you make your own reality. If you think marriage is a prison, then it is for you. If marriage is a commitment, then it is for you. If you view marriage as a lifelong partnership, based on friendship and forgiveness, then that's what it is. If you feel marriage is a business arrangement, so be it. It can be all, some or none of these things. It's kind of like a philosophy on life. If you think it's absurd, and strange that we even exist, and that no matter how hard you try, there can be no meaning found in it, then that's your paradigm. You put meaning into your life, a child's love for their favorite toy puts meaning into that toy. Your thoughts are the only thing you can really control. Ultimately, marriage is what you think or make of it. The trick is being on the same wavelength as your partner. And therein lies the rub.

Andrea: How has your lactation ability given you a new perspective on what women go through? Or has it?

Calder: It's definitely given me a new appreciation for the body changes women endure during pregnancy. I am very thankful and in awe that my wife, Maren, has given birth to such a beautiful daughter who gives us so much joy and love every day.

Andrea: Do you think men will one day be able to give birth?

Calder: I don't know. I hope so. I think it's something every man and Everyman, in the metaphorical sense, should try. I know I'd love to do it. I'm sure it would be very difficult, and it would probably require a nine-month hospital stay, right? There's women's lib, why not men's lib? If both men and women gave birth, I think that would be the best situation, the best of both worlds. And each gender would have a better ability to empathize with the other one. Who knows maybe one day it will happen. We are still evolving you know.

After *The Andrea Peabody Show* aired that afternoon, Calder Boyd became the No. 1 trending topic on social media. A new discussion on gender spread like napalm around the planet. Interview requests flooded his cell phone and Calder had to disconnect his number to have any sanity. He was totally unprepared for this level of fame.

When he arrived at the ad agency, it was half past eleven. Nobody seemed to notice the morning interviews. In reality, his colleagues were too scared to mention it and steered clear of him, not wanting to come fact-to-face with him in the men's room or the pantry when they were fetching coffee or the morning pastries that were always there. Today, though, the pastries—the cheese Danish was his favorite—weren't there. And that was Calder's first subtle clue, like the reluctant high five that had begun his lactation odyssey.

The hammer came down later that morning, two minutes before noon, when Mathos called Calder into his office. Calder's Greek, almost playground consort closed the door.

"That's not a good sign," Calder said ominously.

He was right.

You've become a distraction.

We need to cut some staff to better position ourselves for the future.

It's a conflict of interest.

Last one in, first one out.

I'm selling the firm.

We're being absorbed by a larger as conglomerate.

No hard feelings.

It's nothing personal.

The details of your severance pay are in this packet.

Calder was not surprised. There had been whispers of a shuffling of the ad deck for almost a year. He had been on high alert since being switched to a cubicle. Maybe it was for the best. His benefits and pay would extend for eight months, a rather generous sum more than he had actually earned in his 10-year stint.

This was a blessing in disguise. Calder wished he could pick up his cell and talk to his father right now. He was in desperate need of some guidance. He felt the things he once cherished vanishing like the paint chips under the windowsill.

Whereas in the silent minority of stay at home dads, stay at home moms, lonely housewives and little old ladies Calder was an object of pride, curiosity, worship, desire and wish fulfillment, his burgeoning status created no special treatment at home.

"You finish your job eighty percent. You always leave something out," Maren scolded him. "You have to rinse the bottle out right away."

Calder was on the verge of snapping. He still had not told his wife about work developments, more specifically the fact he had been laid off along with the entire staff. Two weeks later, the entire firm went belly up. Mathos's blustery talk of a breast pump campaign had been a lie. It wasn't the first time Calder had been lied to, nor would it be the last.

That night the temperature plunged to 10 degrees. Too cold to snow. Yet the season's snow accumulation and ice held their grip on the city streets, their frozen fingers a nemesis to safe pedestrian maneuvering among the canyons of glass and steel and the smaller gullies of brownstones and condominiums. Calder often found himself staring in awe at the winter elements. Because he was raised in L.A., the snow fascinated him even though this was his 20th winter in the city.

Jan. 19

6:38-6:58 a.m. Bottle fed Zoe 85 ml of stored breast milk. She pushed it away and was fussy. Changed her diaper (lots of pee). Put moisturizer on her cheeks and lotion on her legs and torso. Burped her. Put her back in her crib but she wouldn't go back to sleep. Kept curling up on her side. About 7:40 a.m. smelled poo. Changed her diaper again (big poo and she started peeing in the middle of the change). Used two new diapers. Changed her clothes (put lotion all over her body) and the changing towel. Burped her again. Put her back to sleep at 8 a.m. with her head facing the way we wanted (looking to her right, left as you look at her).

9

The text popped up on his cracked iPhone at 6:12 a.m. on a late August morning after a heat-abating thunderstorm. He had been up, wondering why the hell his wife hadn't come home the night before—blinding himself to the harsh facts he didn't want to really delve into.

Ignorance is not bliss. Knowledge isn't either.

It came from a New Hampshire area code. Calder had never been to the Granite State. But his wife certainly had. *Live free or die.*

> **Aug. 12, 6:12 a.m.**
> *calder*
> *you don't know me and I don't know you but you deserve to know that I slept with Maren for the last year and a half or so. I just found out about you this morning, and kicked her out of my place*

Numbness, a feeling Calder had escaped since the abrupt collapse of his brief first marriage, swarmed around his head at the head of the bed like the stench of a rotting corpse. If he was being honest, he would admit to a single tear staining his pillow. A bloody tear Calder imagined as a way to cope with the final confirmation. Mr. X didn't even have the decency to capitalize his name. Calder kept the torpid information that he had confirmation from Maren. He had to use the knowledge to his advantage. What if he filed for divorce today? Would that give him the upper hand in any future legal proceedings?

It's cheaper to keep her.

Calder could not afford a divorce right now. He wanted children. What would his future prospects be? He had no inclination to have to meet someone new. Maybe he was being fucking lazy. He truly was a victim of his own hubris and the Internet age. The guy who was fucking his on-the-verge-of-total-estrangement wife had informed him via text message. Text. Fucking. Message.

Thanks a lot asshole. How's that for a slogan?

Calder had suspected since early June, perhaps earlier—his wife's meetings with clients that went well after midnight. Their relationship had deteriorated so much that winter and spring, that Calder used this free time to go out drinking with friends without hearing any complaints from his still-wife. What were they doing?

By late June, he had been certain of his wife's extracurricular activity. His anger so complete that it turned to apathy and then to revenge. He decided to do whatever he wanted for a few months. The aftermath reeked.

That day at work, Calder failed to get much done. He contemplated hitting a bar on his lunch break just to ease his mind. He had no girls on layaway he could call to score the greatest revenge fuck of all time. His longtime friend and drinking buddy Fumiko Sakagura, a high-cheekbone temptress two years his senior, was in Japan. Probably a good thing. With a great rack and a propensity to wear tight clothing and black thigh-high boots, there was a high probability Calder would get sloppy drunk, play a Sly and The Family Stone song on the jukebox and try and fuck her, past failures be damned, and he would ruin their friendship.

Calder let his mind wander to past girlfriends. He reserved a special fondness for the NYU grad student whose flawless touch could make him ejaculate all night long as they performed oral sex in every position imaginable and filled each other's orifices staining walls, bed sheets and the floor in the orgiastic process. Who could he sleep with right now to get even? To make him feel less the cuckolded, impotent male and more the lothario he had embodied 10 years earlier.

His mind approached the dark corners and gladly wallowed in them. Yet in reality, he was overwhelmed by sadness and had Fumiko, the NYU acrobat or any other desirable woman been lying totally naked on the bed begging him to delight them, Calder would have been unable to get an erection. Sadness and sex were not allies in this situation. He and Maren hadn't had sex in months, a big clue. Calder had avoided the subject because of the ugly arguments it begat.

He left work early and was on the early shift at the Kenilworth Theater. He would be back home in Greenpoint by 9 p.m. He didn't even know if Maren would be home, though he dallied in the notion that she might not be expecting him home that early and he would catch her in the act. That was an unnecessary wish. He had his ugly proof.

The three-bedroom railroad apartment was spacious, but they spent the majority of their time in one room, which they had once enjoyed painting the walls—and each other—lime green. The TV maintained the balance in this room. Maren was indeed home, sitting Indian style on the dusty purple futon and watching some mindless reality show.

There are no easy ways to confront your wife about infidelity. No easy ways if avoiding jail was a goal. There was no manual as far as Calder knew, and if there was, it was a path toward darker arts. The games and scenarios playing out in Calder's mind left him mentally exhausted. A shard of his former self peeked through like a dissipating lighthouse seen from two miles offshore on a foggy night. The light tried to keep him sane.

After receiving the text, Calder could not remember much. The immediate aftermath was not something he wanted to remember, though he had the gumption to record Mr. X's phone number and text message for posterity. He spent the next hour thinking about the previous year and a half. Was the joyous impromptu dancing with friends at a bar on the Lower East Side utter bullshit? What about all of the home-cooked meals Maren had made? Were they signs of true caring and love, or ruses to keep Calder off the adulterous scent? Calder imagined how many lies Maren must have told. A year and a half or so? Every other word out of Maren's mouth had to be a lie. With Calder not thinking straight, it was a definite statistical probability.

He did not know how he made it into the agency that morning. The term personal day matched this situation too nicely. On the subway, the rush hour straphangers did not exist. Calder wallowed in anger and sorrow and disbelief. He looked around and the other passengers were not there. He was imprisoned within his own terrible thoughts. His mind turned inward.

Had he been that unhappy in their weakening marriage that he reveled when his wife was out of town or meeting with a potential "client" until late at night? How much was he to blame? Calder blamed Maren and himself. Both conclusions were partially true and partially false simultaneously, together making an incomplete whole. This new system of beliefs burrowed past pedestrian concerns, such as going to work, eating and bowel movements, into the recesses of Calder's brain that could never be wiped clean. In the haze of regret, second-guessing and contempt, Calder trusted nothing.

Now that he was finally home, the tension was colossal. Calder looked at his left ring finger, the gold wedding band glistened, and then at Maren, and blurted it out.

"Are you having an affair?"

The gush of tears flowing from both eyes provided the truth. Neither of them spoke for at least a minute. "Maybe I wanted to be caught," she said.

Calder was too upset to speak and too upset to even sit near her, fearful the anger might bubble over into something worse than a defensive bear hug. A broken neck or other violent episode loitered nearby. Calder rose from the tear-soaked bed and made his way toward the hallowed door, toward the original Sofa Island. Maren's tears, pain, shock and embarrassment she had been found out filled another long silence. Calder stopped and returned to the bed. He knew they had to continue talking, at all costs, and however painful.

"You're never home," Maren said, tears clinging to her face throughout the entire conversation. "You always come home after midnight."

Not true, Calder believed but didn't express. He was early on Broadway four of the eight shows and late on four. Even on the no more than three nights a week he was "on," in the ushering parlance, he was home by 11:15 p.m. He wanted to work. He would rather have a nagging wife with money in his pocket than one without any money there. But sometimes, he plain did not have money no matter the situation. And this was the root of all evil.

He needed the extra ushering money. He was damned if he did work all the shows and damned if he didn't. He was paid—"not much" according to Maren—at the agency biweekly on Thursday and weekly on Wednesdays along the Great White Way, which was a terrible nickname for Broadway that

Calder still didn't understand. The Wednesday ushering paycheck in the non-agency paid week was vital. Financial inaction weighed Calder down. Hindsight, the great prognosticator forever too late to do any good, was brilliant nonetheless. Money made the world go round and in Calder's psyche it was the reason his first "starter" marriage had failed. He did not need anyone to tell him this, least of all Maren. She took a broadsword to his manhood and swung with full gusto.

"Your first wife left you for a reason," Maren sprayed an old wound with a machine-gun fire. "You didn't make her stop dancing."

True, his first wife had once been a stripper but it had no bearing here. Maybe it did but Calder saw no reason to mention it. It was a direct assault.

You'll thank me one day.

Calder rued those words his first wife said when informing him their marriage was over, and rued the fact they were the only words of hers that remained etched in his memory. What more could he do? What more could she do? Questions begat more questions, and went down rabbit holes, past and present, that Calder nor Maren really wanted to traverse. The ground was unsteady, a new tectonic fault line went right through their apartment, and pierced their once strong bond.

Calder tried to listen to his wife without interrupting and without choking her. After 10 minutes, he realized he had to leave before things turned ugly, or before there was no turning back. He wanted to leave wiggle room to salvage their marriage. Maren, of course, viewed it as just another flight from marital danger, from the things that couples thought but rarely vocalized.

"You're just running from your problems, again," she said, penetrating his soul—death by a thousand cuts. "Like you always do."

Calder looked back at Maren, nuclear warheads wished to be as powerful. The look haunted both of them for the next few days. His eyes burned with rage, and one more word and things were over. Maren knew this. And thankfully, or unfortunately, depending on Calder's minute-to-minute fluctuations in mood, she did not say anything further. She knew she had hurt him deeply and he had to take a walk.

Calder wended his way along the East River, amongst the abandoned warehouses and graffiti murals on West St. Each shimmer of light on the asphalt mocked him, each twinkling light atop the Manhattan skyline across the river was laughing.

How could you let this happen?

***

"Are you okay?" Maren asked, noticing Calder was not present. They were sitting together Indian-style on their bed while Zoe slept in the living room. He did not hear what she had to say about what other linens he was supposed to throw into the laundry. He was thinking of something more sinister, a scar that the day's interviews reopened.

Calder stared at his cell phone. He had copied Mr. X's text three years ago and emailed it to himself. It was a record of a terrible episode of the dramedy known as his life. He let the memory pass; he stuffed it back into the unknown areas of his mind where it would remain, waiting to erupt. Maren broke the impasse.

"I've never heard you talk like that," Maren exclaimed. "Those ideas. I never knew you were so philosophical. You never talk that way to me."

"I have. Maybe you just haven't been listening. I've always felt that way."

"So what do you think of our marriage?"

Calder clammed up. He knew any false step could get him killed.

Don't Tread On Me.

Give me liberty or give me death.

And the clincher: *Live Free or Die.*

The bags under his eyes looked like UFOs. Calder's scrambled brains fell back into slogan mode. Newly amongst the ranks of the unemployed—he didn't count the part-time ushering gig—he wanted to break himself of the habit since it was no longer his bread and butter. It limited his thinking, he thought limitedly. There were no easy answers so he fell back on them.

"Live Free or Die," he said.

"What's that supposed to mean?" Maren emoted, her voice rising an octave. "Don't give me one of your slogans."

Maren called him out. It was a mild put down, but spouses could cut their other halves down more quickly and surgically than anyone else. Blink and Calder might lose a brain lobe and not even notice it for a few days, maybe even a week. And after a month, he wouldn't even know it was gone.

"Forgiveness. Remember we talked about that? Unconditional love. Zoe benefits from having both parents around and the unconditional love surrounding her is the best thing in the world, like guardian angels protecting her at every turn. She has brought so much joy to this house. She's a blessing and I am so happy she is here. Thank you for baking her so well. Happy thoughts breed a happy child. Love conquers all. Is that philosophical enough for you?"

Maren glared back. He sounded hollow, nothing like he had in his *tete-a-tete* with Andrea Peabody. His new mantras beamed into the homes across America, and his was the face everyone would soon turn to as the new voice of quiet Stoicism. Everyone in America knew Calder Boyd, yet his wife didn't know him at all.

"I'm not stupid. Don't treat me like a first-year philosophy student."

Philosophy works.

Calder had worked on that ubiquitous subway banner ad when he first joined the ad agency. They broke him in slowly, having transferred from the world of newspapers. Calder was a young man in a dying man's industry. He got out before he received a gold watch, or downsized to inhabit his own floor in a ghost like tomb of once thriving offices. This had happened to a few of his colleagues working at giant news conglomerates whose sole holdings were print media.

Diversify.

Calder had heard this term all his life and as a child had thought it meant having people of all different stripes working together or better, procreating to create a smarter more understanding breed of human being. Calder could not hide his internal humanist.

"I was just trying to give you a compliment, you know," Maren finally admitted, exasperated by the downward spiral of their conversation. It didn't have to be this way.

Why did every attempt at conversation devolve away from its intended purpose? Was it the latent tension of having been together over 10 years? Silence had not been a helpful tactic, Calder realized.

"I'm sorry. I know you were."

"I wish you would talk like this more," she said. "You rarely open up about your feelings. Sometimes I don't understand you."

"Sometimes I don't understand myself."

"Who is Marcus Aurelius anyway?"

Calder embraced his wife and they didn't say a word, their humble moment only interrupted by Zoe's hunger pangs. A faint cry evolved into frenzy.

"I'll take care of her tonight," Maren said. "Your face looks like it got zapped on an electrical fence one too many times."

Calder grinned big and wide. He was on the verge of collapse and his wife saw it clear as day. Anyone could. He realized she had always been here to help but he had been subconsciously shutting her out. He had overturned the apple cart. While he rose in stature, he diminished her. In this moment of clarity, he understood his wife's frustration, about his sullen moods and sloganized view of society. The world was bigger than that.

Life was not a slogan.

That would make the ultimate slogan, he thought, and then stopped himself. This would be a good time to inform his wife that he had been laid off. But he didn't want to ruin the mood. Flawed thinking for sure, but it had gotten him far. If Maren found out, naturally, she would be concerned, though perhaps not. She could seize the opportunity to work more and he would be a stay-at-home dad. Her freedom would explode and his would recede even further.

Zoe's beautiful brown eyes floated into his consciousness. He saw them clear as day, peering back at him as he pondered his course of action. They gave him that innocent look, the look that would break many boys' hearts, Calder suspected. His was already melted. To sustain a modicum of composure in their gaze took a Herculean effort, otherwise his entire body would transform into goo.

There were three simple pleasures he craved doing before he came clean: One, he wanted to see a movie, in a theater. He hadn't seen one in over a year. Two, he wanted to spend a day at the Guggenheim. It was only eight blocks north and two avenues over, but he hadn't been there without fear of having to rush home in a year as well. Three, he wanted to go out and grab a few drinks with his old friends without his wife finding out about it, only to forget his life for a moment, to give himself a day of debauchery.

Calder pushed his daughter's loving stare into the background. He would hold onto his secret for a little while longer, just one or two days. He would leave in the morning and return after his theater gig, operating business as usual. Things—meaning the outside world—were just getting interesting. He had to maintain the upper hand even while risking this new understanding. He returned to the moment at hand.

"Thank you. I've gotten used to Sofa Island."

Maren laughed. She had not heard him use the *nom du jour*.

"Funny. So that's what you call your sofa enclave. It has a nice ring to it."

"You could join me there sometime," Calder replied.

Maren rose from the bed and tended to Zoe. Her cries ceased as Calder lost consciousness as soon as his head disappeared into the lavender pillow.

When he awoke the next morning, Maren was asleep next to him. The door was propped open so they could hear when Zoe stirred; the crib did not fit comfortably into the bedroom. Calder listened to his daughter's breaths stay in perfect cadence. He lumbered out of bed, not even bothering to look at the clock to see what time it was.

There on the sofa lay bare a nice writing journal. It looked identical to the book of titles he had kept at the agency. Wait. A new fear crept into his carefully laid plans. How was he going to move that stuff back home? He had one day at best before Maren would find out anyway. Today, he was going to enjoy himself, give himself a much-needed break from his own life. He might be able to watch a movie without being recognized. He accepted the risk. He felt even worse for the plan when he opened the journal.

Maren had secretly been recording all the things she had done as a record for the doctor and for Zoe's baby book. Calder almost wanted to cry. She had been listening to all that he was saying, shoveling, in against her natural urges, his dogmatic insistence that they record everything for the doctor just in case the information was needed to diagnose some hypothetical malady. Maren believed if Calder worried too much about something it would manifest itself in reality. "I don't want Zoe to grow up around nervousness," she had told him. At last, he saw the logic in it. He opened Maren's baby journal.

Jan. 19

8:48-9:10 a.m. Bottle fed Zoe 140 ml of Calder's pumped breast milk (with the vitamin supplement added). 8:50 a.m. I suddenly sneezed and Zoe got scared and cried and cried. Calder breast fed her for a few minutes to calm her then I resumed feeding at 8:57 a.m. Changed her diaper (pee). Put moisturizer on her face. Her right cheek was especially dry and cracked. Put lotion on her legs and a little on her torso. Burped her (big burp on my lap at 9:33 a.m.). Read *The Snowy Day* on this snowy morning, and several other books. She fell asleep on my lap while I was reading *Brown*

Bear, Brown Bear What Do You See? Put her back to sleep in her crib at 10:01 a.m. Calder left for work. You are a great father (I hope you like my little surprise for you). Zoe is the best. I love her sooooo much!!!!! Thinking about her makes my heart so warm and beat so fast!!! So happy we have her!!!!!

10

The sedulous sun barged into Calder's Sofa Island refuge, its unbridled rays proclaiming hegemony over his apartment and the Manhattan morning rush hour. Outside, in the actual world, away from Zoe's aura of joy and Calder's private island, it was crisp and clear under an azure sky stolen from Magritte. Ten degrees and plummeting with a brutal wind chill, but sunny nevertheless. A "Polar Vortex" moved in to wage war with the sun.

Calder could fight the slivers of light no longer. He arose from Sofa Island and peered through the blinds, creating a crinkling sound as he wedged his fingers between two slats. He looked down at the scurrying New Yorkers in pity. Odd, given the fact he no longer had a full-time gig. For the last five minutes, while Zoe slept in her crib nearby, Calder observed the comings and goings of people getting off from the night shift, the night people, and those who were heading into work, the day jobbers. He'd made a new distinction—an observation rather— during this five-minute respite. None of it mattered.

Sure, money was needed and a day job was the path to said money, but at what cost? People spent their entire lives—their most valuable aspect was time—chasing something that was completely manufactured by the government: currency.

What if money was no object? Yesterday, on his commute home from his last day as a day jobber, Calder read an article about nanotechnology claiming that in the not too distant future atoms could be manipulated to create food, and whatever else we needed. Imagine that. Calder leapt from the notion of abundance to real world applications. Formula approached this on a regular basis.

More milk than milk.

Lactamil touted their slogan proudly, a simplistic example of spot on ad copy. It convinced consumers that Lactamil was a superior product while also rendering its competition—breast and cow's milk—somehow inferior. Milk on demand. Breastfeeding could become obsolete. If everything could be manufactured, would there be a need to work? His revelation—advocated by his father and sparked by the hordes on the sidewalk below—was simple: money is not as valuable as time. For Calder, it was time to do the things he had never had the time to do. He would finish the Great American novel, make a feature film, and make a point to take some time for himself every day.

He hurriedly took a shower and ate a bowl of cereal before Zoe awoke. Maren was still sleeping and he wanted to leave their apartment before she could make any errand requests that might throw him off his path. He couldn't be "late" for work but he could be late for life's adventure. Monotony was the enemy. He pulled on three layers of clothing then his heat tech, black down jacket. He hated brutal cold weather on a clear day. Might as well snow. Thankfully a fresh dusting coated the packed ice below, making for treacherous footing but a beautiful Central Park snowscape.

Just as he was about to leave, the apartment buzzer broke the morning silence. Who the hell could be visiting him at 8:30 a.m.? Maybe it was Astrid. Her cell number had come up on his phone several times last night. He suspected she was angry that he hadn't given her the same spectacular answers he had to Andrea Peabody. She texted her concern sometime after midnight and the tri-tone nearly woke Zoe. Calder would need to change his cell number soon.

The buzzer rang again, waking Zoe. Calder was forced to decide between tending to his daughter and answering the buzzer. He looked back at the crib and noticed that one of Zoe's mittens was missing. Maren insisted she wear them while sleeping because she scratched her face in her sleep, potentially scarring her dry skin. The buzzer vibrated through the apartment once more. Who was ruining his morning "commute" and his last day of leisurely—his wife most assuredly would say "lazy"—pursuits?

Calder pushed the button, and could here the clang of the front door both in the hallway and on the street below.

"You have packages, plural, you need to sign for."

Calder instantly recognized Varick's voice. Calder hadn't seen him in a while. Why the sudden return? Calder sensed he was trying to hone in on the breastfeeding celebrity just like everyone else. He was wrong.

Calder picked Zoe up and handed her off to Maren, who had also been aroused, then loped downstairs.

Varick stood in the foyer, surrounded by a pile of packages, boxes of varying size, and a giant mailbag—all of it for Calder.

"What the hell is all of this?

"For you. From your fans," Varick replied. He tapped the largest, though lightest, box. "This one's from a pillow company. I wonder what this is. They must think you need to get some proper sleep."

"So you saw it too?"

"Man, you need to come to my refresher seminar. You remain completely emasculated. You need to reclaim your wife and your life. I gave you a card, right? In fact, I'm holding another male empowerment workshop at my apartment tomorrow night. I insist that you return. I'll give you the friends and family rate as a post-graduate."

"I don't want this stuff," Calder said, pointing to the mound of mail while disregarding Varick's offer.

"It's gonna start piling up soon. There are even a few leave-your-wife-I'm-better-for-you marriage proposals in there somewhere."

"What? Wait, how do you know?"

"They were on postcards I saw while sorting. You can have your mail put on hold if you like."

"You read my mail?"

"I'm sorry. That's now something the United States Postal Service prides itself on. I didn't pry open any letters or anything like that. The postcard fell out of the pouch and when I picked it up I noticed the lipstick. And the big letters MARRY ME! I'M BETTER FOR YOU. So yes, I read *one* of your postcards. I'm sure there are more letters and cards with similar sentiments. There are a lot of lonely women out there. You probably have a few proposals from men while you're at it."

"What does putting your mail on hold cost? Can I do it permanently? I don't need this stuff."

"It doesn't cost anything. I can set it up for you. Or you can do it yourself online. People usually do it for three to six months. I guess technically you could do it for a year or more. I've never heard anything like that though. We had one guy's mail for five years. Turns out he died a month after putting it on hold. He had all kinds of bills from collection agencies and lawyer's charges. Sad. That's the only good thing about marriage. You die and someone will know usually within 24 hours. If you die single, your body might rot for a few days or even a week. I read about a woman in England who wasn't discovered for over a year."

"That's beyond sad. Anyway, if you could set it up for me, that would be great. It sounds too good to be true. Hopefully, I'm not going to die anytime soon."

"I'll do it today. Any specific date you want to start? Though wait, your wife's mail would be held too. It's not a problem if you pick up every week or so, but you probably should talk it over with the Mrs. before I set it up."

"So you do advocate being emasculated?"

"I'm just trying to save your ass. Nothing more, nothing less. Personally, if it was me, I'd just go ahead and do it. You could spy on her correspondence."

"Why would I want to do that?"

"Why wouldn't you? Everyone in the United States knows she cheated on you. You gotta protect yourself, man. You have a kid now. All bets are off."

"I'm not gambling."

"Suit yourself. Let me know after you talk to her. Sounds like she owns you. You definitely should come to another session tomorrow night. It'll change your life."

The look on Calder's face conveyed the talking his mouth couldn't—or wouldn't—provide.

"You know what, you need to have your mail held," Varick said. "Better safe than sorry. It can only lead to trouble. I'll take care of it for you. Make an executive stand. Be a man."

Calder didn't protest. He wouldn't attend any more seminars, but he knew the mailman was right.

"Here's my card again," Varick continued. "Free of charge. The first session is always free, no matter where in the five-day process it happens to be, but I'd have to charge you for a refresher. Drop in any day. No harm no foul." Varick paused, didn't think better of it, and continued. "I loved watching your dad play, man. Why did he retire so young? He was in his prime."

"And he always will be," Calder said.

"Let me know about the seminar!" Varick hollered as the glass pane in the building's front door cracked from the 10th straight day of temperatures well below freezing. Calder wondered why it hadn't happened earlier. The door clanged shut every time someone entered or exited and was in dire need of repair. That day had come.

Calder inhaled deeply, letting the cold air fill his lungs as if he were a drowning man suddenly infused with life-sustaining oxygen. The morning commuters were down to a trickle, but he had to leave home to maintain the illusion of being a day jobber.

He scanned the horizon in all directions. He even looked up toward the infamous fire escape, half expecting a flash to immediately pop. However, there was nobody with a camera in the vicinity. He had discovered the perfect antidote. The sub-freezing chill kept the paparazzi away. He hoped the snow stayed on the ground until April Fool's Day.

That's what he was, a fool, the haranguing notion he couldn't shake. He didn't have his agency job to depend on and he had a family to provide for, yet he needed a day to regroup? Leaving the building, he paused for a moment, reconsidering his intended plan. The illusion of personal freedom proved too great. He longed to shake Maren's harsh scrutiny, if only briefly. She had mentioned a few of his improper baby-caring methods on his way out the door.

Why did arguments always happen on the way out

KELVIN C. BIAS

the door? He guessed it was the only time he was available. Having warmed one of the bottles from Calder's refrigerated milk store, Maren fed Zoe dutifully though he saw the same longing for freedom in his wife's eyes. Forty milk bottles stood guard in the refrigerator. Calder, he admitted to no one but himself, had not really been forthcoming in his reasons for pumping breast milk well into the previous night. He knew if he pumped a lot it would make Maren feel he was desperately needed and placate her penchant for biting comments.

The biting air matched Maren's frigid sexuality. Their last bout of sex in the past year and a half was last week but it wasn't enough. There was a barrier of insecurity, body consciousness and fleeting affection. He had probably overlooked Maren's cold ways—in comparison to his insatiable warmth of passion and proclivity for deep wet kisses—before they got married. Had she always been this way? Or was that his fault? He was certain how she would vote. The early primary results were tallied two years ago when New Hampshire's Mr. X clouded the picture. The night before, Calder's jag into this Mobius strip of troubled thinking prompted his plan. Now it just seemed like he used it to warrant his self-given hall pass for a day.

Maren's dalliance was extinct as far as he knew. The idea could never be undone. It took true forgiveness. Calder stood gallant, but sometimes he let the latent anger bubble to the surface. He looked down and imagined red-hot magma overtaking the street and melting all of his beloved snow. It filled the space all the way to his chin, the imaginative scene smothering all other senses and Calder pulled back hard against the momentary flight of fancy. He stayed the predetermined course. He kept his feet to the ice-glazed grindstone.

Free from the constraints of fatherhood for just a day—in his own internal logic anyway—Calder beelined for Central Park. He adored the solitude of the snowy winter mornings. The frigid temperature would provide the illusion that the entire park was his alone, a respite from his tempestuous thoughts and livid life. It took him longer than the usual 10 minutes what with the treacherous navigation of the compounded ice and snow, which could hardly be called snow any longer as it too was frozen solid.

Calder had always proclaimed that nothing matched the tunnels and pathways of Central Park after a fresh snowfall. He'd lied. He looked up and discovered something was better after all. The snow and ice clung to the withered trees like a layer of vanilla frosting on a birthday cake, reflecting the sunlight and creating a sepulcher of refracted light. It was a spectacular explosion of cold beauty. The delicate marvel of the wintry landscape swung his convoluted mind toward another white lie.

There was something else Calder did not tell his wife. He was not working at the theater tonight as she expected. In the silence of the first lactation interview with Astrid Persson, she had invited him to an art opening in Chelsea. She assured him she wouldn't tell Maren.

Essy Frisk was a Swedish porn star cum artist and

Astrid whispered the information in Calder's ear during the initial prep while the two techs set up the camera.

"You'll like her style," Astrid assured him. "I know Maren isn't into art, but you are. She told me all about the children's books you've written for Zoe. I've seen your independent film too. It's...interesting."

Interesting. The kiss of death. No wonder he hadn't found distribution and put his budding auteur aspirations on hold until he could afford a more Hollywood-friendly budget.

Calder retrieved his smartphone from the bowels of his winter coat and snapped some quick photos of the wintry wonderland. He had been working on an experimental documentary in his non-existent spare time for the past two years. This had been another reason for his polar Central Park sojourn.

After a few snaps, Calder devolved from the world; he was too engrossed in framing a perfect series of photos, gesturing to the snow and ice above a barren oak tree like it was a sentient being. His documentary idea—he would only have wild sound and instrumental music a la the 1983 Godfrey Reggio documentary *Koyaanisqatsi*—developed out of his love of snow, a fact he pinpointed to his mother, Pernille, reading Ezra Jack Keats's beloved children's classic *The Snowy Day* in sunny Southern California.

Because of this book, Calder yearned for snow growing up in L.A. It, as expected, never came, unless they drove up to Big Bear. Published in 1963, *The*

Snowy Day was one of the few mainstream children's books at the time that featured a black protagonist. Calder's mother wanted to be sure to surround him with knowledge of who he was, secure in being able to navigate two worlds, the one everyone saw him as—both black and white—and the world of imagination cultivated by a little boy making a snowman and snow angels alone in the snow. Her bedtime stories fostered his imagination and tangentially were why he stood alone in Central Park in inhuman weather. Calder realized that was odd, to be a sole stark mark in the all-encompassing white, which reflected the quickly rising sun. There was not another soul. No bundled up joggers, no snowshoe walkers, no other intrepid amateur photographers. It was that cold.

Standing with the entire park as his personal playground, Calder silently thanked his mother's prescience. He read Keats's book to Zoe often, and always on snowy mornings when a fresh coat of powder greeted dawn.

With the snow frozen, Calder would not be able to create instant snow art, nor build a snowman like Peter the protagonist in *The Snowy Day*. If there was a hell, Calder mused, maybe it was ice cold instead of burning hot. The intense chill was equally as bad as lava-hot hellfire. How he wanted to drop to the ground and swath his arms up and down in Arctic semicircles. He searched for a layer of fresh powder that had yet to freeze. Sometimes the city's exhaust pipes, which emerged from hidden pockets all over the five boroughs, melted the ice or kept it from freezing. These portals were easily identified on the street, their wisps of billowing white steam flooding the surrounding air above like tentacles of an octopus. NYC's homeless population knew where the steam grates and vents were. Those unable to find one or a shelter would die in these temperatures.

Duel paths—his line of thinking and the icy path below his feet—combined to make Calder count his blessings. He did not attend church but had found his way back to prayers when he thought of Zoe and her health and safety. He prayed in quiet moments such as this. He prayed wordlessly, the sentiment being please help God or whoever you are, to keep Zoe and Maren safe and help them live long, happy and healthy lives. He prayed for his immediate family and his extended family on both sides.

Caught in the introspective moment, Calder nearly forgot his other unspoken mission. He reached deeper into his down jacket and produced a glistening bottle of his pumped breast milk. He wanted to make a monument of this moment in time. Bury it beneath the snow, and see if it lasted until spring, his private version of Groundhog Day, though that day was still almost two weeks away. It seemed an odd personal time capsule, but how else to articulate the weird turn his life had taken.

He did not need a coping mechanism, he needed someone he could confide in, and that person turned out to be himself. Calder set up a black spider tripod—it looked like a miniature satellite on the surface of a frozen comet—and put the smartphone into its mount. He framed the scene perfectly, reversing the point of view of the phone's camera. He had to take off his black leather gloves momentarily to compete the setup, and his fingers nearly froze. He pushed the red record button, returned his gloves to his numb hands in the same motion then knelt down at the foot of a bench and began to chip away at the ice with his keys.

"I'm leaving this breast milk bottle in the hopes that it lasts the entire winter without being discovered. It's a video art project to see if anyone notices or cares what it means to be alive and a lactating male. Continue watching if you have the courage. I'm not sure that I do."

Calder paused and moved toward the mini-tripod as if to end the recording. He was losing his resolve. *This is for your sake, Calder, he thought, maybe you can save yourself from yourself.*

He crouched once again before the all-seeing smartphone, and wiped a tear from his eye before he continued. The tear originated from the cold, not because he was sad, though he was sad. Why did he feel this way? "It's also because you know that I am not a vocal person. So I hope you understand. Maren, I have to tell you something...."

Calder recited words he had memorized the previous night. Once he had created a hole that was sufficiently deep enough to wedge the breast milk bottle into, he did so. He was grateful nobody was around. He didn't know if he would have had the courage to go through with it and speak freely if anyone had wandered by within earshot. That term was relative given the biting cold. With no one around, his voice carried in the virginal solitude. He concluded with three overused words.

Calder held his crouch for a few moments before a slow smile crossed his face. Then he took his gloves off and stopped the recording. He pushed the share icon, but kept the video as an email draft. As he said, he did not have the courage to send it quite yet. He stashed his smartphone and small spider tripod back into his jacket pocket and left a tiny monolith, a marker for the state of his independent heart. Unseen beneath layers of warm clothing, the e-mail jettisoned toward its destination, accidentally sent when he popped the phone into the bowels of his black winter coat.

Behind him, as he grew evermore detached from this world, two black specks became larger and larger until they were upon the park's lone intruder. Two NYPD officers in full winter gear called out to Calder, but too ensconced in the majestic scene, he did not hear them. He didn't notice them until one of them flashed a hand in front of his face just as he witnessed a bright red male cardinal alight on an icicle.

"The park's closed sir," the chubbier of the two officers said. "For your safety, we're going to escort you out. The mayor has closed all city parks until the deep freeze thaws. Didn't you see the signs? The one that said BRRRR in big black letters?"

The snow covered the ice, which covered the asphalt path that led to the frozen Jacqueline Kennedy Onassis Reservoir about 100 meters west of 89th Street and Fifth Avenue. Calder might have seen one sign. But others were blown over or covered in icicles that stretched toward Pluto.

"I'm sorry. I didn't."

"No problem, this way," the lankier cop said.

"Do you have somewhere to go?" The chubby one spoke again. Then his face beamed with recognition. "You're that guy aren't you?"

"What guy?" Calder answered, hoping the notion would be too fleeting for the chubby beat cop to grasp.

"The Milkman. Son of Bib."

Calder fought hard to prevent his eyes from rolling. He had to make his escape. He glanced beneath the bench safe in the knowledge that his frozen milk bottle had not been discovered. They were well meaning, but 'Son of Bib' was not a moniker Calder nor his father would have welcomed.

"I'm good thank you. I have to get home." Calder even lied to NYPD blue.

These were Upper East Side cops. They might have beaten him with their billy clubs had he been in the South Bronx, thinking him a potential suspect of some crime. A brown man was in the park at this hour? He had to be up to no good. Calder paid more for goods and services and his money disappeared quicker in this neighborhood. He was losing money like a sieve, and now he had lost his main gig. The panic he had experienced when he accidentally locked himself out of the apartment, leaving Zoe alone, returned.

The Guggenheim didn't open for another two hours, at 10 a.m. and Calder needed to find immediate respite from the cold. There were no open cafes he knew of so he had to seek an alternative safe haven. This was not the time to lollygag. Calder's beige Timberland boots navigated the terrain and he looked past the massive oak at the entrance to the park as he walked past it. Just north of the Guggenheim he spied his target.

The stained glass windows of the Heavenly Rest Episcopal church, which could almost serve as a bookend to the museum's famous rotunda, called to him. On account of the frigid weather, the church's main doors were closed and Calder had to enter through the sacristy. Inside, he found a slight respite, but the air still caused his breath to escape in a visible cloud. It was likely in the upper 30s closer to the door. The further Calder wandered into the church the warmer it got. He placed a few quarters in the collection box and continued his unguided tour. He was amazed no one pounced on him or sought to ingratiate themselves to his soul. The resident reverend could tell when someone just needed a quiet place to think.

Calder slipped into the last pew, along the right side, somewhere he wouldn't be noticed. The altar appeared to look like a golden table about two hundred feet in front of him. The rising sunlight cut a brilliant swath across the vacuous chamber. Various hues of gold infused the purples, reds, and blues of the massive panes of stained glass on each side of the church. It was doubtful he would be recognized here but he could never be positive. He chuckled—ever so slightly audible—at the fact that he was escaping scrutiny in a place where people flocked to discover the light.

Since it was a bone cold weekday, the church was virtually empty. A janitor, or vestry member, he couldn't tell for certain, was fussing about the altar. They were probably getting ready for the afternoon service. Calder's time as an altar boy had been filled with various noble episodes and untold shenanigans. Burning his name on the wall of the taper room still haunted him even as the stained-glass light imperceptibly moved across the center aisle at the heart of the church. He never should have desecrated God's house. It was the lowlight, but there had been highs too, witnessing baptisms up close and personal at the back of the church and the occasional celebrity wedding for which Calder was handsomely paid. He fondly remembered the bout of heat stroke, and more so, the alcoholic benefits of assisting Reverend Bowland at St. Matthew's. Calder was thrilled as a 10-year-old boy allowed to drink communion wine. Reverend Bowland had passed away two decades ago, but being back in an Episcopal church made Calder reminisce about his boyhood altar adventures.

Children are close to God, he thought, born with a purity that escaped little by little with each passing day until innocence was lost, never to return. Milton's paradise was not only lost, but a lost cause. Somewhere, too, as he grew older, Calder faded from the church. He half-seriously told his mother he would attend the Episcopal seminary across the street from Northwestern University in winter—to get his beloved share of snow—when he turned 70.

He couldn't recall the last time he had attended church. Calder, like his father before him, internalized God. "Church is just a building," his father used to say. "I don't need to attend to talk to God. It works for some people, but not for me." Calder subscribed to his father's type of thinking about the Heavenly Father, much to his mother's chagrin. When did he last attend? Calder racked his troubled brain. It had been sometime five or six years ago while home in L.A., attending the midnight service with his mother who perpetually sang in the church choir.

Pernille possessed the voice of an angel. Her son believed she could have been a pop star if she so desired. But no, she was content doing God's work in a minimal way with singular focus. Calder often joked with Reverend Morrison that the church should be renamed after her. St. Pernille's rolled off the tongue. It was also easy on the ears. With all the time she donated as a member of the vestry, it was the least Reverend Morrison could do. Calder needed to call his mother like the actor on the Oscars once implored everyone to do. She hadn't seen Zoe since the first month because she was tied up with the church, getting the house ready for sale and looking to buy a new townhouse in Orlando to be closer to her youngest son, Brice, whose family had recently moved to the outskirts of Disney World. Calder would call her as soon as he got the chance. It was just after 6 a.m. in L.A. There was a better than average chance his mother, an early riser, was awake, but concluded it would be best to wait until a more decent hour, lest she worry that someone else in her world had died.

Calder undid the buttons of his coat, which felt less bulky with his milk deposit back in Central Park. He didn't understand why he had felt the need to bury a bottle of his breast milk in the snow but he had been compelled to do it. He so wanted it to be there whenever he returned. It served as his roll of the dice. He draped his coat across the pew in front of him and out of curiosity grabbed an errant Book of Common Prayer from the knee runner and put it back in the pew's wooden shelf in front of him. Calder marveled at people who attended church every Sunday. Did they really need that structure? He guessed they might tell him he needed to go to church more often. He despised when people said this. Church was a private sanctuary, not something he wanted to share with others. Calder stared at the Book of Common Prayer. It mocked him. Finally, he broke down and cracked it open. He read a few familiar incantations.

Lord, hear our prayer.

The next thing he knew, he awoke and 50-60 people chanted that exact refrain. He fell asleep. And now it was half past 1 p.m. and in the middle of the service. An aged man sat in the pew a few feet away and chuckled, in much the same way Calder always did. "Winter will do that to you. I thought I was the only one in here trying to beat the cold," the man whispered.

The man returned to the service while Calder ducked out the back of the church. "Don't worry," the man trailed after Calder. "Your secret's safe with me.

It's between you and God."

Calder nodded and bid adieu, to God. He thought French and Spanish got it right. English was wrong.

Goodbye.

Twenty cautious steps down the sidewalk, Calder sauntered into the Guggenheim's Frank Lloyd Wright rotunda. From the outside, and especially on a normal, *warm* day, it looked like a pile of white tires plastered over with silly putty. But today, the ice coated it like a diamond. This happened only on rare occasions. On the inside, it was serene; the spiral design wound its way toward the heavens. He walked at a deliberate pace, taking in the Italian Futurism exhibition.

Calder was a failed artist, a former writer of untruths who peddled products nobody really needed to keep the economy going strong. Never acknowledging his inner calling, Calder lacked his magnum opus: the Great American Novel, a cult movie hit or a play on its feet. These flights of desire had all eluded him. Chasing things that required the good graces of others, he felt hollow even when his life was supposed to be at its pinnacle, buttressed by the birth of his daughter. Was this his form of a clichéd midlife crisis? Critics would see right through anything he wrote or tried to film at this point, and some would have the gumption to mention it. Calder aspired to something more than being a contagious Internet meme of the week. But art has many forms.

His greatest body of work was Zoe. He and Maren could not imagine what their daughter would look like before she was born. Now that she had arrived, they couldn't imagine her looking any other way. Her tiny nose, almond eyes, sharp jawline, milky mocha skin and wavy golden hair in tresses at the top of her head matched the swirling lines of a jumbled Futurist painting.

There were no boundaries at the edges of the frame in this curated section of the exhibition along the middle tier of the circular ramp leading to the highest floors. Calder looked over the curved edge of the eggshell colored retaining wall toward the lobby far below. If someone wanted to commit suicide, this was an easy and high-profile place to do it. The wall barely came up to his hip. If someone were to accidentally lean into him the wrong way, or give him an off-balance push, he could easily topple over the side. A gruesome imagination belied his heart. Calder never feared death, but Zoe reminded him every day that there was a major reason to live. That was set in stone.

Calder was not feeling particularly melancholy. His leaps within digressions could not be contained. How would Maren react when she discovered he had lost his job? She didn't count the ushering gig. She should appreciate it more now. Calder kidded himself as he circled a Boccioni sculpture.

Furious.

No genius thinking was required. He hoped she didn't learn of his agency's complete dissolution through the grapevine, or worse, the dreaded *New York Post.*

Page Six material absolutely.

Subconsciously, Calder felt like the dynamic

bronze Boccioni figure before him: *Unique Forms of Continuity in Space*. The muscular pseudo-human legs of the contorted gold-colored sculpture stood on two blocks beneath the "feet" that were part of the piece as a whole. Like Calder, the figure was eye-catching and unique. Unlike Calder, the sculpture had definite form, confident in his decisions, in his solitary purpose to be admired. Its musculature pierced the museum's atmosphere as Calder moved on to an adjoining row of Futurist paintings.

He reached the Guggenheim's rotunda and glanced over the retaining wall again. People looked like stray beetles, bumping into each other to find an exit. He envisioned the museum's spiral design rising ad infinitum in the distant future, creating an endless cavalcade of art and even more dizzying heights.

Calder's interior spiral upward from bottom to top took approximately 45 minutes. He could have spent hours in the white New York institution, but his unscheduled nap at the church cut into his movie time. It was both refreshing and panic inducing, like the vertigo an endless spiral into the sky might cause, to enjoy his freedom. He savored the air, had spring in his cold steps and the fatigue of Sofa Island receded into the background. He was the captain of his destiny, the king of bad decisions.

He bought a few postcards at the gift shop on the highest level—he liked to mail them to his friends in the city to keep the lost art of personal correspondence alive—and then instead of taking the elevator, returned back down the spiral interior.

The descent snatched three minutes from his day.

As he exited the museum on the ground floor, the temperature skyrocketed to a toasty 20 degrees. This would be the day's high. He went to the entrance of the park to see if it had been reopened. It hadn't. Several maintenance trucks lined the inner service road near the reservoir and workers dutifully took chainsaws to downed tree branches, clearing the park one acre at a time. There would not be a reopening today that much was evident.

This crimped Calder's feasibility. He wanted to avoid springing for a cab to the Upper West Side where he would catch an afternoon screening of the latest blockbuster on the 100-by-80-foot IMAX screen at Lincoln Square. The crosstown bus was a much less viable option because the chances of being recognized by the elderly-ladies-who-lunch and had infinite free time to watch *The Andrea Peabody Show* religiously, was too great. A movie theater served as the perfect refuge, if only he could get there inconspicuously. For all Calder knew, the Central Park police officers had already mentioned their brush with odd fame on social media.

The cold. It remained his most valuable ally, as did the very show in question. It was almost 3 p.m., *The Andrea Peabody Show* hour. The very people who could point him out would not be out. The bus would work.

Calder walked briskly to the corner of 86th and Fifth Avenue and waited with an elderly man who appeared to have no idea who Andrea Peabody was, nor own a TV. He was dressed all in white, with a puffy white three-quarter length down jacket, and cradled a poodle in his arms like it was a last ditch effort to make it to the veterinarian. The dog's manicured feet and pink hat looked ridiculous. Why the hell was this man subjecting what was obviously his pride and joy to such brutal cold? The things people do for love, or the love of their love. Calder thought of his own inane actions and discredited the old man no further. He probably fulfilled an agenda that kept him sane. The dog, zipped tight in a black doggie case, barked at Calder. "He only barks at bad people," the old man said. "You must be doing something wrong."

Was it that obvious?

Calder turned up the collar to his winter coat to obscure his face, and when the bus finally arrived after an obscene wait in the icebox, he appropriated a seat at the very back.

Ten minutes later, he exited at 86th and Broadway and took the downtown 1 train three stops to 66th St. Two hours later, another revelation revealed itself: the movie sucked, not worth the wait to see it, nor the precious hours away from his wife and family. He could hear Maren's favorite saying in his ear: "Was it worth it?" She asked this whenever he hung out with Fumiko, Gerald or did anything that Calder surmised took time away from her, whether it was true or not.

The art opening would make up for it. And to kill some time and get a good buzz to eradicate any residual doubts, he stopped at an Irish bar for an "after work" drink. In fact, many people inside, there for the "after work" drink, like Calder, had no day job. Calder had not stepped foot in a bar in over a year, and assuredly not before 5 p.m. The workman bartender, Mike, made drinks to request, but Guinness and other drafts were the run of the house. The bar was long and skinny, running the length of the space. Calder went as far away from the front door as he could. It was near the bathroom, but out of the way from the regular "sauce heads," his term for the resident alcoholics or regulars. In this case it was a 50-something-year-old Lincoln Center musician putting an edge on before a performance in a jazz festival, a wrinkled leather-skinned bald man who looked to be no younger than 60 and two female Columbia grad students discussing their latest archaeological dig in Chile's Atacama Desert. Calder brought up the rear. He ordered the Belgian draft, a gauche move in an Irish bar. But it tasted good. The frosty beer met his lips like a long lost friend. As soon as they met, the old feelings and memories came flooding back.

Maren could drink with the best of them, and for that matter, the worst. In the early days of their relationship, they were regulars at the Green Boot, a dive bar on the Lower East Side, near the one-room studio apartment they would soon share. They were sauce heads then, lively in spirit and in spirits.

Calder attacked his beer. His beer curl prowess long since abandoned him but the action was a muscle memory and he quickly fell into a groove. He could finish the drink in one swig but he was too sophisticated for that. He needed to revel in the moment, smile devilishly as he broke societal norms.

He was breastfeeding. How dare he taint his fountain of lactate with alcohol? It would be gone in a few hours. Mix it with a glass of water here and there and he was good to go. Besides, he had the pumped breast milk on grand reserve in the refrigerator. He could take one night off, if not two. Calder was a mere mortal, but he was thirsty. This little taste of his pre-baby self quenched sparingly but created new problems. His tolerance level had declined sharply and he began to feel a buzz. He was a cheap date.

His tongue reacted favorably to the cool missiles rocketing down his throat. He hadn't even taken off his coat. He planned on having no more than one beer—another recalibration—just a little pick me up, an oxymoron given that alcohol was a depressant. If he took off his coat, Calder thought, it would signal intent to consume more. He didn't want to give that impression. He never knew when eyes were on him.

The bartender wiped down the counter and changed three taps in preparation for the Thursday night rush. In 30 minutes the place would be teeming with Manhattan single life. In the midst of an intimacy desert, Calder reminisced about past girlfriends.

The Columbia grad students, five stools to his right, reminded him of his former NYU paramour—finance was her game. Man, she had been good to him. She put up with his shit and that alone was worth its weight in relationship gold. And she was the only one who satiated his every sexual and intellectual urge, though they had never actually had intercourse. She never let him penetrate her because

174

he was with other girls and not fully committed to her. It was an unspoken barrier, but it had served only to make him want her more. Was she even aware of that? The rubbing and baby oil of their naked bodies was the usual sexual position, and he had fingered her and/or gone down on her for days at a time, ratcheting her into a frenzy until she came all over the sheets leaving a massive wet spot. He loved those wet spots, and smiled at the recollection, but there had been that one major sticking point. She made up for the lack of intercourse in other ways. Who knew blowjobs and hand jobs could be so pleasant and produce such orgasms—the make you want to squirt across the room and see how far it goes variety. Thinking of her now excited him. He would have to stop thinking about it lest he would be trapped until it subsided. Add it to the list of life's paths not taken.

His raw sexual digressions were not without purpose. They floodlit the glaring fact that sex deepens relationships. The most primitive of human connections was urgently needed, but how had Maren lost the urgency to engage in it? They desperately had to work on this aspect of their marriage. It was the key to everything. That was Calder's motto. It reduced stress, which killed, and was a great form of exercise to boot. Sex kept Calder—like most other men—happy and more imaginative. Its regenerative properties were an added bonus. Men don't think straight when they are full of sperm. Too much testosterone in one place can be toxic. Every nag and even innocuous household request became amplified beyond the level of annoyance when there was little physical intimacy.

Calder had used sex to stay in shape for years, but in its dearth, had let himself go. This last point he knew was weak, if not all the others, but it was true on its face. He could work out more. All he needed was the hardwood floor of their slightly expanded jail-cell size apartment. Pushups and sit-ups were easy in this environment. Maren claimed she would feel like having sex more if he had six-pack abs. Calder did not believe it, and so, made little effort. Maren, he felt, should want to have sex with her husband in any case.

Desire.

Lust.

Ecstasy.

Bliss.

The concepts made Calder immediately return to the previous forays into past sexual liaisons. How would his life be different if he'd just rammed her and stuck it in, without regard, making a commitment to the NYU brainiac back then? Or to the Bolivian girl he had treated terribly and who had definitely loved him like no other? Or what if his first marriage had lasted longer? Or the Norwegian girl, who broke his heart a decade earlier, hadn't?

Drinking alone. Calder did not wear it well. But it made him appreciate what he did possess. His family. He would skip the art gallery show and go home. That's where he belonged. He fought once more to wrest these troublesome sexual memories from his skull forever.

Zoe returned to the forefront. A happy-ending path with any of the aforementioned women and Zoe would not exist. It gave Calder pause, even in a slightly inebriated state.

He stared at the last few ounces of his Belgian white. He still refused to take off his coat. His fingers trembled slightly as he nursed the dregs of his beer. Time stood still in bars and when tending to babies. Minding his own business, Calder finished his pint and prepared to leave when it happened.

"Take off your coat. Stay awhile," the bald old man said while sliding another draft down the bar. "I know you can use a cold one. Don't worry. I'm not paparazzi."

The person Calder least suspected had watched *The Andrea Peabody Show* made him. The whispered wails into his cell phone were a diversion; the old man finished his alleged cell phone conversation abruptly with a series of grunted "yesses" and "I knows". He was wearing all denim like a misplaced Calgary stampeder. All that eluded him for full Marlboro Man emeritus status was a mustache and white Stetson hat. Spilled beer and a large glass of water surrounded him. His eyebrows brimmed with anticipation as he formulated a sentence like a hibernating bear stuck in molasses.

"Pardon my interruption. A man should never drink alone. Not in my bar."

The bartender shook his head. Noble untruths regularly spewed from the regular's mouth, an unregulated line of approach that left the gentleman where he still remained: a bar stool on the Upper

West Side. Calder could not leave now. That would be rude. He lifted his new beer stein to the stranger.

Today, Calder died. Or maybe yesterday...

Camus jumped into Calder's head. Each moment, whether he acquiesced or not, equaled a slow march toward the big sleep. Calder scanned the bar. It reeked with anticipation. The jukebox went unused. The cries of drunkards from previous night's glories echoed under its beer-stained surface.

The grad students each wore a turtleneck top and tight jeans, a bulwark against the frigid exterior. One of them, the brunette in the black turtleneck, had bangs, the other didn't, her beautiful red hair flowering out of the back of her head and over her white turtleneck like an eternal fountain of youth. They were both pretty. Their saucer eyes sunk into chiseled cheekbones.

Did they know their future was rigged? What brought them to this moment, on the brink of being accosted by a laggard drunk and a married man? If this wasn't meaningless, then the word had no meaning. Existence was a blessing, yet in the gaps between everyday moments and profound ones, also banal and futile.

Political correctness sucked the wind out of the fleeting time inherent in this setting. If everyone spoke their mind, bars and clubs might well be perennial ghost towns. No one could take the brutal honesty.

Am I fat? Yes, you are.

Liquid courage run amuck, defeating the purpose.

Feed the beast.

Buy this product, not that one.

Calder couldn't give up his passion for slogans, no matter whether he tried or not. Everyone wanted lies. Lies were the bedrock of America. Etiquette aside, why was he giving this man two cents of his time? Because he felt sorry for him? Calder was no better because he was right there with him. The loneliness permeated the bar. He could very well have been at another of Varick's seminars.

The old man made a motion to the Columbia grad students flanking him, shaking his head back and to the left in a coordinated arc. A we-can-do-this type of look carved his face into a devious mess. He picked up his own beer, something Irish but Calder didn't know what, and sidled up next to the lactating poster child for emasculation. Calder noticed the black hawk with piercing red eyes tattoo—between the index finger and thumb on top of the man's right hand—but thought nothing of it.

"I need a wingman. And there's nothing better than a semi-famous one. Better than a washed-up old janitor who moonlights as a professional barfly. Come on man. Help an old head out. I turn 50 in two weeks. Think of it as an early birthday present."

Calder hesitated. This man had zero chance with the pair of late 20-something, future-published archaeologists. The past semester they enjoyed a threesome with a vagabond Spaniard who was researching the poetry of Pablo Neruda. They had no need for an aging playboy and his lactating new father slated to run interference. They were quality catches and expected quality in return.

Still, the 49-year-old with 60-year-old wrinkles tried. Calder shook his head. He had to give the older—he was no longer old—man credit.

"It'll feel good, I promise," he said.

The man leaned in toward Calder like he was whispering a trade secret or divulging the location of a CIA mole. "My name's Jacob and we met at an NYU symposium on the brain five years ago. Let's run with it."

Up close, the man appeared much younger. The dim light of the bar did not flatter him when Calder passed by upon entering. Calder, detached from non-baby-feeding people, took the offer, an involuntary response he could not deny.

"Ladies...."

This was already bad.

Twenty minutes later, with the bar buzzing from the after-work insects, somehow it wasn't. The girls, seemingly lost in their own world when Calder arrived, blossomed under Jacob's strangely effective charms. They opened their hips to him and Calder and maintained eye contact. Though, Calder noticed for certain seven seconds into introducing himself that both women immediately saw his wedding ring. He was thankful they didn't make an immediate point of it. Calder liked to exist in a free possibility zone. He hated when women at a bar mentioned it forthright. Let a man be. Some, to be true, viewed a wedding ring like a talisman, attracting their competitive side to see if they could hold a kept man's interest, as if to fortify their own insecurities. Hogwash, they might say if they could read Calder's mind.

"Aren't you supposed to be at home?" Susan, the brunette, asked.

The redhead, Rhea, remained attentive, but strangely quiet for most of the conversation. Beware the quiet ones. Her eyes fixated on Calder's vanilla mocha skin. Then it came.

"What are you?

"My mother and father are both humans. So I guess I'm a human being," Calder replied with his standard line.

"He's got jokes," Jacob responded, then reclaimed his Lothario-like mastery of female prey.

Calder was distracted. For the past five minutes, his phone vibrated. He pressed his thumb deeper into his pants pocket. His phone vibrated again. Maren was definitely trying to reach him. Why today? She rarely called. Most of their communications were via text to avoid any miscommunication, or denials of what someone thought they had said but really hadn't. The proof was in the wireless pudding known as the cloud. Words mattered. Putting them to paper, or an electronic screen or a video diary made them beyond real into the aura of supposed extra meaning.

Bullshit.

Available at a moment's notice, 24/7 365 days a year? The 1970s represented the golden age of men drinking without care or contact—the old ball and cell phone—unless your wife called the bar in question. Afraid to look at the screen of his phone, Calder let the phone simmer in his pocket like a hot coal that had to be extinguished at some point, preferably quickly, before it left a scar.

The suspense injured his peace of mind. What if something had happened to Zoe? He was being an irresponsible parent and husband. Then he thought of his traumatic text from Mr. X. Its force came to bear. The armies of guilt and defiance marched onto the field of battle. But neither proved the difference maker: the foot soldiers curiosity and necessity won the day. Calder had not yet reached the don't-give-a-fuck plateau. Forced to acquire knowledge, he excused himself to go to the men's room.

The cramped room reeked of sweat and urine. Calder took refuge in the lone wooden stall, a hoped for barrier against the stench that instead led to the source. He remained standing, thank you very much. He swiped his phone, punched in the code and an illuminated text greeted him.

Where r u?

It wasn't from Maren; Astrid was inquiring. He was safe for the time being. Eris and Eros, the Greek goddesses of chaos and love, fought gallantly at his side, foreshadowing disorder and lust in equal measure. As he splashed water on his face, he noticed a slight lightheadedness. A faint nausea gave birth to itself in his bowels.

Calder returned to the fray, nursed the dregs of his second beer and mostly listened as Jacob worked his magic. The milkman wasn't a wingman; he was a prop. Better to be aware of it than gullible.

Tread lightly and carry a big stick.

"We're heading to an art gallery opening in Chelsea. Would you like to join us?"

Jacob blurted the question out, but with his piercing blue eyes the grad students couldn't resist. He wasn't a janitor either; he was their union's legal representation. Susan had eked it out of him. Another lawyer, it figures, Calder chuckled under his breath.

Jacob otherwise quarterbacked the discussion back onto the two grad students. What did they do? Rhea was actually a psychology major who had only volunteered for a educational two-week archaeological vacation to join her friend in Chile. This revelation led to another 15 minutes of discussion. They had forgotten about the opening. Calder barely spoke until Jacob asked if they had seen *The Andrea Peabody Show* or seen yesterday's *N.Y. Post*.

They hadn't. Jacob asked Mike to fetch a copy behind the bar. As a regular, Jacob knew that's where he kept the current *Post* and a few days backlog to hand out to bored patrons or to the gamblers who often dropped by with mysterious—i.e. illegal—wagering slips. There was something of an underground sports picks circuit in NYC bars and restaurants. Calder had won a few bucks himself. He was merely up $100 though and only bet small amounts to potentially win big in 12-team parlays. He currently participated in his biggest gamble to date: a brunette, a redhead and a female game-theory proponent.

Mike, the barman, handed Jacob a stack of *Posts*. They were in chronological order so it took little time for Jacob to find yesterday's edition. He held it up proudly, like a beaming father showing his baby to friends for the first time.

"Is that you?" Susan asked, even more intrigued by the new drinking quartet and its later evening prospects.

Calder nodded.

"Can I see? You know, a demonstration."

"Maybe later. Somewhere private."

Jacob was proud. He smiled, secure in the knowledge he had made the correct wingman call. Seizing the moment, Jacob mentioned the Chelsea gallery show again, though the women had tacitly given their affirmative answer the first time by continuing the conversation, indulging Jacob's relentless focus-on-them tactics. He couldn't have said more than 10 words about himself in a 30-minute span.

They simply asked perfunctory questions about what they were supposed to see.

"Who's the artist?" Susan blinked, temporarily forgetting about the lactation show she might see later. Jacob already had his right arm strategically placed around the small of her back, ramping up his game into an erogenous zone.

Calder was on. The art show was his provenance. Jacob focused his gaze on his accomplice.

"Essy Frisk, a Swedish porn star, painter and performance artist. She's painting a live sex act and assorted nudes. It's her thing. Sometimes she asks for volunteers."

Rhea's eyes lit up.

"I heard about this. Sounds like an excellent field

experience on human sexuality. That's my focus. I'm doing my doctoral thesis on the Coolidge Effect."

"What's that?" Calder took the bait and then guzzled half a glass of ice water.

"Humans naturally find it more appealing to engage in sexual activity with a new partner than one they are in a relationship with, long term or otherwise."

"I see."

"What about your wife and kid?" Susan asked.

"Men need dreams and fantasies to make it through life happily," Rhea piped in, the battlefield having shifted to her domain. She paused, took a final swig of her beer and added: "We all do actually. According to Chilean love poet Pablo Neruda."

"Let's get out of here," Jacob interjected, regaining control.

Two minutes later, the foursome was in a cab going at a snail's pace down the icy West Side Highway. Jacob, Susan and Rhea, the redhead, sat together in the backseat while Calder brought up the front. It was now 5:45 p.m. He replied to Astrid's text, while Jacob began kissing Susan, and sliding his free hand onto Rhea's knee.

On my way.

As if subconsciously trying to join in, Calder asked more questions about Rhea's field. Happy to expound, Rhea did not make any mention or exhibit an uncomfortable vibe from Jacob's advances on her and her friend. She spoke through the barrier glass, which was intended to separate the driver from the dangers of his passengers, but in this situation made the conversation awkward. Calder felt another surge of dizziness; however, he did not display any weakness. He'd only had two beers. He used to put back bottles like they were water. "What is this?" His friend Gerald often goaded him into guzzling his beer. One of the main things Calder learned in college was the ability to down beers in seconds by letting gravity allow the liquid to fall straight through his esophagus into his belly. He would tilt his head backward and the beer would slide down.

The physics of inebriation.

It was an early slogan Calder never found useful. But it would look good written down somewhere.

"Do you know about the term refractory period?" Rhea asked, knowing the topic would arouse Jacob further.

"Enlighten us," Jacob belched.

"It's the recovery phase after orgasms, in which it's physiologically impossible for a man to have additional orgasms. The older a man is, the longer the period of time is," Rhea said with clinical aplomb.

"What's the average length of time?" Jacob queried.

"Not long at all if you can separate ejaculation from orgasm. If not, it's about 30 minutes for a 20-year-old and it's all downhill from there."

The rest of the conversation swirled with words such as dopamine, oxytocin, and prolactin and each of the roles the human chemicals played. Jacob fell silent as he and Susan tongued each other, oblivious to anyone else in the vehicle. Rhea continued talking, mostly to allay any nervousness that might creep into what could have been an awkward coupling. Yet to Calder, it became a mélange of nothingness. He drifted off to sleep.

Eternity was on the brink of every moment. Or maybe Sappho's phrase was: *every moment we stand on the brink of eternity.* As he dozed, Calder would find the answer deep in his memory.

11

Streaks of red, orange and rust rendered the horizon a kaleidoscopic display of ancient history. James, Pernille and Calder Boyd stood on the precipice of a billion-year wonder. There was no hint of time as they stared into its maw.

"This is God's country," James "Bib" Boyd whispered. As soon as he uttered the words, he recognized his mistake. They stared across time's grandeur in silence. Pernille grasped her husband's hand and squeezed it tight. Looking back, Calder wondered if she had known something was ailing Dad then. The aura of the Grand Canyon distracted such ideas, a blaze of brilliant colors blended together to form an angelic glow around James, Pernille and their eldest son.

Each sandstone layer represented eons in geologic time. Calder would spend eternity here with his father. The moment in time captured in their last trip together in the Great American West. The sky transformed from powder blue to equal shades of sunset hues, making heaven and earth appear as one.

The Colorado River snaked through the ground, cutting closer and closer toward hell, with no nemesis but man and his water-diverting quests preventing it from succeeding. A lone passenger jet pierced the panorama. The contrail divided the sky into hemispheres with the canyon's reds mirrored in the hot sunset light above the zooming plane. If it weren't for the jet, it could have been ages ago on a primitive planet long before mankind arrived.

This wasn't Calder's first trip to the Grand Canyon, but it was the most spectacular. Sunset on the Mogollon Rim would forever be etched into his brain. Thirteen months before his father's death and two years before Zoe's birth, he joined his parents for a week in Sedona. They made the requisite pilgrimage to the big hole in the ground. Since the day was nearly over, Pernille suggested they catch the sunset on the rim of America's gaping beauty.

She knew nobody in their family was afraid of heights and believed the drive and, by extension, the entire trip would be a diversion from the everyday follies of their business-dominated lives. James Boyd—Calder never referred to his father as Bib—had sold the flagging laundry business long ago, and for the past 25 years had been the proprietor of a community-based pest control shingle in Pasadena, the city of Calder's birth.

Pernille excused herself to use the restroom, a good walk about a quarter mile along the canyon's edge. It would take at least 15 minutes there and back. She left her men to themselves, perhaps arbitrarily creating a moment or more than likely orchestrating it.

"If I ever become medically incapacitated by stroke or heart attack, or whatever, and wheelchair-bound, please do me a favor and bring me here and accidentally push me over the ledge. I wouldn't want to be alive anymore."

"Dad..."

It was a strange opening salvo. Something was not right, but Calder did not know it at the time. He revered his father and the long conversations they often had, but this conversation was stranger than all of the others. Calder found the preoccupation with death awkward, even though he too wondered about it.

Like father, like son was the patriarchal slogan to end all slogans.

James Boyd had turned 70 on Groundhog Day so the fixation on all things mortal was understandable, if not unappreciated. He earned the right to reminisce and flirt with the specter of leaving his legacy behind. It was a legacy filled with love, humor, humility and grace. Calder couldn't help but wonder if he harbored darker secrets. The deathwatch conversation smacked of a detour on the road to greater revelations.

"I'm serious," the elder Boyd continued. "Park the wheelchair right near an open section of the rim and if I'm able, put the electronic motor switch in my hand and I'll do it myself. That way you won't be culpable."

"You've really thought this through."

"Not with your mother. Not yet."

Calder was not sure if he believed him. He had never known his father to be anything but forthcoming.

"She conveniently left to go to the restroom. What have you told her?"

"Son, I'm fine. I just sometimes think of the finality of life. It would be a glorious death though, wouldn't it?"

He peered down at the majestic red pillars crisscrossing the Grand Canyon.

"It's beautiful. My father took all of us here when I was a kid."

It was one of the few times Calder remembered his father speak about his own father. The son did not push his father on the topic any further.

"It's 18 miles across at its widest point," Calder said.

"So you do remember our first big family trip here when you were eight."

"I remember when you lost your wallet at that KOA Flintstones-themed campground and Alan thought there was a snake in his sleeping bag and it turned out to be your wallet."

"We were about to turn around and go home too. I was one minute away from using the pay phone to cancel all my credit cards. No cell phones back then, son. The good old' days."

The elder Boyd put his hand on his son's shoulder.

"I'm proud of you. But when I do go, make sure I have on clean underwear before you push me over the edge."

Laughter floated into the air like children's bubbles.

"I thought I wasn't going to be culpable."

"I'll have to write up a new will absolving you of any wrongdoing."

Then, as the sky illuminated in a brief flash of rocket-exhaust orange before the sun dipped below the horizon, the silence moved in to fill the vacuum. The pretense dropped along with the sun.

"There's something else I need to tell you."

Bib Boyd, though age had taken a couple inches off his stature, still stood well over six feet, a good three inches taller than his son. Calder watched as his father's vulnerability peeled away layer by layer like the Colorado River cutting into the sandstone over and over throughout time to leave a giant spectacle of beauty.

"I hesitate to even tell you this. I'm doing it in the hopes it might help your current situation."

What was his situation? What did his father know? Calder didn't think their marital discord oozed from his pores plain as day. His father never spoke ill of anyone. Calder's apprehension skyrocketed; and if he possessed it, daredevil Evel Knievel would never have considered jumping the Grand Canyon on a motorcycle. It was a good thing he never attempted it, saving another trip to the hospital for shattered bones.

There would be no jump today. Calder's canyon of life unfolded in his mind, wondering what news would demolish his standard. There was no parachute.

Maren had declined to join her husband on what would prove to be the last family trip for James "Bib" Boyd. Calder had no idea it was because she was spending time with a mystery man from New Hampshire. The text from Mr. X was a future event. Then and there, however, Calder's father, prompted by the stunning landscape before him made a startling admission.

"I love your mother with all my heart and as you know she has been a wonderful mother...."

His dad fought back tears. Calder had never seen his father cry. Bib Boyd wrested control of his emotions and subdued a deluge that could have filled the immense rift staring back at him.

"Bottom line is, I forgave her," he said. "Forgiveness is the key to marriage. Forgiveness, then forgetfulness."

"Forgive her for what?"

Calder turned his head to his father. Tears flowed, winding down his father's cheeks creating their own canyon.

"This is not the legacy I wanted to give you."

"What is it, dad? It's okay."

Choking on his words, Calder's father reached into the pocket of his slacks and produced a small silver key.

"About a year before you were born, your mother and I were having marital troubles. I essentially told her to get lost. I couldn't stand her anymore. Every problem became a whirlwind, every argument, a hurricane. I was working three jobs essentially. The self-serve laundry chain, the pest control business and a car dealership, I was being pulled in different directions, all away from your mother."

Bib Boyd paused and wiped the sweat from his brow. The sunlight was nearly gone and the majestic glow of the Milky Way arched the sky like a starry rainbow.

"I told her to leave if she was unhappy. And she did for a few weeks. I was so stupid. I found out that she had been seeing another man on the side. She slept with him only once."

Calder didn't want to know the answer. He asked anyway. "How many months before I was born?"

"About nine."

Bib Boyd looked away from his son as the tears streamed down onto his Hawaiian-print shirt.

"We had slept together too all through her affair, so we didn't know who the father was. I loved your mother and felt to blame for her indiscretion. I didn't want to start a family with someone new. I wanted to start it with her. I stayed with her hoping the child was mine. I sold the Laundromat and car dealership and focused solely on the pest control business. When you were born, the moment I saw your big brown eyes, I knew you were my son. We forgave each other. We had a paternity test done, but when the results came in the mail, we never opened the envelope. This key opens the safe deposit box at the city credit union. One day maybe you'll feel the urge."

Calder did not know what to say. Silence, a dependable friend, was eternally ready to step in. The last hints of sunlight burned like dying embers in the night sky. Finally, Calder placed his hand on his dad's shoulder and tossed the key into the jaws of carved mesas overcome by darkness.

A thunderstorm approached. Two minutes later, Calder, Pernille and the patriarch all hugged as they gladly became soaking wet.

12

"Where have you been?" Calder's question loitered in the morning light that filtered through the long windows overlooking their bedroom. No answer filled the ensuing silence. Sitting on the edge of the bed, here and now, Calder became forever suspicious of silence. Two months after his trip to the Grand Canyon with his parents, Calder knew the real reason Maren did not make the trip.

Calder often returned to this moment. He relived it, analyzing his response, his surprising lack of outward anger. Despite the time that had passed and major life events, his mind could not escape it.

Time heals all wounds.

Time is relative.

Calder stayed in the maze of his memory; he hoped for the final time. The waking sun illuminated the scene of the crime like an overconfident detective shining his flashlight into the dark corners where no one dared venture. The old window blinds, left by the previous tenant and always ineffective, offered no extra sleep. Lies and deception ripped the bedroom—

once a sanctuary—in two, each side equally unappealing. The text message from Mr. X rattled in Calder's skull, confirming his haunting suspicions. Calder left for work and nothing was resolved. All day, he practiced the talk he knew had to happen. That night it would.

While waiting for his wife to return home, she also needed to get away from the apartment, Calder steeled himself to confront her. That August morning, instead of a "gotcha" moment—showing Maren the offending text from her paramour—he blurted out the hackneyed response of a cuckolded husband. There was no appropriate slogan for this. Maybe there was but Calder did not have the wherewithal to think of one. His memory flagged; he knew they had talked when Maren returned, but nothing substantive. She wanted to be caught? Calder wished he could rewind time, erase this moment, and remain ensconced in happier times. He left the apartment and walked along the East River, mind racing as fast as the glistening black water.

When he returned from his self-imposed exodus, Calder retreated further into the railroad apartment past the detritus of a former room that now resembled a forest of cobwebs and had become a storage space. Beyond that, Calder plopped himself onto a dusty futon in the TV room, which also contained additional storage space above two closets. Of course, Maren's hair products, clothes and shoes dominated the closet space, Calder's life relegated to three drawers in an oversized, blue particleboard dresser standing watch in the bedroom. It was sometime after 3 a.m.

Maren followed him.

More silence ensued, then tears.

"Who were you with?" Calder quickly recalibrated. "Don't tell me. If you do, our relationship will surely fail. The name will eat away at me until I cannot continue to be with you for all I will view you as is that name. The less I know the better."

"I felt so lonely. I've been telling you for months. You are never home. You're always coming home late at night. Other husbands cook dinner for their wives. You never cook for me. You come home after midnight every night."

"That's not true."

Why had he even allowed his wife to spend the night at her girlfriend's every now and then? He was too lenient, too aloof, because he expected the same courtesy—the ability to be trusted—in return, even if he never got it without blowback.

The next few weeks and months the couple went through the motions of marriage, the words "divorce" and "lawyer" and "separation" bandied about like overused children's toys. Calder buried himself in his work but found it difficult to concentrate, his mind consumed by Mr. X's text. He reexamined every episode over the past year and a half. How many nights Maren said she was working late had she, in fact, not been working at all?

They talked and argued and talked and tossed around about more legal terms—Calder needed an "affidavit of separation" to apply for a new apartment. The hurdles to a divorce, namely his finances, kept them together and living under the same roof.

There, in the wallows of sorrow and betrayal, things slowly began to improve. Small things, like laughter, watching movies again on the laptop side-by-side in bed, and having dinner together more often, became the bricks and mortar of a new Tower of Marital Babel. And babble they did.

"If we are going to continue as husband and wife, we have to trust each other," Calder said one night about three months after Mr. X's revelation.

"I trust you."

"I haven't done anything to betray that trust but if I go off the reservation, if you catch my drift, it's warranted."

"Don't tell me about it if you do." Maren uttered the unthinkable, but realized her position of weakness.

In the two weeks immediately following Maren's outing, Calder hung out with his friend Gerald two or three times, both weekends. One night, while Maren was overseas on a London photo shoot, Calder made out with a beautiful blonde Dutch woman, even fingered her in the club in a drunken state of ecstatic misery. He would sleep with her and he would hold onto this white-lie secret forever. He felt no guilt, shame or remorse. The sex was spectacular. God placed temptation, affirmation and redemption into a Dutch package. He never spoke of her to anyone. He felt alive again. And now he and Maren were even.

When she returned from Europe, Calder hugged his wife, the first time he'd really touched her in two months. He wanted to keep her, and he wanted it to be anything but cheap. A fissure opened in the fortress of certain divorce, and a small sliver of light became trapped. In the Pandora's box of love, light is all you need.

13

When they sauntered into the Chelsea art gallery a tornado of curves, gorgeous hair and male bravado, Calder's coat collar went up. So far so good, nobody noticed. Calder's present company notwithstanding, the cops had been the only ones to recognize him today.

Astrid and the striking blonde accompanying her with size 36C cups and svelte figure spotted him immediately. Only Astrid was free to move. Essy Frisk was in the midst of de-robing, walking nude around the gallery and taking impromptu selfies with unsuspecting patrons. A deejay played electronic background noise—unusual for an opening, yet oddly suitable—and white-jacket-clad Chelsea boys served hors d'oeuvres. In one corner, two women were body-painting volunteers, one a 20-something female art student with a spectacular figure, and in another, a man gyrated on a stripper pole as part of Essy's "live sculpture" Adonis. A late 19th century carnival vibe percolated. Calder half-expected an elephant to ramble past at any moment.

This orgiastic circus was not without an even more stultifying entrance. The frigid weather did not deter this expectant crowd. Two armed and uniformed security guards—off-duty NYPD—manned the door. At one of Essy's early shows in Stockholm a zealous protestor had showered three patrons and one "living nude sculpture" with blue spray paint and stabbed another patron with a six-inch hunting knife. Ice stalactites clung to the awnings above and appeared posed to slice anyone who tried to rush the door or stepped too far out of line, if that was possible given the clientele.

Calder and his motley crew had entered the gallery through a gauntlet comprising of the two beefy security personnel, a metal detector, a wending line that got progressively narrower the closer it got to the front door and a table occupied by two twenty-something terrors who checked names on the guest list like a pair of secret service agents, complete with communication headsets. Rhea, Susan and Jacob were not on the list; however, in Calder's presence, they entered like royalty. It created an added layer of excitement on top of the already pulsating throng.

The presence of two unknown women—a pair of curious flies with tight turtlenecks exposing the curve of their bosoms—surrounding Calder, confused Astrid, but it did not deter her from approaching. Nothing much would, Calder surmised.

Doing his best to remain incognito, his own fly on the wall, Calder and his pickup troupe headed for the catered bar. The pungent aroma of wine swirled throughout the gallery. He still felt lightheaded but believed a glass would calm his garbled nerves. He was going into darker psychological corners with possibly murkier people.

Astrid circled the bar cautiously, a pantheon of blue. Her sky-tinted stiletto heels, cobalt dress and sapphire eyes cleared an easy path for her. Calder overheard another woman say, "I'd love to see her naked." Despite her powerful outward appearance, Astrid's true hidden feelings were rendered opaque against the canvas of controlled chaos inside the Eisenstein Gallery.

Calder recognized clearly that Astrid harbored an attraction towards him. He had sensed it at the St. Regis following his interview, but the competition caused her lust—straddling a fine line close to contempt—to blossom.

"You seem to be doing well for yourself," Astrid broke the ice as she passed dangerously close to the nude living sculpture. "Who are your friends?"

Jacob, who up until that moment had been dead set on bedding Susan, suddenly lost his mind.

"We should volunteer."

Astrid gave a gnat more attention.

"Don't trust Essy. No matter what she tells you."

Astrid calmly, yet with a deliberate grace, placed her right hand on Calder's left cheek as if staking her claim on Antarctica despite the treaty banning such practices, and her left hand on his right one. Calder clasped her fingers and she slowly redirected his right hand back down to his side. She did not let go.

"Your hands are freezing but your face is burning up. Are you OK?"

"Are you here to save me?"

Calder, forgetting he had invited others, suddenly remembered.

"The unrepentant Lothario is Jacob. These two are grad students at Columbia. Susan, an archaeologist to be, and Rhea, a sex researcher."

"On a field trip so to speak," Rhea interjected.

"You've come to ground zero then," Astrid replied. "And here comes Patient Zero, the maiden of honor."

Frisk—obviously not her real name—abruptly ended her conversation and stalked the lactating celebrity. She burst past Astrid, breaking her friend's grip on Calder's hand. Astrid and Essy were friends in the every now and then sense. They didn't go to each other's social functions all that much, or attend church or sporting events together. They existed as each other's darker half, if Essy could have one. Darkness to her was being seen in a more normal light. Astrid's respectable job on air in Sweden provided Essy an air of legitimacy, and Astrid was afforded the street cred Essy provided.

Essy was her real first name, but she added the "Frisk" after she appeared in her first "erotic"—in her mind, none of her films were porn; art but never porn. The film, *Blue Sunday*, about an aging painter who hires a nymph to pose nude for him, had been a cult hit and even screened out of competition at the Cannes Film Festival. Essy had been named after a similar Swedish actress, Essy Persson, no relation to Astrid, who had appeared in the 1968 film *Therese and Isabelle*—about two girls' sexual awakening at a Swiss boarding school—and gone onto a modicum of fame. Raised by her father—her mother abandoned Essy when she was two—the film was a totem for young Essy, and she viewed it as her destiny. It infused many of her ideas for installations, and performance pieces.

Astrid met her at a Stockholm nightclub, when *and* where they both discovered they were sleeping with the same man. They became sisters-in-cheating-arms.

A low-grade buzz of hushed whispers whipped through the assembled art, and sex, lovers. Calder was a cause célèbre.

"You're going to be my next art project whether you know it or not," Essy purred. "You're bigger and much more handsome in person."

"Thank you."

"Don't fall for it," Rhea said. "Classic gambit to win your affections, steal your status and then throw you by the wayside. In my sex researcher opinion."

Rhea made air quotes on the words "sex researcher." Calder whispered into her ear: "I didn't know what else to call you. Sorry." Seeing the floating photographer documenting the event—he ran a blog that posted photos from art gallery openings—Rhea kissed Calder full on the lips just as the photographer snapped his grab.

"The Coolidge Effect," Susan said.

"His manhood is under debate," Jacob returned to the fray, defending his newfangled friend's actions.

"I think it's beautiful, you could probably use some different femininity." Susan spoke and slid

Jacob's hand away from her waist in one fluid motion.

"I'm just joking," Jacob defended himself. Susan ran away, providing the illusion of playing hard to get. Jacob followed and a minute later they were fondling each other in front of one of the videographers in the corner, kissing like beasts. Calder would never see them together again. But he was happy he had provided Jacob exactly what he needed, even if it was lacking in his own life.

"Lucky for you I have to run," Essy said. "The show is about to begin."

Nobody knew what she meant by show. She could strip naked, or pile on clothes, or release venomous snakes in the corner. Her volatility was her performance. She hired five videographers. Four manned each of the gallery's corners while the fifth floated through the madness pointing the lens on the intimate encounters that ensued when beautiful naked bodies abounded. *PRETTY PEOPLE PROCREATING*, that was the name of Essy's show, the nomenclature being hers of course. Essy had instructed them to "document the art of flirtation."

Essy clapped her hands loudly and emitted an ecstatic moan to garner the ravenous patrons' attention, as if her bulging figure and ostentatious aura did not suffice. She sauntered to the center of the room and immediately disrobed. The moment her blue cotton robe hit the sleek white floor, the lights went dark and a blue spotlight cracked on, illuminating her body from above as if she were a spectral Greek sculpture. Gasps of longing and excitement punctured the air.

Essy became a living nude statue.

Over the next two minutes, she contorted her body so that any movement was imperceptible and transformed into the Venus de Milo. The light above her rotated from blue to green, to red, to purple and back to blue. Essy began to heave her chest up and down sucking in large blasts of air.

Calder, Astrid and Rhea stood on the periphery, at the front half of the circle that had formed around Essy. An amused older man with a trimmed white beard and black and white striped gold hat resting backward on his head voiced his opinion to no one in particular. "The NYC art scene is dead. It's about time somebody shook it up." An older woman standing next to him, presumably his wife, added: "It reminds me of participating in Yayoi Kusama's Happenings in the 1960s. I want to take my clothes off." The amused man retorted, "Nobody came here to see that, my dear."

Calder wiped the sweat off his brow. He'd only been at the gallery for 10 minutes and he was overheating. He looked back, searching for a way out, but the wall of art hipsters would not budge. Claustrophobia lurked. He had not had a bout since the aborted bus ride he attempted post-Hurricane Sandy. Calder took deep breaths to calm down.

He and the amused man were forced to move when Essy's art accomplices—the other living nude sculptures; all female except for one—wafted their way through the crowd in slow, choreographed motions. The people parted like a mob dodging the rancid, mid-July smell of a homeless man on an empty subway car with no air conditioning.

The male living nude sculpture, Adonis, waved his milky white hands across bystanders male and female. Calder and Astrid were anointed. Adonis circled Essy as she chanted a hypnotic incantation.

"Suckle at the bosom of the goddess of love, suckle in the throes of passion, suckle on the orgasms of the universe!"

Adonis draped his legs around Essy and began to slowly gyrate. Their intertwined nude bodies transformed into one fluid entity. The blue light, filtered now with intricate patterns of projected images of people making love, danced across their skin, which became a living movie screen. In the rapturous climax, just as an aroused Adonis entered Aphrodite, the gallery went completely dark. Then the images returned, one, then another and another, displayed on Essy's back as Adonis' throbbing figure could just be discerned in the shadows.

"Is there any other man amongst you who is worthy of my love?"

Essy reveled in provocation.

There were a few random shouts from the intrepid, testosterone-amped guys who had come for the kink not the art, but Essy ignored them. She continued to breathe heavily, an influence to engender passion in her audience, but Calder thought it was too exaggerated. The flickering lovemaking peaked in intensity.

"Calder Boyd! Suckle at the bosom of Aphrodite!" Essy cried.

A spotlight illuminated above him. Calder looked up and for the first time realized the ceiling was rigged with rows upon rows of lights. They flicked on then off in a strobe effect until only one remained—an actual strobe—that gave Calder and everyone else in the gallery a bit of anonymity. Enough, Essy hoped, to cause clothes to come off.

"Calder Boyd! Suckle at the bosom of Aphrodite!" Essy repeated her command.

The living nude female sculpture, representing Demeter, the goddess of the harvest—fertility in Essy's case—started to wail uncontrollably. The sea of nameless art denizens parted once more as Essy floated through the crowd carrying a glowing white bauble. Calder became transfixed, staring intently at the orb. The nude woman walked in a zigzag pattern around the inner edge of the circle holding the orb up to onlookers' faces like a jack o'lantern.

The nude Demeter stopped in front of Astrid, and then, with the care given to a newborn, swiped the glowing sphere, which was the size of a bocce ball, across Rhea's left cheek. Demeter spontaneously kissed Rhea, and at the same instant, in a clever feat of misdirection, opened the radiant ball at about waist level.

Distracted, neither Calder nor anyone else in the gallery noticed what Demeter accomplished elsewhere with her lowered hands. She cracked the orb open, each half made of light plastic like a giant Easter egg, and produced a pair of chained cuffs.

Before Calder knew what was happening, and while his strange sensation of disorientation reached a crescendo, she clapped the cuffs around his wrists. Helpless to stop her, Demeter finessed his shirt off button by button, moving in a ritualistic manner while Essy throbbed in the darkness. Images of orgies and breasts and real and phallic symbols passed across her back, a sexual kaleidoscope of lust, pleasure and sin.

Calder's shirt fell to the floor like a lifeless doll. Demeter moved on to his trousers, unzipping them as dizziness swirled through his body. The pants too fell by the wayside, but mercifully for Calder's sake, Demeter went no further. Essy intervened.

Essy unclenched from Adonis and strode in measured steps to her ultimate target. She stood on her toes like a ballerina and stretched until her breasts were level with Calder's.

She squeezed with all her might. A jet of white milk streamed over her face and down her breasts.

"The milk of lust. The milk of love. The milk of life!" Essy chanted.

Calder finally mediated on his behalf and ended the proceedings in a blink.

He smiled just before passing out. A fleeting image gripped his mind as he fell. His face kissed the floor; blood became the fruit of their union.

Zoe.

14

Rivulets of rabid rain pelted the windows at the far end of the hall on the 12th story of Roosevelt Hospital. At 5:55 a.m., the labor and delivery floor was unusually quiet. Maren doubled over in pain and all Calder could do to remain calm was to focus on the menacing downpour flooding the city.

The 19th of October was the rainiest night Calder could remember. It was a Wednesday. Maren's labor began—at least contractions of some unbearable pain—48 hours earlier. In fact, doctors admitted Maren only to send her home when what they said in triage was six centimeters dilated turned out to be five. Now two days hence, Calder found relief in the knowledge Zoe would not be arriving in the back of a taxi.

Calder experienced neither the irrational fear, nor the complete expectation of the inevitable. He existed in the middle, on the outer limits of meaning. Because, he realized, he was nothing without his wife, and her endurance to deliver a beautiful child was supreme. He was without meaning until Maren delivered. He had never been sure of anything but he was sure about that. Yet, when it came to the nuts and bolts of the actual birth experience, Calder was naïve.

After Monday's false alarm, his confusion deepened. With every contraction, he wasn't sure if it was a disobedient Braxton-Hicks or the beginning of the beginning. At 4:30 a.m. that morning, Calder knew from the look on Maren's face. They hopped in a cab on the corner of 81st Street and Third Avenue at 3:54 a.m. and were being entered into the system on the ground-floor emergency room 10 minutes later. Calder only remembered passing the illuminated Metropolitan Museum of Art. The large drops of rain smashing into the windshield kept perfect rhythm with the windshield wipers. Everything else was a haze of memory.

In triage, Maren was measured at five centimeters dilated. Aware of her false alarm history two days earlier, the presiding doctor advised Maren to walk the maternity halls for two hours until her labor was further along.

This brought Calder to this extraneous moment, staring aimlessly at the God-size buckets of rain being dumped on Manhattan. He rubbed Maren's neck and shoulders, wishing he could vanquish her pain in a deluge of love. The immediacy would be a permanent Etch-A-Sketch in his skull.

"Yeah, right there," she cooed, a brief respite from the happy hurt.

Maren winced in pain, not from his unprofessional attempt at a massage—she never thought he did a good job, but trying was a gigantic first step—but as waves of life-giving contractions shuddered through her torso like muscular earthquakes. Calder implored her to try to keep moving, in a voice that was a mélange of concern, apprehension and thankfulness. Love was the given in the geometry equation.

Maren shimmied into a white hospital gown and a pair of slippers. Or maybe she was allowed to keep on her Nikes. Calder could not remember every small detail. Births and deaths have a way of consuming everything in the room around them.

About 10 minutes to eight in the morning, Maren's long blonde hair flirted with the back of her gown as she was admitted and wheeled into Room 32—the same chamber they had been in two days prior, thinking Zoe would pop out any moment. Would the second time be the charm?

At 9:09 a.m., Maren's pain became unbearable— a nine on a scale of 10—and Calder dutifully suggested the epidural. Calder kept copious notes, so much so that he risked not being present. He realized this and stopped taking notes in that same palindrome minute.

The anesthesiologist, a resident, pricked Maren's back and soon the good stuff flowed. The attending doctor asked Calder if he had eaten. "No."

"You might not get a chance for the next 18 years," the doctor deadpanned. Calder chuckled at the joke. It brought much-needed levity. Nonetheless, Calder did not want to leave his wife's bedside. Upon further doctoral imploring, and after Maren convinced him it was okay—"Zoe isn't coming out right this minute. I'm the mother. Trust me."—Calder escaped the hospital, absconding with a cheeseburger and fries from the bar across the street on the corner of 57th and Tenth Avenue. He couldn't recall its name to save his life.

Just after noon, Maren went into active labor. The doctor informed her with smiling eyes that she could push with the next contraction. Calder and Maren spoke very little. Holding her hand tightly communicated all. Every tiny moment became its own universe. The clouds outside blended so the streets and sky appeared as one, the small of the nurse's back looked like a volcanic crater. Dr. Sorenson's frizzy blonde hair obscured her face and the monitors and whirring sounds they emitted became a battlefield of nervousness versus elation.

Maren's tight grip loosened by the same force applied to a soft turn of a screw. Her eyes focused on an object on the far side of the room—a technique she learned courtesy of Jackie and her weekend Lamaze class.

Who, who, who.

Not a question, it was the sound of Maren's rhythmic breathing. The pattern she couldn't forget and never would. Catch that breath. It won't be your last.

You'll never have that contraction again.

Jackie's voice filled their ears. They both thought of her at the same—and sane—time.

Joy, Maren's mother, arrived from Norway on the same day as the false alarm. Her flight across the

North Atlantic left her a bit tired but she did not remain at the Upper East Side apartment for this reason; she had a more altruistic agenda.

"This is your moment," she said. "I'll be there when she arrives, of course, but this is your time. Share it together as if you are the only two people left alive. For all that matters, you *are* the only two people alive. The only three people alive. You're truly a family now. Remember each moment and welcome Zoe with open, loving arms."

Maren half-heartedly objected, but Calder knew the wisdom in his mother-in-law's choice without any prodding. They were the only people alive saving the world with the birth of their child, who in turn could give birth herself in two decades extending the eternal cycle. Zoe would be born with all the eggs for her entire lifetime, as many as two million.

In the taxi ride to the hospital, Maren slid toward the same opinion. Her husband was the only other person alive. The pounding rain on the windshield had hypnotized both of them, marking time like a metronome.

"It sounds like Zoe's heart monitor," Calder recalled saying. The raindrops smashed into blotches upon violent contact with the windshield, then disappeared in the first instant of their fleeting life streaming down the glass past the black blades.

"This is a beautiful night. I will never look at rain the same way again." Calder knew his wife wouldn't. Neither would he.

The rest of the cab ride transpired in silence. All that was left was the heartbeat-mimicking rain and wipers. And even as Calder waited at Maren's side in the delivery room, the pelting rain metronome and the erasing windshield wipers echoed through his mind. Later, Maren admitted to him that as Zoe's head crowned, all she heard were the raindrops outside the window until a brilliant cry from tiny lungs filled Room 32.

There were no notes taken and Maren forgave Calder's mythomania. Zoe Indigo Boyd, weighing seven pounds and four ounces, bounded into the world with her dark eyes—they would turn gray in three weeks—peering into her mother and father's gaze. They didn't notice the nurse when she slipped on a pink and blue striped knit cap and placed Zoe in Maren's arms. Tears fled her eyes and she breastfed right away, no matter that Maren's breasts lacked the required level of nutrients. Skin to skin, a bond formed that would last beyond the death of the universe. Calder watched in awe. The sound of the rain outside—or maybe it was an echo of the taxi ride—matched the beating of all three of their hearts.

And a few minutes later, when Calder had his turn, he never wanted to break his staring contest with his baby daughter in his arms. Calder heard and heeded his mother's advice: "Think about the first words you want your daughter to hear as she comes into this world. They will be the words that shape her entire life. Choose them wisely."

Calder bent down and whispered in his daughter's ear. She smiled. There was no documentation and Calder's penchant for embellishment would render it hard to believe, but it was true. As true as he fit his new moniker: father.

15

The itinerant gash streaked across his forehead like a comet, spewing blood and inducing vitriol. Though his head throbbed, Calder could hear two women arguing in the background. It wasn't the nurses; they sounded rather put together and not prone to such outbursts. No, the highs and sighs of a pitched battle waged somewhere nearby.

He recognized both of the voices as he slowly came to in an unfamiliar antiseptic environment. The glass separating his Hill-Rom adjustable gurney from the outside hallway bled into the familiar figures of first Astrid, then his wife. They floated like phantoms trapped in fog, disembodied arms, hands and heads bobbing up and down.

Zoe wiggled in Maren's arms until she calmed her down and put her in the stroller, aka the Sleepmobile. Calder saw the whites of Maren's eyes and teeth as she clenched them. If she could grab a scalpel at this instant, she would slash the right side of Calder's forehead out of spite to keep it symmetrical. She brandished her right index finger an inch from Astrid's face.

All of this transpired through the prism of pain medication and hazy vision. Calder tried to move his right hand, but he couldn't. He tried the left. Same thing. A bundle of cords weaved their way from his temples into monitors and other electronic equipment behind, and to the side, of his hospital bed. Crystallized thoughts began to form. He was in a hospital. He remembered hitting his head. Calder made intimate love with the hard studio floor at the art gallery, and seconds before that, Essy's erect nipples poked his eyes.

Pretty People Procreating.

A shot of additional worry flooded through Calder's mind. Where was Rhea? There was no sign of her. His desiccated mouth craved liquid. Calder knew he was in enough trouble already. He didn't know it was worse. He had been exposed, and the shrill beep of the monitor, which indicated he had come to, would not save him.

"Nurse, nurse! I think he's waking up." Calder definitely recognized Maren's voice. His daze was numbered.

Maren barged into the room; Astrid remained a fuzzy figure. As Calder came to he realized he didn't have blurry vision at all. The glass itself was frosted and only went halfway up the wall, to allow patients, in this case Calder, to be seen by medical staff.

Even before the nurse arrived, Maren's first words weren't, "I love you."

"What were you thinking?"

Calder tried to answer but a breathing tube had

been inserted into his gaping mouth. That accounted for the dryness. The nurse finally made an appearance.

"Where were you? Get these tubes out of him!"

There was no need for that. Calder wasn't sure if she wanted them off out of concern or so that she could berate him further. He deserved it. He resigned himself to taking the high road—or perhaps the low; he recalibrated—and just nodding his head. Keeping your mouth shut worked best in this situation, Calder agreed with himself.

"Ma'am, we have a monitor at the nurse's station. We know exactly what's going on with all of our patients at all times."

"Is he OK?"

"The doctor will be in shortly. He'll explain everything to you."

"Everything?" Maren vocalized Calder's concern at the same instant he had in his mind.

The five minutes between the nurse leaving and the doctor arriving felt like a three-hour Super Bowl halftime, the advertising day to end all ad days.

The doctor was younger than Calder. He looked more handsome and clearly had six-pack abs hiding beneath his white coat. His skin was a light golden brown, not unlike Calder's. His brown hair flowed down the back of his neck like a lion's mane. His presence immediately ended the rancor between Astrid and Maren.

Calder groaned.

Not because he was in pain, but because he dreaded continual blowback for the next several days, weeks, months and possibly the rest of his lifetime, which he may have significantly shortened. He wouldn't be able to live this one down, or up. He had to take it.

Astrid retreated outside the room while Maren berated Calder in a harsh, but loving whisper; there was still the fact that he had evidently suffered a traumatic injury. He had that paving his way. The doctor interceded, placing his hand on a Maren's back, calming her with his charisma and good looks.

"How are we feeling, Mr. Boyd?" The doctor wasn't expecting an answer. "Let's get that breathing tube out and unbuckle the restraints," he continued to the nurse, who had mysteriously reappeared from the shadows.

The doctor checked Calder's stitches.

"It was only a precautionary measure. He kept pulling the tube out in his sleep so we restrained him. His breathing was shallow and very labored when he was admitted last night."

Last night?

How long had he been unconscious? Calder's thoughts became riddled with new concerns. How much did Maren know? Not of his medical status, which should be paramount, though oddly wasn't, but of his first day of "day job" unemployment. Did she know he had been laid off the day before? Maybe it was two days ago. Calder again tried to recalibrate but his internal logic circuits did not comply.

He had to call the head usher. He obviously would need to take a few days off—forever if Maren had her wish. This wasn't even important in the immediate aftermath of his hospital room awakening. Calder regained some semblance of command, and the synapses under his skull returned to worrying about the latest ice storm hitting his existence.

Wait. Espera. Attendez. Chotto matte. Vent.

He thought of the word in every language he knew. The shock of what Calder saw—and his scrambled brain—as the nurse removed his ventilator inspired the minor polyglot in him to emerge.

Another familiar face was slumped over in the corner of the room on a chair: his pseudo friend, nay nemesis, Varick. He had been keeping a dormant vigil while dreaming of Astrid—who didn't? It may have been his loud snoring that roused Calder out of his deep slumber.

"Mr. Varick Williams was kind enough to track down your wife. The paramedics found his card in your wallet and figured he was a friend," the doctor said. "I apologize. I'm Dr. Uxbridge."

Varick Williams? The mailman had transposed his name for dramatic effect. Calder lifted his hand and Dr. Uxbridge made contact in a perfunctory matter of fact manner. Maren was staring at his flowing brown hair.

"You two could be brothers," she observed.

"My father's British and my mother's Jamaican."

The doctor broke the tension in the room. Astrid peered through the glass, her mascara running down her face like a defiant streak from a black magic marker. The suspense had killed someone else and moved on.

"What's the prognosis?" Calder interceded, taming the elephant in the room. Then he noticed the creamy substance all over his chest. He lifted his aquamarine hospital gown and pressed milk between his fingers. Instinctively, he licked them.

"Bring Zoe to me."

"She's asleep."

"I need to feed her."

"I don't think that would be a good idea," Dr. Uxbridge advised. "You should wait until the Rohypnol is entirely out of your system. An endocrinologist will be speaking to you as well. He's part of your medical team."

Wait.

Calder contorted his face into a myriad of confused states. Jacob must have accidently passed him the wrong beer, the beer intended for Susan, or Rhea, or both.

"Were you at a bar?" Maren inquired.

"I, Calder Boyd, under the advisement of attorney, plead the fifth, on the grounds I may incriminate myself." His sense of humor was still intact, but at what cost? Dr. Uxbridge saved him, of sorts.

"We did an MRI, and while you have no major effects from the fall, other than a mild concussion, we did find something rather unusual," Dr. Uxbridge explained. "You have a pituitary gland tumor. The tumor is causing the abnormal release of prolactin, hence your lactation. Which is called galactorrhea."

"What?" Maren expressed genuine concern, shock and awe. Calder felt cared for. Or maybe she did know about his unemployment status. Now he knew she did, but she was saving that gem of a conversation for a more appropriate time.

"Galactorrhea," Dr. Uxbridge reiterated. "It's the correct term for your husband's condition."

"No, I mean the tumor. Is my husband going to die?"

Dr. Uxbridge looked beyond her.

"Yes, Mrs. Boyd, you're husband is going to die. But not today, or anytime soon. We hope. We caught it relatively early and it doesn't appear to be metastasized."

"Well, at least I've got that one going for me," Calder couldn't help but interject his foot into his mouth.

"We're quite surprised you don't already know about it. It's in your electronic medical history. Dr. West entered it into your record one month ago. Our scan just confirmed it."

"You knew about this?" Maren's face split.

"No."

"Let me explain." Varick was awake, almost as if on cue. His overcoat might as well have been a superhero cape. He sprang to his feet in one fluid motion and went into his patented sales pitch mode. However, would Dr. Uxbridge and more importantly Maren, who were likely each in the midst of their own black sand beach fantasy, buy the story?

"I had our mail forwarded," Calder blurted. He thought it was best to stay ahead of this one. He cut Varick off before he began.

"You did what?" There was one more thing justifying Maren's ire. "I've been looking for two paychecks."

Exit Stage Left.

Calder had no easy out.

"I suggested it," Varick copped. "So I take the blame. There's a big bundle at the post office. I'll stop the hold tomorrow. Well, today. Shit, I'm late for work."

Varick began to run beyond the frosted glass, from the room's frosty aura and into the frost outside. As he brushed past Maren, Varick remained fixated on Astrid.

"And I invited him to the art gallery show," Varick added. "Essy Persson is a close personal friend of mine, if you know what I mean."

"No, I don't know or care what you mean," Maren glared, then rescinded. "I'm sorry. Thank you for looking out for my husband last night. I got here as soon as I could."

"No problem," he said, then turned toward Astrid and changed the octave of his voice. "Do you want to share a cab?"

It was love at first, second and third sight. Calder was the inadvertent wingman once more. The dynamic duo vaporized.

As soon as she could?

Suspicion, once suspended, but no longer, crept into Calder's mind.

Where had she been? Mr. X calling.

"Am I interrupting something? I can come back later," the endocrinologist, Dr. Alston, knocked on the open door and entered the room from behind the frosted glass.

"Thankfully, the tumor has not grown since it was

first diagnosed," he said. "There are several options for treatment. Surgery usually being the most effective but drug therapy and chemotherapy, or a combination thereof, are additional options."

"I don't want surgery," Calder said as Zoe began to wail in her stroller. "I don't want to stop lactating. Zoe needs me."

In truth, it was the other way around. And Calder was the only one in the room who didn't know it. Zoe was a living breathing person, complete with her own personality, but she was also Calder putting on tiny pink gloves at 4:41 a.m.—to prevent her from scratching her head-to-toe eczema—and feeding pumped breast milk or latching to a nipple at 5:55 a.m., and engaging in staring contests replete with unconditional love at any hour and wiping her cute, poop-covered buttocks during the eighth diaper change in a 24-hour period at 6:56 a.m.

She was love, a reflection of the love radiated toward her.

And even in her father's time of rescuing, she aided his quest for peace despite his poor judgment.

Zoe glowed whenever she basked in her father's adoration. When he walked in the door, she stared big, dreamed big and cooed big. Maren admitted once to being jealous. "Dads are usually less strict," Calder had said two months ago. It was this bond that made home relevant and that kept the doghouse relatively at bay.

With his breathing function back under his control, Calder inhaled deeply, a cleansing and centering breath he had learned from an ex-fling. He couldn't remember her name. Zoe superseded all other names.

16

Jan. 20

4:12-4:52 p.m. Breast fed Zoe for 20 minutes on each breast before we left the hospital. She fell asleep sucking on my left nipple so broke the suction with my right index finger. Changed her diaper (she finally pooped!). Put lots of lotion on her legs and a little on her torso. Put moisturizer on her face. Her rash is nearly gone. The prescription the dermatologist gave is working. Will give her a bath tonight. My nipples aren't as chapped. The nipple cream is thankfully starting to show some results. After feeding, Zoe fell asleep in her stroller on the way home.

The floorboards creaked as the Boyd family entered their cramped apartment. It was the lone sound breaking the afternoon chill. The air outside was no match for the air inside, a feat Calder didn't think about when he embarked on his Homer-like odyssey back to Sofa Island. When Maren glared at him, Calder stepped into a pre-designated dead spot on the floor. The meaning in her eyes was clear. Walk in the safe zones and do not wake Zoe at all costs.

Two pairs of eyebrows sweated in the silence between them, a foreboding stillness in stark contrast to the moments before Zoe's birth. A thin, but noticeable, layer of dried blood obscured one pair; the other pair disappeared behind the bedroom door.

What with Zoe sleeping in her arms, Maren closed the door gently. Calder heard Zoe stir. A series of muffled whimpers slid beneath the hollow plywood door directly into his ear. He felt like he was on Mars and the transmissions took several minutes to reach Earth.

If men truly are from Mars, Maren is from another galaxy. Maren sang several lullabies in an attempt to quell Zoe's fussiness.

Row, row, row your boat, gently down the stream. Merrily, merrily, merrily, merrily, life is but a dream.

Maren possessed a keen sense of humor; the song served as both a baby pacifier and a warning shot of sarcasm. By the end of her fifth rendition of the children's standard, quiet reclaimed its throne in the crowded apartment. A thick tension rejoined the fray. There was a vacuum of understanding. Calder knew he was sleeping on the sofa tonight—hey, that's where he was anyway—and the tumor reveal was no reprieve.

Strangely, Calder and Maren did not argue. The

roiling anger, however, crept into every crack in the white brick wall behind Sofa Island. White, the color of purity, reflected the fading sunset light that poked through the open blinds. Icicles stretched down the window like the fingers of a doctor's scalpel forming an ominous lattice against the backdrop of the black blinds.

Come to Sofa Island. Let all your troubles fall away.

Calder realized—he always had, but suppressed the idea—that it was all a lie. Sofa Island was no luxury. It was a low-lying barrier island that protected the shore from hurricanes, preventing real damage further inland but racking up insurance claims at the forefront. It did not prevent flooding from occurring. The bile would spew forth in due time, but now he needed rest. For one night, there would be a truce.

The stitches zigzagged across Calder's forehead. He had taken the large butterfly bandage off to let the wound breathe as the doctor ordered. If he bothered to leave the misguided safety of Sofa Island and look in the mirror, he would see pus oozing from the grisly cut.

Let it air out.

The doctor's advice was equally appropriate for their marriage, which was also in need of bandages. As he lay on the sofa, the last glint of sunlight disappeared and darkness blanketed the room. Calder wallowed in the absence of light. Every past argument flooded back into Calder's cerebral cortex.

Once, after Maren had worked a Fashion Week show, the designer had mailed her a dress to show her gratitude. The box sat in a clutter near the trash repository at their dank, old Greenpoint apartment for weeks. Mistaking it for trash, Calder discarded the box that unbeknownst to him was needed to return the borrowed dress; it had not been a long-term situation. When Maren discovered what he had done, her face split into a gargoyle.

"I hate you now," Maren said at the time.

Why would the word hate even be uttered? There were other words to express anger, but she hated him? She made Calder buy a new box. Months later the sting of her harsh words upset him.

Believing they had escaped arguments about faulty appliances or other woes when they moved into the Upper East Side apartment, another conflagration occurred when Maren insisted the refrigerator, or something else, caused an annoying electrical hum. Calder didn't notice the hum, and it and that fact perturbed Maren to no end. "You are ignorant," she said.

The dust-up devolved from there. "You're too self-centered. Why don't you take care of me?" And later: "Most wives leave because their husband doesn't listen. I'm so glad I'm finally saying this now."

Four months later, Maren was pregnant. An immaculate conception caused by three months of conception sex. Calder wondered if tonight's State of the Union was about the nation or the state of his marriage. The stitches jagging across his forehead made Frankenstein look handsome. Maren hadn't spoken to him since he was discharged from the hospital.

There had been no need. Another *N.Y. Post* headline said it all: BREAST MILK. No question: she knew about his job status. Lactation would be his saving grace and his death. Zoe cried in the other room. Daddy to the rescue.

"I'm going out."

"Where?"

"I'm having dinner with a potential client, to discuss a shoot," Maren said. "Somebody has to work around here."

The stinging rebuke was all that was said as she grabbed her overcoat, kissed Zoe on the forehead, which had no effect on her cries, and bounded out the front door. Maren didn't say when she would return and Calder didn't press his luck and ask. He only knew that when she was gone peace would reign. The storm would come, but she was too angry to even let it begin. Calder was both impotent—she treated him with kid gloves—and important—he was the perfect daycare provider. Calder hated the term. It wasn't daycare. He was taking care of his daughter. Happily. Daycare was when you were hired to take care of somebody else's kid, a brat to which you had no real attachment. Zoe needed little work. She cried when she was hungry and when she was tired, but tranquility was her basic mode.

But when the door slammed shut, Zoe was still crying. Feeding time.

Ten seconds later, Zoe was at his left tit, and milk trickled down the sides and onto the sofa. He didn't even try to wipe up the mess.

Oxytocin.

Delirious tidings of joy emerged as Zoe suckled. Calder enjoyed the hormone's release undeterred, unbeaten and unbowed by neither the latest scar on his forehead nor the full disclosure its summoning unfurled. In addition to his abnormal production of prolactin, Calder's hypothalamus and pituitary gland worked in a relentless fervor that he had no conscious control over. He didn't want to give up his power. That was his only explanation.

Surgery was not an option he wanted to entertain anytime soon if he could help it. Doctors could monitor the tumor's size and postpone any procedure until it became larger. He had refused the doctor's recommended medication, bromocriptine, because it would suppress his lactation. Give me a month, he bargained with Maren. Maybe it would go away on its own just as unceremoniously as it had arrived. Maybe he could control it with his thoughts.

Calder wouldn't have believed it three months earlier. Today, anything seemed possible in his distorted mind. And his wife would vouch for the fact that it was warped before. It was one of the quirky factors that drew her to him in the spark of meeting cute at Rockefeller Center.

Sometimes, though, he went too far over the edge of the Earth, spinning into the blackness of space, divergent from the rest of humanity. In his own headspace, he believed male lactation was the one thing keeping his marriage intact. A misguided notion, but the idea burrowed deeper into his internal labyrinth with every feeding.

Alone in the room, he was king. The pixies in his

skull would not let him come to harm. They did provide some sidelight entertainments from time to time amidst Zoe's smiles, babbles, as well as the loving staring contests she engaged in repeatedly with her dad. He could look into her orbs for minutes at a time without a need, or desire, to blink.

Calder dozed off for a few long seconds mirroring the effect his milk had on Zoe's 15-pound frame. In the half-awake resurrection state, images his visual cortex stored weeks and years earlier passed into his waking life as if a computer were rebooting itself. Maybe his brain needed to play the images or they would be lost forever. Calder found this phenomena peaked while breastfeeding. He interpreted it as another blessing. He found comfort in the art books he had perused during his last volunteer shift at the information desk at the Museum of Modern Art six months ago, in Maren's last trimester.

He imagined himself bobbing on a calm sea in Magritte's painting "The Seducer." He was captain of a tall ship formed out of the horizon's seawater set against a powder blue, cloud-filled sky. It symbolized his once calm existence. He had left his volunteer position at MoMA and craved artistic inspiration. The images raced in uneven patterns like watching a disjointed experimental silent film.

Sitting alone in the living room with his daughter once she fell asleep, his thoughts then drifted into intricate fantasies of art installations, videos and films he wanted to see but no longer had the time. Inspiration struck at odd times, and with Maren out of the house, he should take advantage.

He had already done that in a non-artistic sense, accounting for Maren's abrupt "meeting" with a client. He hadn't used his camera in some time, though his cell phone was filled with pictures and videos of Zoe. Calder needed to upload the photos to the ubiquitous "cloud" so he could clear space and take more.

Calder's mind continued to wander, traveling to the most remote sections of the universe and circling back inside the molecules of desire. He'd seen a science documentary about oxytocin's love effects on YouTube and wondered how his tumor affected him beyond the blunted attempt at sex he and his wife had shared weeks earlier; Calder now viewed that bout of erectile dysfunction as an anomaly, more psychological than physical given his new information about the tiny mass latched to his pituitary. But despite increased oxytocin levels, he wandered sexless in the Sahara Desert.

A day without sex is a day wasted.

Despite the fact he was in the doghouse—tumor be damned—Varick's mantra played in his head. The phrase had gotten him in trouble yet he saw some logic in it. Cardiovascular exercise relieved stress. Viewed under that rubric, he was wasting a day. Viewed with the prism of the byproduct of a loving union between two souls, he would not waste a day for the rest of his life. One side effect of the tumor lodged deep in the crook of his skull was the diminished sex drive from a physical standpoint. If he delayed treatment, Maren might quench her urges elsewhere.

Fuck Mr. X.

Forget him. He was Mr. X no longer. He was Mr. Z, and the Z stood for Zero, a non-entity, a specter that would no longer guide Calder's mind. He already forgot the moniker.

A mind is a terrible thing to waste. No more Mr. Nice Guy. Pussy is stronger than God. Actions speak louder than words.

No. More. Slogans.

Calder was Mr. X—the new Omega man in a rebranding of the ghost—and he wanted to fuck his wife. Not just fuck per se. Reclaim. Reconquer. Reconsider his position. He had been an equal partner in their bedroom apathy. How much can you really do if someone says no on a regular basis? He wasn't a criminal. Maren, and all women, held the power. Calder could do more to set the mood.

In her absence, when his dreams ended and the vision of art inspiration blurred into the reality of his life, a plan crystallized. Recalibration, his defense mechanism, would be his new marital weapon. He would bend his will into hers, making it seem that his ideas were hers, that what she wanted was what he wanted and vice versa. But first he must examine the entire environment, like a forensic pathologist at a crime scene, forgetting his scarred forehead and bulging pituitary.

He turned his head and stared for what could have been three seconds, three minutes or three hours. The white brick wall behind Sofa Island became an infinite horizon with his silhouette cradling Zoe the only blemish. What would this wall say? He imagined he was the wall, listening to every argument, seeing his every action from a detached perspective, without any mercy or fear. Calder studied every item on the far wall, Zoe's section, a panoply of children's books, bottles and baby wipes.

There was also a blank wall. Above the Container Store shelving, there were no pieces of art. Zoe's name was not there in wooden letters or any other alphabetical incarnation. The picture frame still had the random pale baby in it.

Behind him whiteness. Above him whiteness. Across from him, interrupted only by the baby emporium, whiteness. The room closed in around him, the latent claustrophobia crept upward surrounding his brain. To combat it, Calder sprang to his feet, in as much as he could. He cradled Zoe like a precious egg. There would be no cracks. He was adept at holding her with one arm while simultaneously putting on his shirt and jacket. Streets of ice be damned. They were going outside. A copy center rested catty corner to the Boyd domicile.

Calder turned once again, placing Zoe on Sofa Island to prepare her for the fierce cold. In Scandinavia, newborns were out in subfreezing temperatures as a rite of passage. The cold was their friend. It made them strong and filled their lungs with a ferocity they wouldn't relinquish until death. This was Calder's template. His Nordic blood emerged in flashes and coursed through his brain.

He bundled Zoe in layer upon layer while he seemingly at the same time finagled her into the ergonomic baby carrier. He saw the future, a giant frozen milk bottle in the Central Park ice metastasizing as an illuminated core lit up everything in its vicinity. He had closed his eyes for a split second in his moment of clarity and seen it, its meaning clear to him.

Make the most of his gift. Do not squander it in the snow. He felt no throbbing veins. No pain. No obstacles. No trepidation.

Zoe looked up at him and cooed her tacit approval. Her serene eyes bathed him in love.

Let's go outside daddy. Don't worry. I can handle it.

The man smoking in front of the Korean deli froze. The look, mouth agape, broadcast 'What the hell are you doing to this child?'

"Are you crazy? Get that baby inside," said the man with the cancer stick dangling from his lips. Calder paid him no mind. Zoe smiled up at him. She approved and she was fine.

In one minute, they reached the safety of the copy center. Calder reached into the dark recesses of his pocket and produced a USB drive. It contained several pictures of him and his family. He took his place at his assigned computer and three minutes later a six-by-four-inch kaleidoscopic image on extra glossy photo paper fell from the color printer into his waiting hand.

The trudge back to the apartment proved anticlimactic. Calder begged for someone to look at him sideways, to recognize the Milkman and chastise him. He was ready. He was a new man. He was a family man, and he stored this cold journey in the lobe reserved for special memories.

Back in the warmth of the radiator-infused one-bedroom domicile, Calder placed Zoe back in her crib—the cold had eased her into a peaceful slumber—and clutched the picture frame. He snatched the store model photo of the random blonde-haired, blue-eyed kid and replaced it with his version of happiness.

A small moment surpassed Mount Everest, a plinth in his way of thought that would never erode. He fell asleep staring at the new photo: newborn Zoe, Maren and Calder staring at their reflection in the bathroom mirror the day they brought her home from the hospital. It was the first day of the rest of their lives.

When Maren arrived home, it was well past three in the morning. Why was it called morning when the sky was pitch black? She noticed the photo immediately—nothing gets past a mother's eye—its small detail beamed like a poltergeist rearranging Sofa Island. In their small apartment any change, however slight, emitted an unmistakable radioactive glow.

She picked up the frame and tears began to flow. Two wet splotches landed on the glass casing and she wiped them with the diligence of a palace chambermaid. She couldn't bear to wake her husband up and have that conversation now. Before she retired to the only other main room in the apartment, Maren glanced at her wondrous daughter in her crib. Zoe smiled in her sleep and Maren melted into the sheets.

Lost in the folds of his subconscious, Calder had no idea the profound impact his tiny action had on his wife. He dreamed about milk bottles and perfection. A new him stepped out of his frozen milk bottle lighthouse. When this new Calder emerged, the giant Central Park bottle shattered into a million pieces, absorbed into the waiting ice.

Jan. 22

7:42-7:51 p.m. Snowing again. Bottle fed Zoe 130 ml of formula (concerned about the painkiller interaction). Put moisturizer on her face when she slept after drinking milk. Changed her diaper (pee). Put lotion on her legs and body. Put healing ointment on her legs. 8:34 p.m. Heard her poop. Changed her diaper (poo, a normal brownish yellow color). Read several books to her, including *The Snowy Day*. She played in her crib and fell asleep at 9:35 p.m. She woke up at 11:11 p.m.

The familiar squishing sound as Zoe bounded up and down on his knee indicted a soiled diaper. His work had begun again.

***

Calder fidgeted in his seat at a high-end midtown bistro not far from the United Nations. Worried that the maître d' recognized him—the infant-filled stroller was an obvious giveaway—Calder needed some diplomatic immunity. He burrowed his nose deep into his menu. Nobody could out him if he revealed nothing.

A cascading fireplace billowed from an adjoining wall nullifying the stultifying cold that remained entrenched over Temptation Island, otherwise known as Manhattan. The dark, out-of-the-way place on the corner of 50th Street and First Avenue epitomized anonymity. The assortment of bankers, divorcees, visiting athletes and diplomats filling the spacious dining room were dignitaries in their own right and couldn't care less about the infamous lactating cult hero in their midst.

Calder's lunch companions might stir the pot a little, but none of this clientele would speak up, not wanting to reveal their secret porn addiction by recognizing Essy and her ex-husband and business partner colloquially known as The Rabbi.

The Milkman couldn't explain why he had agreed to this. The quest for new revenue streams circled him. For three days, Essy stalked his Upper East Side digs, buzzing the buzzer when she would see Maren leave.

"I want you to shoot your breast milk all over me in my next film," Essy said on the first, second and third "chance meetings."

"You don't even have to take your clothes off. Please consider it."

"Will you stop harassing me if I say I will."

"You'll do it?"

"No, I'll consider it. A big difference."

When Essy mentioned the word negotiable, it led Calder to a wall-hugging table where he was face-to-face with a legend. The balding man looked nothing like a porn mogul. Admittedly, Calder had no idea what one would look like. He did not consort with those types on a regular basis, on any basis to be exact. Older than Calder by at least five years, The Rabbi remained handsome like a statue of a young Socrates. The man's *nom de porn* was Malachi Blue. He guarded his real identity, Jonathan Silverstein, like a state secret, though everyone who knew Blue's Films knew the former rabbi was the moneyman behind Essy Frisk's oeuvre. He operated under an alias but didn't need to. It was an open secret known by everyone who imbibed of skin flicks.

Essy brokered the lunch meeting between The Milkman and The Rabbi and blessed them both with her presence. The mischievous duo had a proposition. The Rabbi wore a blue pinstriped suit, white shirt, light blue tie and a white fedora, like icing on a cupcake. His handshake scared everyone and five minutes into the luncheon the fingers on Calder's right hand still ached.

"Fifty thousand dollars." Essy blurted. She turned to The Rabbi. "Tell him. Tell him."

"I will pay you fifty thousand dollars if you appear in *Swedish Milk*. All you have to do is fake it. We can shoot around it."

"Shoot around what?"

"Your penis. We can hire a body double. Or we don't have to show your face," The Rabbi said.

Calder considered it even as he vehemently protested.

"I can't be seen with you. Please, I appreciate the

offer, but I just can't do it."

"Did you ask your wife?"

"You think I'm that foolish. I don't have time for this."

Zoe cooed in the stroller at Calder's bidding, a way out of the scene. He had no choice but to bring her along for the wayward diplomatic trek. Essy stopped the proceedings momentarily to peek into Zoe's stroller. Calder had convinced the maître d' to allow the stroller inside the bistro. Luckily, he too, was a fan of *The Andrea Peabody Show*.

"She's so pretty," Essy said.

"Don't even say it."

"Understood."

And that was that. Essy placed her adult offer back on the table.

"You can use an alias," she said.

"Cornucopia Jones," The Rabbi interjected. "It has a nice flow. Or how about Milky Way? You can't trademark the name of our galaxy. Maybe we'll use Milky Ray just to be safe. No copyright infringement there. You can never be too careful."

"You're not hearing me," Calder raised his voice above the din of knives and forks stabbing into steaks and clattering on hot china. "I am not going to do it. My life is not a joke. I lost my job, and if I push my luck, I'm going to lose my wife."

"I had no idea you lost your job," Essy said. "I never would have made you a part of my performance piece. I'm only trying to make it up to you."

"Fifty thousand dollars richer and I think your

wife won't say a thing," The Rabbi pleaded.

"She'll say nothing less than fifty million. But that's not going to happen."

Calder got up and left, the chair screeched—and surely someone recognized him now—like fingernails on the blackboard. He and Zoe screeched their way out the door.

***

Over the next four weeks, Maren and Calder reversed household roles. He became intensely angry when Maren acted single, as if she didn't have a kid, going out three or four times a week with girlfriends while he took care of Zoe and pumped milk like a world champion cow. Calder's exhaustion reached a breaking point, but he was too stubborn to ask his wife for assistance. But this was a dangerous gambit. What if he fell asleep while breastfeeding and Zoe toppled to the floor? The specter of hurting his daughter, combined with his rational uncertainty of his wife's whereabouts, drove splinters of insanity deeper into his brain stem.

He wondered if Maren was in the midst of another affair, though this time there was no smoking text. He should trust her. Without proof, any accusation could incite the end-all-be-all argument. One night after a long photo shoot, a new conflagration emerged.

Maren didn't want to change Zoe's diaper at 3 a.m. the night before Calder met The Rabbi. He said she was being lazy by not waking Zoe up to clean her. "I'm fucking lazy, what about you?"

"You didn't carry her inside of you for nine months," Maren retorted. "I'm not being lazy, I'm being selfish. I need some me time."

The Me Decade: coming soon to a shoebox apartment near you.

17

Phantasms of blue-green light pierced the Icelandic night like God's hands rending the firmament in two. On the left side, total darkness demarcated by the sperm swirl of the Milky Way mixed with an independent green band of luminous molecules that dominated the right side of the heavens as Calder looked north.

He looked up naked; Maren's arms, legs and breasts draped all over him in a private geothermal pool at the popular Blue Lagoon. He searched for the constellation Orion, and realized it was slightly behind him. He craned his neck to get a proper glimpse, but Maren pulled his head back toward her and planted an eternal kiss on her husband.

When their lips parted, Maren moved her face back precisely five inches from Calder's and stared into his swirling eyes. This trip represented a reset on their relationship nine months prior to Zoe's debut. There was only love. It steamed from each of their bodies as the thermal waters caressed and lifted them toward the watchful heavens above.

"I'm ready."

Calder, without translation, understood. "We'll have beautiful children."

"Let's start with one and see how that goes," Maren replied. Calder didn't even mind her tempered expectations. They were moving in the right direction as a couple. If their sex life still needed work—and it did—so be it.

That night, a year after Mr. X's revelation and two months after James Boyd's death, Calder and his wife made love for the first time in a month. Their sex life was a work-in-progress, and more than once he did not pull out.

Calder was almost 40 and he wanted to have a child. He loved children. Part of the reason he wanted to repair his marriage was a desire to help raise a child of his own. Maren wanted kids as well and, at 36, did not want to wait any longer.

Calder often fantasized about remaining the resolute bachelor, forever free to come and go as he pleased with no hindrances, unencumbered and carefree. However, if he believed his inner truth, the threat of no offspring always moved him away from that lifestyle.

Neither of them had the desire, not the energy to go through the entire process of meeting someone new, having to relive the whole dating and courtship process all over again, to speak nothing of the nuances, pet peeves and compromises said person would thrust upon each of them and they upon the new partner. A cynical reason but the entire kernel was true.

The grass is always greener.

The lovemaking night led to an inconsequential morning sleeping in well past noon. When Calder and Maren stumbled out of bed—and Calder actually stumbled, hitting his head on the bedpost—they drove southeast to the town of Vik and spent the day walking along an immaculate black sand beach as majestic whitecaps crashed under lazy patches of sublime cumulonimbus clouds. The glasslike waves eroded the snow and an occasional mini-iceberg bobbed on the crests until it made landfall. The winter utopia of undisturbed snow and tantric ice drew Calder and Maren closer, literally to stay warm and figuratively as they reveled in their joint love of winter. They had the entire 10-mile stretch to themselves. The basalt sea stacks near Reynisfjara Beach and the Dyrhólaey arch kept watch. There was nobody else around because no one else was foolish enough to brave the cold and wind. They didn't care. The cold shaped the flesh of their mortal bodies from God's clay into something livid. It made them feel alive. Each night they made love in a different small Icelandic town along the Ring Road, a shamanic frenzy of procreation.

Calder loved Iceland. Though he always thought it was misnamed. The volcanic island in the middle of the Atlantic, straddling the North American and European tectonic plates, was verdant, especially in the warmer months, while Greenland was ice-covered. He proposed the two North Atlantic islands swap names as part of a tourism campaign, but the Icelandic tourism board rejected the idea. He'd been here once before to coordinate a car commercial at the glacial lagoon, which was their current destination after one night in the tiny black sand beach hamlet.

At sunset, the orange glint of the dying sun rendered the dark Atlantic waters and the encroaching spray from the pounding surf into a kaleidoscopic mix of amber grandeur. The Crayola sky was somewhere between Atomic Tangerine and Burnt Orange. The sea and sky kissed with almost no way to distinguish where one ended and the other began.

Maren fell gently onto the snow and flapped her arms in wide arcs, revealing the black sand beneath. She arose to admire her work, a single dark angel compromised of trillions of grains of eroded volcanic rock. Then she and her husband returned to their inn and resumed their conception paradise.

***

The OB/GYN estimated the conception date as somewhere between Jan. 27th and Jan. 31st. Calder and Maren snickered when they heard this news. This meant that little Zoe—already bicycle kicking like an Olympic champion—had sprung into the world on the sofa, not amidst the blue icebergs of Iceland. She was a product of the best sex her parents ever had as a couple. Each of their essences combined in an ecstatic flurry.

Calder was right. Iceland was beautiful but the warmth of a sofa that dominated the entire living room, nee kitchen, proved the fait accompli. Before conception, Maren thought they should go to a fertility specialist and check Calder's sperm count. He bristled at this suggestion, an affront to his virility. She claimed, falsely in their case, that they might have trouble getting pregnant. She was over 35 and it was a first pregnancy. No, that wasn't true. He was surprised to learn that Maren had had an abortion while a student at Columbia.

He argued they should just start trying like rabbits. It would be fun *and* great exercise. Calder knew something his wife didn't. He knew his sperm was good, having impregnated two long-ago girlfriends. Both resulted in abortions, and both left volcanic sorrow in their wake. He wasn't proud of these facts, and harbored a lingering sense of guilt. Would they be punished? Deemed unworthy because each had terminated a previous gift? Those decisions had been foregone conclusions. But what if he had a 20-year-old child now? He probably wouldn't have ever been with Maren. He momentarily thought of the paths not taken and then the moment passed and the guilt dissipated like morning fog.

He heard his father's words: *Never sleep with a woman unless you would be happy and ready if she got pregnant.* It was a great rule of thumb and one that Calder had (mostly) followed. He thought of the little life growing inside his wife. This time he was happy *and* ready. However, a return to the city, and the millions of hazards to a pregnant wife, transformed Calder's eagerness into a form of madness. He longed for Iceland's calming beauty. The snow-covered black sand beach, lapped at the edge by the Atlantic waves, would not make it in New York City. The masses would ruin it with footsteps, urine and vomit.

He wanted to return to the country with which he couldn't argue, and to the euphoric bouts of sex. Calder possessed an acute understanding that his love life would suffer over the subsequent nine months and into the foreseeable future as the baby sprouted into being a toddler, and soon enough, an adolescent. He decided to pretend he was in Iceland.

After jags of lovemaking and geothermal bliss, the city was jarring. The dirty sidewalks, the teeming masses and the lack of open space all conspired to temper his enthusiasm. Was this the best place to raise a child?

Prospective fatherhood was a foreign sensation that blossomed as the first month of Maren's pregnancy closed. He felt he needed to work more, save money when he could. He opened a savings account for his child-to-be two weeks after he found out. He hoped it didn't jinx things. Now, every health fear kicked into overdrive.

18

Varick summoned an evil thrill as he dumped nine rubber-banded bundles of held mail at Calder's doorstep. "This is my last week working for the postal service," he announced unceremoniously and left in a flurry of creaking stairs and the incessant sound of errant apartment buzzers.

Three weeks after the gallery incident, catastrophe or enlightenment—depending on your perspective—he didn't have the courage to ring Calder's buzzer, but had no problem using the others tenants'. The awkwardness of the situation was too fresh, bleeding into every background thought.

Calder intended to stop the mail earlier but it had been lost in the myriad tugs in potentially dystopian directions: tumor abatement, marriage readjustment, financial security and superseding all, baby rearing. Maren forgave him.

Varick must have used 5D, the go-to buzzer. When Calder passed him in the foyer two days later, Varick apologized and said he had been in a rush to meet Astrid. An odd couple pairing, the two had been dating for two weeks. He would have left a note but there was just no time.

"What about being mysterious?" Calder hit his pseudo nemesis with a line from his own burgeoning male empowerment empire. Without asking for permission, Varick placed online banners on his website and a few strategically placed ads in skin magazines—Essy's idea—featuring Calder in a state of in flagrante delicto at the art gallery. He traded on Calder's name recognition.

Own your own life.

Varick Williams male empowerment seminars, available online or get the entire video series downloaded to your personal device. The ads were strangely professional, nothing Calder saw in Varick spoke to a mailman cum mogul. He should have known.

Everyone in New York City had a side gig, the job they hoped to be paid handsomely for someday, from the motorman on the 6 train to a ticket taker at the Guggenheim. Calder was no different. Like eight billion others in the City That Was Asleep—hyperbole was an ex-ad man's true nemesis—he sought fame, and as a writer. Calder could learn from Varick's audacity. At the end of the ad, the kicker kicked in: Graduates include The Milkman, Calder Boyd.

Graduate? He had attended one free seminar inside Varick's equally cramped apartment with men desperate and, he thought, possessing the vibe of losers, like gamblers who squandered away big winnings because they couldn't walk away from the table. He had walked away after one session, without saying a word to Varick as to a reason. He must have felt slighted and the ads smacked of retribution. Varick tried at every opportunity to get him to attend again, to "brush up on his man skills and commiserate amongst men."

Calder was tempted to buy a skin flick magazine if only for masturbation purposes. Varick's ad provided the perfect cover story. No, a man on an usher's salary with a young child could not splurge to quell an urge. Varick's boldness irked Calder. He could hire a lawyer and draft a cease and desist letter but he had no liquid income. It wasn't a necessary expense, but if other people were profiting on his name, why not him? He owned the narrative to his life. There must be a banner ad he could write about himself. He was the product and he needed to profit from it.

Surprisingly, Maren, out again on a styling job at a remote, but beautiful mansion location in upstate New York, held her tongue in regards to her husband's poor judgment. She reserved most of her ire for Astrid and Essy, a shadowy duo she saw in a new dark light. Maren disassociated herself from them both, and nobody thought Astrid was serious about Varick. She would go back to Sweden at some point, her interview superseded by Andrea Peabody's. Maren concentrated on work.

Calder hated the fact that his wife now took every single job she was offered. Yes, he was on thin ice and financially Maren worried, but his family was rarely in the same room. He still received two months' severance, and the employees filed a pending lawsuit to recoup the six months' severance they had been promised upon hiring, but it could take years before he saw any of that money, if ever. The family unit was fractured into two camps: father and daughter, and mother and the Manhattan studios or exotic locales she frequented without her family. They weren't spending much quality family time together except in the mornings when Maren would kiss Zoe on the forehead—if she was in the city—on her way out the coat-rack-obscured apartment door.

With Maren's diligent overdrive, the tables, already financially askew to begin with, flipped wholesale. Calder cooked, cleaned and catered to Zoe's every need. The doting milkman breast-fed her every two hours, though the pediatrician recommended she should begin eating solid foods. Violent green, orange and yellow jars and intricate packaged boxes of Japanese baby food filled the kitchen shelves after Maren's insistence on using them—the Japanese had the world's longest life spans, she reasoned.

Mother knows best. Father knows to keep quiet.

Fill her needs and subjugate his own. Those Technicolor Japanese baby food-stores lining the refrigerator, kitchen and windowsills—anywhere there was free space available—represented a threat to Calder's power. Once Zoe started drinking regular milk, Calder's lactation would end, tumor remission or not. He would then rely wholly on his wife or the generosity of others; he was not a good cook, nor was he proficient at preparing a child's meal to the standards of FDA enrichment.

Zoe became fussy and Calder looked at his watch. Noon. It had been three hours. He lost track of time inspecting the backed-up mail of the past month. He searched for precious envelopes known by the proprietary business names peering through the plastic envelope address window, needles in a junk mail haystack. There was an unusual presence of white handwritten mail that, at first, Calder took little notice of because he sought a more important treasure.

Six checks. Totaling $8,760.

Maren wondered where they were. The held mail was an unwise option. Finding the checks provided Calder respite from the benign, but caustic comments Maren made about her husband always making a mess of things. Calder let the rivers of low-grade rancor run right off his back, paying them no heed and focusing on his new harmonious directive. In her eyes, the retrieval of the missing checks completed Calder's rehabilitation from his latest *N.Y. Post* banner headline, though he knew it was but a small step on an infinite journey.

The new man walking through a field of snow toward a grove of snow-covered Norwegian spruce trees, lonely in winter, reeked of beauty now. The recurring vision appeared to him every few days. He understood no meaning but enjoyed the serenity it symbolized.

Peace. What the world needs now. Calder was its purveyor.

Love was also afoot. Not just between him and

Zoe, Varick and Astrid and tepid blooms between him and his wife. There was a more benevolent—some might say crazed—cause for the unusual slew of held mail. It was actually 10 bundles, not nine. Calder hadn't received more than 10 handwritten letters his entire life and surpassed this ignominious record easily. Finding Maren's checks required the patience of a master puzzle maven because there were hundreds of letters from lonely women, *and* men, married and otherwise.

After the litany of TV interviews, Calder's enduring 15 minutes of fame spawned an inundation of marriage proposals from strange women. Rivers of heartfelt emotion trickled from the red lipstick oozing at the spot they had licked and then clasped the letter firm like a vault. He felt like an infamous killer on death row. One lactating woman offered herself in a threesome with Calder and his wife or "the woman of his choice."

Calder splayed his legs next to Zoe on her green, pink and purple heart laden foam play mat in the living room, his daughter on one side and a mountain of letters on the other. He spent hours reading through them while Zoe played happily with her plush toys and musical button contraptions. His legs served as the Maginot Line, keeping Zoe from reaching over with her rock climber's grip and placing dangerous envelope glue or ink into her mouth.

The first letter Calder opened was adorned with red lipstick. It reminded him of Oscar Wilde's kissed-covered tomb at Pere La Chaise cemetery in Paris. As soon as he broke the seal, a glossy photo of a nude, 26-year-old California blonde fell to the floor. Zoe snatched it in the same instant and Calder endured a brief tug-of-war to extricate the crazy-eyed woman's prize.

> *Dearest Calder:*
> *Marry me! As you can see, I have the assets you are looking for in a mate. I don't care if you're married. We can all move to Utah and I'll be your second wife. I think your wife would love me and let me cater to your other needs (if you know what I mean). Please call. Anytime.*

The letter continued, detailing her psychology degree, as other contents spilled forth: in addition to another nude pic of herself standing astride the Pacific at sunset, a photocopy of her Mensa membership card and a condom. The letter was signed with a big heart, followed by a series of X's and O's and her name: *Brook Holster, San Diego, California.*

At least somebody wanted to have sex with him. Calder laughed and continued his morbid fascination into the heartfelt desires of unknown admirers.

There were hundreds more like Brook's, yet a scant 20 or so included photos of any kind, and only one other woman, a 67-year-old grandmother from Topeka, provided a nudie pic. He didn't need to see that one, but saw it nonetheless. One man from

Pittsburgh proposed in flowery prose that Calder wouldn't even have to sleep with him, or even live with him. Just tie him up and tickle him with a pink feather once a week.

Some envelopes contained the overbearing scent of perfume. Hints of jasmine and lavender made Zoe sneeze. Another letter displayed ominous black hieroglyphic-like markings on it. The envelope itself was red and was hard to the touch. Anthrax? He'd be a martyr. He opened it anyway—without recognizing the clasp symbol: a black hawk with piercing red eyes.

A formal manifesto writ on white parchment bored its way into inclusion. Across the top the words Militant Men's Society, a shadowy underground network of disgruntled husbands, bankers and military officers who saw no place for gender equity and wished it was still 1950, or even 1750.

Dear Mr. Boyd:

Hereby, by decree of the grand elder, we advocate for the return to dominance of the male human species by any means necessary. Women control your economy, your wallet and your sex life. Warriors must return to their natural state....and you must return to the fold. Stop your nonsensical clinging to a gift God reserved strictly for women immediately or pay strict consequences. We cannot stand idly by while you make a mockery of our manhood. We are watching you. Do the right thing. End your charade.

Sincerely,
The Militant Men's Society Brotherhood

Maybe he should notify the proper authorities. It was likely some harmless fringe lunatic working as a "lone wolf." He paid it no further attention. Calder tossed the red envelope into the trash, the succession of plastic supermarket bags Maren insisted on using instead of a traditional kitchen garbage can.

He would be more discreet in choosing other letters to peruse. He discarded any letter that weighed more than usual or contained any strange markings. Calder couldn't keep them anyway; there wasn't enough room. He tossed an unusual letter with a UFO logo and two that seemed a little too sticky. He read the ones that smelled nice. Those, with one exception, were from single women who supported his transformation.

When he'd had just about enough of the mostly positive fan letters, there it was: a letter from Dr. West's office dated two days before Christmas. What a gift. It had been part of the held mail and he never received it. He opened it, though given his some would say fortuitous tumble at Essy's kinky "performance art," he already knew what it concerned

*Dear Mr. Boyd...*it began.
We tried reaching you.
Left numerous phone messages.

We've discovered a clinical finding that you should get checked immediately. The MRI revealed a small growth in your pituitary gland.

Calder's second moment of clarity in as many days arrived. He opened the cabinet drawer beneath the sink and pulled out two large supermarket bags. He filled them with letters, tied them and left the bags by the door.

He kept just one. Sweet Brook Holster. Posterity assured for a future son, or son-in-law, whichever came first. His communion with fans couldn't last, however, and he knew he had to get rid of the letters before she returned. The questions and possibilities for conflict concerning them were rife. Why create another mountain to overcome that wasn't necessary? He felt little empathy with the letter writers—Brook notwithstanding.

He placed Brook's letter on the inside lip of the bamboo-lined basket that housed Zoe's picture books. There, he noticed a more prominent anomaly. One letter he still hadn't opened sat wedged between Dr. Seuss' *The Cat In The Hat* and Eric Carle's *The Very Hungry Caterpillar*. He was thankful that Uncle Davis had passed it along, but Calder still couldn't bring himself to read his father's letter. It was a white whale. Once he read it, its power would fade and he could go on with his life. He wanted to keep his memory of his father as he had experienced it.

More than once he'd considered destroying the letter, but common sense and curiosity formed a formidable bulwark. He wanted his version of history to remain valid. He feared what truths his father would divulge. He would save it for a low point, when his faults overwhelmed him. And then, he would read it, and put it in the safe deposit box next to his letter to Zoe, a signpost from the past to help pave the way to a better future.

Calder leapt from one stray thought to another, pushing the letters into his mind's background. He remembered how easily Maren pointed out his faults, often in an abrasive tone. He could be a saint one minute and some small inconvenience, based upon a miscommunication—give me this or give me that was not specific enough when Maren called for a baby's bib to wipe milk from Zoe's smiling face— would ruin it the next. His temper shortened, and he saw the logic in her snipes. In some ways, he relished when she was out of town. He could watch whatever he wanted to on television—meaning sports, the hometown teams he wistfully rooted for, the Lakers, L.A. Kings, or the denizens of Madison Square Garden, the Knicks or N.Y. Rangers—and wash the dishes or do laundry at his pace on his timetable. Maren was no exception in that, like many women, she wanted things maintained around the house the way she dictated, meaning now not later. There was no room for deviation. Calder didn't mind if it kept peace in the household. Any wrong moves might break the skeletal ice.

Calder thought of the insidious mass infiltrating his hormone-producing gland. He had to live a long time for his daughter, Maren correctly told him that night at the hospital, and he knew excising the tumor through surgery or medication was the endgame. He also had to live for his "fans."

Again, like an aging king or seven-term senator, Calder did not want to abdicate his power. Breast milk was the ultimate super weapon, a weapon of mass consumption. He pondered his position because an aide de camp was on the way.

Joy waited in the wings within the corridors of power. She was flying back to the city from Oslo for a week, ostensibly to help Maren with Zoe, though it was her son-in-law who needed it, and for whom she harbored more understanding. She could be his biggest ally. Joy always took Calder's side in arguments, imploring her daughter she would never find anyone as nice as him. Well rounded and protective too, Joy said, since *nice* had pejorative connotations.

None of this mattered when it come to homemaking. Maren made sure Calder knew. Ad nauseum. He heard some rendition of this every few days: "You don't know where anything is because you didn't pack it. It's easy to say what to do, but meaningless when you don't know where anything is and didn't help me put it in its place. You don't do anything."

Calder was put in his place like a barking dog. Where? He did not truly know. Maren's words bled from the white brick walls buttressing Sofa Island. Joy was a welcome addition to the tiny home even if her presence would render the shoebox smaller than it already was. With Joy around, the chances of Maren displaying open hostility about something

Calder was or wasn't doing approached zero.

Nevertheless, one thing he heard precisely every day like a fixed gear inside a clock was lament over the size of their miniature Manhattan home. Maren was right, but she hadn't even bothered to view the apartment with him, leaving the decision entirely up to her husband. Had she been too busy extricating herself from an affair? Or was she still engaged in one? Calder's ignorance was not bliss. Ignorance was ignorance. Bliss was bliss. More of the latter needed fertilization.

They had a buyout from the Greenpoint hellhole. All the tenants accepted it except for the scary lady below them who seemed to try and suck their youth when she placed her hand on their back or forearm at every staircase opportunity. The clock was ticking so Calder wanted to pounce on the apartment location more than its size. Neither of them were home much pre-Zoe anyway. Post-Zoe, Calder lived in a sedentary world. He silently seethed over the constant apartment ribbing—as if it were his penis size—because she hadn't helped pick it.

This was a minor issue; stick to the high road. Essentially jobless, Calder benefitted from the fact Maren worked hard. The seeds of her constant working were quite evident, and he didn't need any reminders. He would be and have nothing without Maren.

***

After the latest cold snap and another snowy day, which he watched through the frozen shut window,

Calder welcomed Joy like a long-lost sister. When she stepped through the portal into Tinyland, he hugged her deeply as if to say 'thank God you are here.'

"Everything OK, Calder?"

"I was afraid you were going to ask me that. Everything is as fine as it can be, all things considered."

Calder regretted his cryptic answer while the words still meditated in the air. He didn't know whether she knew about his pituitary tumor. Maren kept secrets from him, so Calder assumed she buried a few in dark chasms far away from her mother. Joy traveled light, clutching only a package of Swedish massage oils, which she plopped onto the only free space next to Sofa Island, perhaps a bit too close to the radiator.

"Where's Maren?" she asked, knowing the answer. She didn't press the issue of Calder's glum response.

"Working. Somewhere upstate. She was supposed to be back today. But I expect her within a day or two. We'll see."

"What is that supposed to mean? You act like you don't know. Or even care."

Calder wasn't certain her response didn't apply to his previous statement about his overall wellbeing. Aloofness knighted its pawn; it was not his best quality. He tried to erase its manifestation. "I wish she was here. I really do, but you know her better than anyone. She does not like being told what to do, and doesn't respond pleasantly if suggestions are made. She has a habit of extending jobs or taking new ones while away. She's a workaholic."

"She has to be, doesn't she?"

Joy held her gaze. This silenced Calder. It was a hint that he was losing his charm with her.

Then Joy added: "I think it's the best thing that ever happened to you both. You can be a stay-at-home father while also having more time to work on your novels. And Maren can feel financially secure while also seeing the necessity of a patriarchal home. She will appreciate you more. You'll see."

The subject of his job loss was never discussed again. Calder moved the massage oils to a safer, under-the-bathroom-sink location—Zoe's well-being foremost in his thoughts—washed the bed sheets and prepared the room for Joy and Maren. He would remain entrenched on the shores of Sofa Island. He doubted he could sleep anywhere else. The folds of the upholstery greeted him nightly like a beloved friend and he fell into dream-filled comas.

Calder and his mother-in-law became fast friends, handling baby cleaning, feeding and home maintenance in equal parts. She schooled Calder in the finer points of breastfeeding, as well as bathroom and kitchen cleanliness, and pitched in a few pointers on how to cook and prepare Swedish meatballs.

Their only problem stemmed from her beauty. She was a clone of Maren, albeit with her all-white hair now braided into a long ponytail, and remained sexually attractive at age 60. In the two days before Maren returned, there were a few awkward moments in the bathroom or when Joy changed clothes in the bedroom. At 3 a.m. of their first night together, Calder awoke and accidentally caught her stark naked sitting on the toilet. Like her daughter, she slept in the nude; unlike her daughter, she didn't believe in closed bathroom doors. Joy and Maren grew up with spas as a common part of life and familial nudity wasn't extraordinary but it made him uneasy.

Calder thought he had left the bathroom light on and investigated, but no, there was Joy in all her exquisite glory. No wonder she had a boyfriend 25 years her junior—she had divorced Maren's now-deceased father 10 years earlier—and talked incessantly of their coital exploits. She smiled and ended her business, and then stood up, exposing all, as Calder froze and stammered, then quickly ran away.

"Sorry."

"Can't sleep? Where are my massage oils?"

Calder was already back to the nocturnal safety of Sofa Island. Was Joy flirting with him? He did not want to find out.

The next morning, nothing was made of their nocturnal pas de deux. But the image stained Calder's brain. Her body was flawless and looked like a 35-year-old fitness instructor, not a grandmother. She reminded him of what he was missing, the pleasure of Maren's stunning skin lying next to him in bed. He craved her touch and started to think it would be okay to seek it elsewhere, so long as he otherwise remained a good father, but certainly not with Maren's mother. He banished those deviant thoughts.

Joy and Calder created a mini-Utopia. Things were in their proper place and all good tidings of Zoe and her laughs permeated the two rooms and kept them light. Levity returned and set up camp.

Maren returned the second night and Joy could no longer resist, unloading her true mission. Joy told both of them they needed to spend more time as a family and agreed to babysit Zoe while they went out on date night.

Feb. 13

11:00-11:20 a.m. Maren fed Zoe yogurt and a mixture of rice and milk. Then I breast fed her. Zoe didn't take the nipple well, almost as if she's bored with it, and I stopped to change her diaper. She pooped right in the middle of changing it. Finished changing her diaper with Joy and Maren's aid. 11:49-11:54 a.m. Bottle fed Zoe 75 ml of formula. Joy put her down to sleep in her crib at noon. She slept for two hours. It must be the cold (20th straight day below freezing and according to Punxsutawney Phil there are six more weeks of winter).

Despite Joy's unabashed body openness, Calder was especially grateful for her encore trip. Mother-in-law's initial Zoe visit, which covered the newborn's first month, allowed for scant interaction between the two. Joy had arrived in mid-October so Calder could work as much as possible at both jobs, saving a cache of money for formula and unplanned fussiness, or as fate would have it, the unforeseen agency layoff. When he came home, they had perfunctory conversations but nothing noteworthy before Calder escaped into the folds of his low-thread-count bed sheets to sleep.

The process repeated for five weeks and in that time he had only seen Joy in the mornings—she cooked a mean omelet and other breakfast delicacies—or briefly in the evenings, where her meatballs temporarily soothed any "lacrimony." Then, they had not been in each other's way. They were two well-hydrated camels passing each other in the Sahara, knowing they would have to join forces at some point if they were to find water and survive.

Today, they epitomized a well-oiled machine full of human interaction in its myriad forms. In their two days without Maren's domineering presence, Calder formed a deeper understanding of his wife through the woman who raised her. They discussed Maren's grade school projects, her bold high school claim that she would be Norway's ambassador to the United Nations one day and the college boyfriend, Magnar, who had soured her taste in men until Calder's immaculate arrival. All of them were new revelations.

Joy was the first adult he'd had a meaningful in-person conversation with in untold days. He was a child, losing his verbal audacity and skill, to the scourge of e-mail, which he felt fostered said regression. He couldn't knock it; e-mail was his last link to the outside world, to people who had sex and had no kids. Via cyberspace, Calder pontificated with his closest friend Gerald about the issues of the day: another white girl missing, another black man killed by the police, another white girl named Emily being born somewhere, another political scandal.

Calder was a chameleon mulatto, equally versed in Ebonics as he was Shakespeare—his father wanted him to be able to live well in any world—but the son longed for respect at home and in the writing field. Debauched past glimpses of erotic encounters danced as he enjoyed a quiet interval in near solitude. But Calder was too tired for dreams. Exhaustion stalked him like a fast-moving plague. It was three in the afternoon, and he knew if he faded into dreamland now what little sleeping pattern he did possess would shatter. Before he dozed off, or tried to doze off, he received a text missive from Maren.

I'll be home tomorrow. I think u lost so many socks my mother bought for Zoe in Nov. New ones! How Sade.

Anger mounted. Then laughter. He chuckled at the auto correction misspelling of the word "sad." There would be no bondage tonight or any other night.

Husband and wife texted back and forth for 15 minutes over the alleged missing socks. The silver lining existed nowhere. No hello. No how are you? Calder had apparently lost his wife's favorite pair of Zoe's socks—allegedly in his last visit to the Laundromat. It was another transgression. Don't get mad. Take a deep breath.

Patience is a virtue.

Commendations were lost in a bleak realm. Wait. Anger rose again. Maren's phone autocorrected sad to Sade. Who was she trading sadomasochist references with?

Zoe napped in the bedroom; Joy dozed in the bed next to her. The door was cracked open a little. Calder bounded from Sofa Island and shut it fully, the floorboards let out menacing sighs as his long feet glided over the uneven surface.

Two minutes later, Calder confirmed a married man's ultimate sadness. He succumbed, but no longer felt shame. He needed a release and relied on an Ame Aikawa link. Two stunning Japanese women—one mature with spectacular breasts, Ame Aikawa, and one younger protégé, who ejaculated multiple times across the tatami floor—induced a rock-solid erection. He scrubbed to the 66-minute mark of the 76-minute clip and came at the same time they did.

"Concentrate. And make sure you clean up the mess," Joy said from behind the door with the tone of a knowing schoolteacher. "You should do it in front of Maren. Let her see the physical manifestation of your loneliness and need for physical contact with her."

Calder wasn't even mortified. He finished masturbating. He didn't care if Joy heard him. It was practice for tomorrow's big reveal.

Maren returned the next night.

Joy and Maren slept peacefully together in the bedroom. Despite the fact that Joy slept in the nude and flaunted her figure, Maren perceived no threat.

She was content in her own spectacular shape. Like mother, like daughter.

In just one night, Joy had more intimate contact with Calder's own wife than he had in over a year. Calder was an asexual dad. If he received an inviting glance from an attractive female passing on the street—if he happened to stumble into a free moment walking by his lonesome—he might explode. He didn't want to view his wife as the enemy any longer. She wasn't. He vowed to do better, to aim higher, to transcend the din of diminished expectations. Sex was overrated.

Calder believed none of this. He struggled with his new affirmation, and it had only been two weeks of his Maren reclamation/renovation/renewal project—pick one's choice of nomenclature, Calder thought. He was losing his mind and it had only been two weeks since his head injury. He aimed for frenemies as a stopgap measure while he kept his upbeat plan intact for long-term success. Do as she needs, not as she says.

Maren awoke in the middle of the first night. Calder pondered his purposeful self-satisfying display intended to shame his wife into sex per Joy's instruction, but he could not go through with the big reveal.

"Calder? Calder, are you awake?"

He acted like he was asleep. The glow from his cell phone screen ruined his ruse.

"What are you doing? Looking at porn?"

"No." Maybe Joy delivered the untoward message for him.

"Why is your cell phone still glowing?"

"I'm writing my novel. I'm up to page 200. Another month and I'll be finished."

"You've been saying you'll finish a novel, but you never do. You had lots more free time before Zoe was born. Why now?"

"I have a family to support and have no major source of income when my severance package ends."

"Thank you Captain Obvious."

They both laughed in the dark, each barely able to see the other in the shadows. The sound filled the room with metaphorical light.

"The book is inspired by my current situation. Actually, it's non-fiction. I should be profiting from my blessed malady."

"And what is your current situation?"

"You should get your rest."

"We've been avoiding the elephant in the room."

"Mr. Tumor or Mr. X?"

"Both."

"We need to work on our relationship. You have to come back and sleep in our bed at some point."

"Are you suggesting a threesome? Well, it would still be a twosome." Calder didn't care if his sarcasm was out of place.

"You're being an asshole. What's wrong with you?"

"We fully committed to trusting each other and nothing has changed. I have been a bit nasty to you."

"*You* should go back to sleep."

"Why are you in such a hurry to get rid of me?"

"How do you think I feel? Not being able to

breastfeed while my husband becomes a minor cult figure for it. And I should have lost the baby weight months ago. I don't feel sexual at all. I'm sorry."

"So I should find a mistress," Calder joked. "Use her only for sex. Maybe we should hire a French nanny. The *N.Y. Post* would have a field day. MILK MAID. FRENCH MILK."

"PASTEURIZED!" Maren interjected.

Calder loved her wicked sense of humor. He longed for more of it as well as the intimacy of physical contact. He put his foot in his mouth moments later, ruining the rapport.

"You don't seem to enjoy sex. At least not with me."

"Stop playing the victim. You were equal party to that. Past is past. Let's focus on the here and now."

"Okay. Fair enough," Calder saw an opening. "You need to spend more time at home with Zoe. She needs her mother. Not her grandmother."

"I've booked a three-day package to the Cayman Islands. Just the two of us. We need to rekindle the spark that drew us together in the first place. Plus, I can't stand another day of winter. My mother will watch Zoe. Sound good?"

"What if I said no?"

Maren ignored him. The premeditated determination dripped from her entire persona.

"Now tell me. What were you really looking at on your phone? My mother told me about your little encounters while I was away."

"I missed you. What can I say?"

Calder held up his phone, touching the screen to

renew its neon glow screaming in the darkness.

There was a picture of a radiant and six months pregnant Maren, standing beneath an ebullient Puerto Rican sun at the Old Fort. Her face blossomed as the still photo seemed to come to live. The Caribbean Sea fluttered as cotton candy clouds passed like cargo ships.

In the black of night, husband and wife felt like they were atop a majestic mountain peak. There were no valleys.

And Maren melted.

19

Calder could not see the light. Two days beyond the winter solstice, the early 1980's sun was somewhere above a blanket of low-lying coastal clouds that hovered only a few feet above the snow-covered, downy birch trees, *Betula pubescens.* Also known as the white birch, the trees combined with the abundant snow and ice to create an infinite white field that conquered the horizon. The all-encompassing trees with their spindly structures reached into the gray, lining the highway on either side to create the illusion that no matter how fast their vehicle traveled they were standing still. And standing still might have been the optimal speed. The effect was hypnotic, and Pernille had to take special precaution as not to doze off. The green Volvo looked like a butterfly hopelessly out of place in the wrong climate.

The motionless effect mesmerized the six-year-old Calder as he clutched a copy of *The Snowy Day* with both hands in the front passenger seat. He stared at the blizzard-like final page, wishing he had a friend to join him in the snow along the side of the road, and then closed the book and tossed it onto the dashboard, which he could barely see over, and looked ahead to the mesmerizing pavement. Alan, then 4, and Brice, 2, occupied their car seats in the back of the sedan. Their father remained hospitalized in the States, the victim of a broken right thumb that required immediate surgery. He broke it one night earlier attempting to dunk in a Lakers victory over the Atlanta Hawks. He would meet them in Bergen in a few days—if the ferry resumed its normal schedule.

"I'm bored," Calder said, his future love of snow had not been solidified yet. He was more preoccupied with his existence minute-to-minute and blissfully unaware of the final stricture imposed by death. Pernille did her best to try and simultaneously keep her eyes on the road and stimulate her young charge.

"Why don't you practice your Norwegian? You can impress *mormor*."

"*Hvordan har du det?*" Calder enunciated the words slowly. His Norwegian was rusty, bordering on the nonexistent. This fact was not his mother's fault. English was his first language but she had spoken Norwegian to him ever since he was born. He always seemed to understand her when she spoke in Norwegian but almost never spoke himself.

"It means how are you?"

"Good. What might you say in response?"

"*Jeg har det bra.*"

"Where do you want to go? I want to do something nice."

This was Calder's third trip to Norway. The Jespersen family Volvo, a Swedish import betraying the hypnotic landscape, traversed a black line piercing the snow on either side. Mormor, his Norwegian grandmother, awaited them in Bergen.

"How do you spell aquarium?" his mother inquired, trying to play word games to keep her precocious son in good spirits. "In Norwegian," she quickly added.

"A-K-V-A-R-I-U-M," Calder didn't hesitate.

Pernille drove west from Oslo, where she had visited some old artist friends, professors at the Norwegian National Academy of the Arts, *Kunstakademiet*, for a night to avoid a nasty winter storm. They were a lively group. Calder loved that his mother took him to all the art parties; though, he had to beg to be included to this one, a tag along who subconsciously found inspiration surrounded by much older, creative types. In theory this is what Pernille hoped, but it was a tenuous idea at best. The current class of students had hosted a party for the famous graduate and while his mother was being toasted, Calder frolicked amongst the work-in-progress sculptures as a-ha radiated from the speakers of a boom box. His mother only went as a courtesy for an hour while another college friend babysat Calder's younger brothers.

Despite the festive atmosphere, this pilgrimage to Norway was not a festive one. The students did not know her father, *morfar*, had died. This was the first time Calder knew someone who had died. Accidentally boiling his angelfish in its aquarium did not count because they were a presumed lower species. Pernille informed her son that *morfar* would not be the last dead person he would know; it was just the natural progression of life.

Calder hoped they would stop at the aquarium in Bergen. Located on the Nordnes peninsula, the aquarium was once the standard in all of Northern Europe. Calder didn't care if it had fallen into a bit of disrepair. One of the penguin pools was undergoing renovations, and the carp pool was being restocked, but that didn't deter his desire. He loved the tropical fish tank. He could stare through the glass hours on end if his mother let him. It was closed during the winter, and especially after the storm had left five fresh inches of powder on top of the already formidable snow banks.

Going from sunny Southern California to the damp air of a Norwegian winter was enough of a shock. Two days ago, Calder rode his bicycle along the Venice Beach boardwalk amongst happy scantily-clad beachgoers worshiping in the sun. That morning, he watched bundled-up winter sports enthusiasts in snowshoes shimmy past Vigeland Park's eerie naked men, women and children sculptures before departing to attend his *morfar*'s funeral.

Morfar was 78 years old. He had slipped and hit his head on the ice while out marking the borders of his farm on the outskirts of Bergen two days ago. His funeral was scheduled for Friday, and Calder and his mother both hoped his father would make it on time. The flight from Los Angeles, including a two-hour layover in London, took approximately 15 hours.

Calder's last trip to Norway, at age 3, was likely his earliest childhood memory. But the events of this trip would supersede it, not for the better. Now that he was a father, he often looked back at this event as a window into his own identity, a splintered recollection that could not be removed. The snowiest winter in NYC's history paled in comparison to the Norwegian winter. He looked at the jagged scar on his forehead and returned to the memory.

It had all happened so fast. The book Calder had nonchalantly thrown onto the dashboard slid across the front and stood upright, momentarily blocking his mother's view. A split second was all it took. As they approached the Norwegian coast, the low clouds had given way to a floating layer of fog.

One moment the horizon was clear. The next...a fast-moving layer of morning mist shrouded the road and white was all there was. It was akin to driving through an aquarium filled with milky water.

Crash. Hundreds of molecules engaged in an underwater battle.

Then came silence, the harbinger of desperate evils in Calder's young and future life.

Seconds after impact, Calder wished he were at the aquarium. His imagination kept him safe. He was a deep-sea diver tethered into his mini dirigible as he was bombarded by thousands of air bubbles. Nothing could harm him or his family.

The Volvo—Calder's invincible submarine—stopped, the weight of the water crushing it at 10,000 meters deep. The warping sound of bent steel pinged like an active sonar, the molecules realigning themselves.

Every moment beyond the moment of impact became an underwater panorama, seen through the milky paste of octopus ink—Calder had seen it at the aquarium once before, the defense mechanism, and he appropriated it as his own. The milk he had been drinking spewed up from his gut and from his mouth in the same moment that Calder's audio and visual perception intensified. He heard the crash and saw the aftereffects as if they took eons to develop. His memory of this indelible day was etched on a granite plinth that splintered his mind.

Calder's seatbelt sprung into action, a safety net guarding the boy from an icy calamity. However, it could not prevent the tiny projectiles aiming for him. The shattered glass catapulted into Calder's forehead, miniature daggers inviting pain.

Later, they did not know if it was a single shard or multiple that carved a line diagonally just between the boy's eyes above the eyebrows. The cause of the accident had been invisible, a killer waiting to strike. The green Volvo was a solemn casualty of a 25-car pileup triggered by a 10-ton lorry that jackknifed on black ice. The veil of fog moved in—up one of the fjord valleys—and blanketed the road on a slight decline as the road began its descent toward the North Sea. Pernille drove into this white sea.

When his ears returned to normal, Calder looked around as if in a dream. His mother's wails, muffled by the searing metal, began to rise in both urgency and tone. The sound of dripping fluid, moaning strangers and his mother's cries, broke the still whiteness engulfing them.

"Calder….Calder! Your brothers! We have to get out of the car as fast as we can. Someone else might hit us. Quickly!"

Pernille tried to open the driver's side door but it was pinned shut by a metal barrier hidden behind the wall of fog.

"Calder, can you open your side?"

He struggled, pursing his small, undeveloped body into contortions of beautiful vigor.

"No, mommy. I'm scared."

Blood trickled down his forehead from the two-inch gash. A pane of glass had sliced it clean. If he wiped the blood away and lifted the flap of skin and flesh, the bone would be exposed. There were no mirrors intact and a controlled fear beat hysteria. Pernille tried to distract him once again.

"Think of the snow," Pernille said. "The way it falls quietly. After the storm, it's beautiful and quiet, like today. And when it's quiet, you can focus on anything and accomplish anything."

Calder kept trying to open his door. He did not want to let his mother or brothers down. In spite of his mother's soothing voice, it was impossible.

"It's going to be OK. Can you climb into the back seat and protect your brothers? Can you be my prince?"

"I can't unbuckle my seatbelt."

Neither could Pernille. She could not move if she wanted to. Her left arm was pinned against the door, and furthermore, she didn't know which direction the

Volvo faced. North, South, East, West, sideways, backwards, forward, these were all abstract ideas with no sight lines, or better, the sun, to guide her. If she or Calder got out of the car, they might be struck by oncoming traffic from the other direction—from Bergen that is—or be crushed against whatever vehicle was in front of them. They would have to wait until the fog lifted or an emergency crew came to their aid, whichever came first. Chance was a ruthless dance partner.

Thankfully, Alan and Brice remained asleep and unaware in the safety of their rear-facing car seats, snug like a pair of itsy bitsy spiders clinging to the wall in a deluge of water from an overflowing waterspout. They were safe so long as no other cars joined the icy horror.

With her free right hand, Pernille was able to unbuckle her eldest son's seatbelt. But instead of immediately crawling into the back, he searched the dashboard for his book, *The Snowy Day*. For the moment, he was unaware of the blood. The red drops had not yet fallen to his lap.

"Where's my book?"

"Sweetie, please get into the back seat as quickly as you can," Pernille insisted while reaching over to the glove compartment. She fumbled until she found the first aid kit. She opened it and gauze bandages and Band-Aids ejected onto the floor mats.

"Your book isn't important right now."

"But I want to read it to Alan and Brice. It will calm them down. They are waking up now. I have to find it."

"It's down on the floor. Can you pick it up and

hand me the red plastic box?"

She didn't call it by its proper name, not wanting to tip Calder off to his own blood. Her son scrambled under the dashboard blindly grasping.

"I found it."

In that moment another car found them. The force of the blow blew open Calder's door and he went flying into a snow bank on the side of the road. Alan and Brice screamed awake, their car seats bent sideways.

Calder clutched the book even as he began to feel numb. He couldn't move at first, but then felt a surge of energy, and his arms and legs began to work again.

Pernille's screams echoed throughout the white birch trees. The blow freed her left arm but she had no peripheral vision. The fog ruled.

Calder finally saw the blood, a deep red strata in stark contrast to the icy white. He scrambled to his feet and called out for his mother. He heard her voice imploring him to stay where he was.

"Can you see anything?"

"Yes, I can see trees and lots of snow. We're on the side of the road. If you come to my voice, Alan and Brice will be safe."

"Run into the woods. Get as far away from the road as you can."

Calder moved toward the trees like a ghost on a scavenger hunt. He could still hear his mother's voice, but he resumed his search. The book was his safe haven. Lost in its pages and within his imagination, danger and cold did not exist.

As Calder zigzagged toward a grove of ominous

birch trees, the drops of blood fell in an intricate path like a line of ants marching in the snow. He felt slightly dizzy. His head throbbed as the wound faced the brisk air. He heard his brothers' muffled cries wending their way through the din of rebounding metal and then he heard other moans, other lives struggling to escape the wreckage.

He realized he was no longer clutching his beloved book. It must be somewhere near the broken door, hidden in the creeping white shroud that hovered nearby, begging him to enter if he dared. He looked back and there was a patch of clear air where the fog had broken.

He looked down at the ground and began to track back toward the road, back toward danger. The book filled his mind. The cut was a painful inconvenience. His brothers now wide awake and their screams became louder and louder. His mother's cries fell silent. What had happened?

"Are Brice and Alan okay? Follow my voice, mom. It's clear up by the trees. It's only about 10 feet."

"Keep looking for your book. Look in the trees," Pernille said, her voice reduced to a raspy whisper. "Don't come back this way. It's safe where you are."

Calder was frozen. He thought something was wrong. Instinctively he reached down and scooped a handful of snow and put it to his forehead. The cold sting felt better than the roiling drips pages out on every heartbeat. Then he spotted something between his chilled fingers.

The Snowy Day, open to the last page, with its mountain of snow piled high, and nestled in a puddle of fresh blood. Two feet beyond it, a woman thrown from her vehicle breathed irregularly, in great gasping whoops that sounded like a punctured airbag. Her head was tilted sideways pressed against the snow.

"Mom?" Calder uttered, just able to get the sound from his lips.

He looked around the other side, knelt down and placed his head even with hers in the snow. His book was no longer important; his innocence fluttered away with it.

Her eyes, a deep blue like his mother's, were hollow. But it was not his mother. She was dead. This was not supposed to be the first dead person he saw.

"Mom? Mom, this way."

Then, a gentle hand took his away, away from the destruction and toward the birch grove. He heard two tiny voices giggling, unconcerned about imminent danger.

"Snow," Brice said.

"Snow," Alan echoed. They were kids, and the fog blocked their view of the horror. Pernille led them away from the Volvo's twisted green metal. The foursome ran up the hill into the safety of the birch trees until they could no longer hear the moans. The quiet forest, flush with snow, was their sanctuary. Pernille told her eldest son years later that they formed a cathedral, the sunlight filtering through and erasing the pain and damage. She hugged her boys tight, the family forming a ring of safety where neither blood, nor broken bones could shatter them. Yet, Calder's eyes wandered toward the distance, across a snowy field beyond the birch trees. There, a grove of six Norwegian spruce trees, stood watch alone on a slightly inclined snowfield. It was an image of sheer beauty. The clouds broke above them and three splintered rays of sunlight illuminated the grove, God's rays. Calder's numb hands and arms felt warmth.

They waited until a man in uniform emerged from the fog, and placed them in an ambulance and took them to a big building that was completely white with lots of windows. Calder remembered the hospital more than *morfar*'s funeral. His father met them at the hospital; Pernille had suffered a broken left arm and fractured two ribs. Brice and Alan received nothing more than a few superficial cuts from the shattered windshield. Calder held his father's hand while they swapped injury stories. A somber mood that *mormor* didn't want to allow crept into the farmhouse barn despite her best efforts. The crunching sound of metal and the red blood oozing into the snow at the side of the road curdled Calder's mind more than 30 years later.

20

"Why haven't you responded to my letters? I thought a man in your position would welcome the more than generous speaking fee."

Calder heard the probing female voice before he saw the body it was attached to. He had just run out to the supermarket, Zoe bundled in tow asleep in her stroller. The woman looked familiar, possessing wavy hair down to her waistline and parading in the habitual Arctic chill in a tight-fitting white sweater and similar colored turtleneck. Clearly she had on several layers lurking beneath to vanquish the elements. The overall effect hid her curvaceous figure.

She was the bohemian, blue-jeaned woman he had seen at Duane Reade the day the *N.Y. Post* paparazzo finagled his money shot. The woman bent down and stared at Zoe, who was hidden in her protective plastic cover cocoon. "She's so cute."

Calder has grown accustomed to total strangers approaching him in the store or on the street, marveling at how beautiful his daughter was. She was beautiful. Numerous people recommended he submit Zoe to a children's talent agency. Some recognized him for his breastfeeding notoriety. One man even thrust copies of the first *and* second *N.Y. Post* front-page banner headlines in his face seeking an autograph. Calder obliged if only to make him go away faster and prevent anyone else who was on the fence about approaching him from potentially noticing the milkman in their midst.

"I've seen you before. At the pharmacy."

"Yes, that's when we first became aware of you. My name is Olivia Finebaum," the bohemian introduced herself, thrusting her non-gloved hand into Calder's black leather palm. "Sorry to accost you, but we are beginning to get, for lack of a better word, desperate."

"Who's *we*?"

"The United Feminist Organization. U.F.O."

"What?"

"U.F.O. We hold our annual conference in Atlantic City next weekend. We want you to be our keynote speaker. You can stimulate a sea change in the perspective of men toward women's issues. It's too cold out here to debate. We'll pay you a significant fee. Please say yes."

***

Across town in a vacant midtown building appropriated for nefarious purposes—the director wanted an authentic view of the Empire State Building out of the office window and not a green screen somewhere in the San Fernando Valley—Essy worked on her money shot. She opened her legs and mind to the performer who stood in for Calder, her morose attitude bringing down the proceedings. Calder's absence and his saying "no" to her—nobody said *no* to her—affected her performance.

"Wait a minute. I'm not feeling this," she said as the male performer continued to thrust until the director halted the proceedings.

Essy marched across the makeshift set without bothering to put on any clothes or wipe herself clean. She dug into her purse about 15 feet across the room. The pink-frilled accessory teetered on a stack of plywood beams at an office building that was in the midst of a wholesale renovation. The director was a newbie trying to make a name for himself under the pseudonymous moniker Corey Light, his de facto "porn star name." His friend was the building manager and had allowed him access for only one hour to conduct the illegal shoot, the penultimate money shot in an opus entitled *The Empire State Has No Clothes*.

It was half past eleven in the morning when Essy extricated her smartphone from her cluttered belongings—condoms, lubrication and makeup clogged her purse—and punched in the numbers to Calder's phone.

"Pick up, pick up. You selfish bastard."

Calder was back at home in the safety—and warmth—of the apartment, sitting on the newly rechristened sofa "Lover's Island" and contemplating UFO's offer. He looked down at his vibrating phone; he always kept it on vibrate as not to disturb his potentially sleeping daughter. He saw it was Essy; her guilt must be getting the best of her. Calder made her wait, answering just before it disconnected; his voicemail remained full.

"Thank you for the generous offer; I'm not interested," he cut Essy off before she could get a new plea in edgewise.

"I'm not trying to convince you otherwise, could you tell me that thing you mentioned one more time?"

"What thing?"

"You said I was beautiful then mentioned something about recovery time after male ejaculation."

"What are you talking about? I never said that."

"You did. At the hospital when I came to visit you."

"You didn't visit me."

"I did. Before Maren arrived. You were sedated. I am so sorry for what happened. I wanted to make it up to you. So the Rabbi and I thought you might like to make a little extra cash to help support your family. Our offer is still on the table. I don't think you would have come to my show had you been thinking straight. To men, losing a job is like getting castrated. And trust me, I know men."

"Maren didn't take your offer so kindly. On the bright side, at least I know about the tumor."

"How can my scene partner withhold coming?"

"I really don't remember this," Calder replied.

"You might have been remembering a previous conversation you had that night. But you mentioned something about the medical term. I want to Google it. We can't continue this scene unless I find out what it is. Truth be told, I find you very attractive. No man has ever turned me down."

"I'm married."

"It's just a state of mind. You're already infamous for shooting milk in my tits and this shoot won't lessen your good graces with Andrea Peabody. That afterglow will never go away. Everybody in America is still on your side. Maren is painted as the villain who pushed her husband too far over the edge."

"The edge of what?"

"Sanity perhaps."

"We've worked things out. I love my wife and daughter both very much."

"More power to you then. Just tell me the term. So we can nail this money shot. I'll be thinking of you by the way."

"I can't remember," Calder paused as he thought. "There was a grad student at Columbia. She was there at your show. The refractory period. That's it. Google Coolidge Effect while you're at it. We all have a propensity to seek out sexual relationships with a new partner. Now goodbye. Please don't call me any more."

"Thank you."

Before Essy hung up, there was one more thing. Calder caught her just ahead of the expected dial tone.

"Wait, have you heard of UFO?"

"Yes, some anarcha-feminist organizations hate my guts, well most of them do. UFO has been fair to me. There are a few pro-sex and sex industry feminists hidden in their midst. We AV stars have our spies too you know. Why do you ask?"

"A woman by the name of Olivia Finebaum has offered me a twenty-thousand-dollar speaker's fee to address the UFO annual conference in Atlantic City in two weeks."

"You'd be a fool not to."

Suffer fools gladly.

Calder would take the money and run—to the Cayman Islands.

***

Calder and his wife awaited the welcoming Caribbean sun, and sought an end to any stubborn acrimony. He didn't mind a little "lacrimony." It was good for the soul. He needed the right button to push, like finding the proper side to open on a milk carton. Maren would soften around the edges and all would be well.

The following weekend, Calder and Maren kissed their daughter's forehead and left her in Joy's care. They enjoyed the taxi ride to the far eastern end of Grand Cayman with a dreadlocked Jamaican cabbie named Adonis, who was no such thing, his legs as skinny as a flamingo's. The normal 30-minute ride took over an hour because he honked the horn at and said hello to *every* woman he passed. Maren joked that he must be escaping a horde of other women in Kingston, and a few little Adonises.

Calder and Maren jested about Adonis long after the trip was over. He might have been the highlight of the trip. After only a couple of hours of sunset tanning and one dark and stormy, Maren ate some bad shrimp at the resort bar, and was incapacitated the entire remainder of the trip.

Row, row, row your boat, gently down the stream. Merrily, merrily, merrily, merrily, life is but a dream.

Everything you need to know in life, you learned in a children's song. Calder thought, as Maren vomited again into the toilet. Playing nurse, he catered to her every need, feeling guilty he had not been more attuned to her sufferings in taking care of Zoe when he still had a job, and was gone from morning until *almost* midnight. He called the front desk no less than eight times. It was for his wife's benefit. However, if he called, Calder knew it gave the appearance that he was actively on the case. No matter what else he did, if he didn't call the front desk, it would be interpreted as not trying hard enough. He also called Joy to check on Zoe, who was peachy. Joy held the phone to Zoe's petite ear and her parents beamed upon hearing her coos.

On the final day on the island, Calder snorkeled by himself beneath the hotel's private pier. All the colorful tropical fish hid in the shadows to avoid the sun, and to avoid being disturbed by meddling humans. They were trying to stay incognito, much like the man who stared at them. All Calder wanted was to return home. He got sunstroke the last day and joined his wife in a makeshift sick ward. Bottles of Gatorade and water lined the bed like a post-apocalyptic garbage dump. Calder closed the blinds to construct a cave worthy of a Neanderthal king. He and his wife held hands and fell asleep, side-by-side, partners in grime.

21

Oct. 19

Dear Zoe:

Please don't read this letter until I have died. I don't know why, but it took me three hours to write that first sentence. I guess I just want this to be a pristine document when you see it for the first time, with the full perspective of a life well lived (I hope). I wrote that sentence first in case you are tempted to read it before I am gone, though I am going to put it in a safe deposit box as part of the will I have drawn up. You will only be able to read it then. I am being cautious. Don't worry. There is nothing earth-shattering in this letter, no secret revelation. You are not adopted, born out of wedlock or any other mystery. I simply want to express how I feel now, on the day you were born, the day of all days, and how you may feel about me after I am gone.

This letter is a monument to love. The death of my own father, your grandfather, prompted me to write this letter as an heirloom you can pass on to your child, or children, one day. I hope I have raised you well, and given you nothing but unconditional love that stays with you long after I leave this world. The term 'unconditional' almost begs the question of whether I am withholding some love, tucked away somewhere where no one can find it. That is not true. Words cannot even describe how much I love you. Words are too simplistic. Actions do speak louder than words, and I hope the actions we shared in life leave you with a "God's house has many rooms" sense of wonder and that you can turn to when both your mother and I are gone. I did not tell her I was writing this letter. This is our own private document, a last testament time capsule from the glory of your laughs, and your cries (I love those too—they are so tender and sweet). I love singing ABC to you to lull you to sleep. You bore holes into my soul with your unwavering gaze. Unblinking, you are a beacon of all meaning.

Your mother and I are so blessed to have you. And you are perfect. Your smiling face breaks all clouds and lifts my spirits to heights I never expected, and will do so long after I have left this mortal coil. I never thought much about my legacy. But it is abundantly clear: you are my legacy. I hope I have been a good father to you. I hope that the joys of life, art, love, family, travel, curiosity, adventure and freedom are yours and you wield them well, and pass them on to others and to the world. I could go on and on listing the good qualities I think make a life, but as your grandfather would say, "You know what to do. You know what the right thing is."

I have failed in my quest to discover the meaning of life. Failed in the sense that I am utterly in awe that humans exist at all. The heart beating in your tiny chest will never stop pumping blood until you too die. It is an amazing organ. How does it last for so long?

You might be alive to see the year 2101, the dawn of the 22nd century. Men may living be on Mars by then, or siphoning water from two of Jupiter's moons, Ganymede and Europa. That's amazing. That is the meaning of life to live and to keep living, to move the human species forward. I hope the choices I have made in this life were good ones, and hold sway in your current life, influencing you in a positive way.

I hope your mother and I make it, made it rather. Truth be told, two years before you were born, things looked dubious at best. We weathered the storm and are stronger for it. Persevere. Never quit and always love. Those are the three mantras I will pass to you. The first two are essentially the same, but I'm not changing them. These are key words in my new life since you arrived.

If I am rambling, please forgive me. It's only a product of the immense happiness your arrival has awakened. I cannot imagine life without you, and I will do my best to give you and your mother my best. There is meaning to be attained in family and in love. Seek it, and you will succeed. If you stop looking, even if the exercise seems futile and no meaning can be found in the absurdity that is the human condition, you will have succeeded through the trial and tribulations of trying.

If I failed you in any way, it was not intentional. I hope you don't resent me for anything that may happen in the future. Well, it is the future for you, and anything, if it has happened, is already your past. Don't let the past affect your present or your future. The future is always happening. And life imitates ads. I saw that on a woman's handbag in the ER admittance room. It stuck with me, and I hope that isn't true. As an ad man, I don't want ads to take the place of reality, of the meaning of life that you must discover for yourself. I shower you with kisses. Your coos are the manna that gives my life purpose. Eureka! I have found it. That's the California state motto. Your father will always be a Californian at heart. Simply put, you are the meaning of life. It is now 3:39 a.m. on Oct. 20, I can't sleep, and I don't want to sleep. Your cries fill the room with adoration. I love you very much.

Sincerely,
Calder O. Boyd, Your Father

22

The outside world, at least the world outside Manhattan, mystified Calder Boyd. The crystal blue sky suffocated the snowdrifts piled high on the edges of the New Jersey turnpike. He hadn't driven a car in years. He almost forgot how to do it and accidentally stepped on the brake instead of the accelerator as he left the rental car garage on East 50th St.

Open space, after the daily crunch of skyscrapers, held infinite possibilities but constant exposure. The claustrophobia of the city gave way to the agoraphobia of too much chance. Other cars on the highway had greater leeway to cause greater damage. Calder drove like a senior citizen and didn't care. He carted a very special passenger.

Zoe nestled happily in her rear-facing car seat, the first time they had used it since bringing her home from the hospital, and Maren guarded her in the backseat. Calder felt like a chauffeur. Maren appeared happy. The United Feminist Organization's decision to invite him as the keynote speaker—more pointedly the prospect of $20,000—

allayed all other concerns and she noticed the apprehension Calder normally displayed receded into the background, lost among the spooky rows of desolate pines as they plodded toward the Jersey Shore.

"The speed limit is 75 you know," Maren pointed out, a gently ribbing backseat driver. "I've been wanting to say that for an hour."

"I know you have," he answered, the memory of his Norwegian highway nightmare clouded his thoughts. "But you know, fog can creep up at any moment."

Maren knew what that meant and did not press the issue further. She loved her husband's bent for keeping her and Zoe safe. She accepted the position of strength it afforded him.

The Pine Barrens soon gave way to the coastal plain and the drive toward the gambling mecca took on an Armageddon-like tone when the sun dipped below the horizon. In the distance, the line of casinos jutted into the darkening sky, their lights a pantheon to sordid possibility.

About a decade before Zoe was born, before they were married, Calder and Maren drove across the country to Wyoming. The sky's patina reminded him of the glowing sunsets of the Great Plains and the basin and range region as they made their way west, Horace Greeley-like, toward Yellowstone. Before the trip, Maren jokingly referred to it as "Whyoming", as in why would anyone want to go there or live there? She scuttled that joke as soon as she saw its end-of-the-world beauty. Calder hoped Atlantic City would do equal wonders, magical thinking perhaps. The neon gambling palaces contoured against the indigo heavens reminded him of the Tetons piercing the last glint of the Wyoming sunset.

When they drew near the second-rate casino at the far southern end of the strip, they passed two women loitering on the street corner dressed in red heels and neon dresses, one green, one blue. Loitering, yes, that's what Calder imagined them doing, though he assumed otherwise.

"Why did UFO choose Atlantic City? This represents everything they are against. Exhibit A of everything wrong with society, a place synonymous with the subjection and objectification of women."

Through the rearview mirror, Calder saw Maren motion to the green- and blue-clad temptresses. They weren't standing on the corner in 30-degree weather to boost their immune systems, and any time spent with them might diminish yours. If Zoe ended up in those circumstances, no question, Calder thought, he failed as a father.

"I'll have to ask Olivia."

"Olivia? You make her sound like Albert Einstein."

"Be nice. She's the one who makes sure I get paid. She's the executive director. They must have gotten a good deal."

Zoe coughed, a dry cough that sounded like a wounded seal. Neither Calder nor Maren noticed the changed cadence of the cough.

"You always assume I'm going to say something negative. Maybe they are just trying to make a point."

"And that would be?"

"Men require sex, gambling and liquor to quell their thoughts, their troubled minds," Maren hypothesized. "Women partake too but they don't require it. They wanted to come into the den of sin and shine a light on the warmer aspects of the fairer sex."

"You sound like Olivia."

"Maybe I'm a card-carrying UFO member, waiting to be abducted," Maren laughed, cutting the building tension inside the rental sedan.

The rows of casinos went from elegant, to serviceable, to decidedly low-budget. Then there was the Atlantic City Hotel & Casino, headquarters of UFO's three-day, weekend bonanza. The sign on the marquee blazed the unwelcome welcome: UFO Sighting, A Warm Welcome to the United Feminist Organization. It sounded, and without question was, hollow.

To get to the front desk to check in, the Boyd family of New York City, as they would be welcomed as, first had to navigate the casino floor. It was filled with women. Calder was the only man in sight apart from the blackjack dealers and pit bosses. He noticed eyes on him like lasers and fingers pointing. He swore the din of slot machines and conversation lowered a few decibels with his arrival.

At the front desk, they waited in line for a good 20 minutes behind a gaggle of 32 housewives from Pennsylvania, each of them wearing a black UFO T-shirt with a flying saucer on the back and the words "Men Are Aliens" across the shoulder blades.

"Olivia couldn't get you V.I.P. treatment, I take it," Maren's voice dripped with sarcasm.

The assistant manager of the hotel welcomed them with a haphazard smile, giving the Boyds the luau suite, a supposed Hawaiian-themed enclave on the 15th floor. Two complementary piña coladas materialized in their hands.

"A token of our appreciation," the assistant manager grunted. He handed Calder the key card and then greeted the next party, a group of lesbian radical feminists called Purple Peril, each of whom dyed their hair a Day-Glo shade of periwinkle.

Olivia later informed Calder that the hotel manager refused to work the convention and was on vacation in Key West. "This is exactly the type of sexism we are trying to eliminate," she said. "Your presence is part of the process. Thank you for being here."

As they carted their shoulder bags through the casino floor to the elevators—Calder already sucking on the pineapple chunk at the bottom of his complimentary piña colada—a cocktail waitress approached him like an oasis in the deep desert. Her nametag revealed her working name: Lolita. Calder imagined her actual name as Kate or Lisa or Cindy. She handed Calder an all-you-can-eat 24-hour buffet coupon and thrust another drink into his one free hand.

"Two-for-one insomnia special from four to six a.m."

"Who the hell is going to be there at that hour?"

"You'd be surprised," "Lolita" ignored Maren and

addressed Calder directly. "I'll be there."

She thrust her breasts in Calder's face in a deliberately provocative move, a revolt against the conventioneers. The cocktail waitress mastered her trademark action when she worked terrible hours and clientele, and she disappeared as quickly as she came.

"I'll be here," Maren thrust her bosoms into Calder's chest and squeezed his ass. Her sense of humor had not suffered.

The luau room existed in a Twilight Zone between tacky and ridiculous; Calder called it ridiculously tacky. The wallpaper was the only Hawaiian touch in the Spartan suite.

"What are you going to talk about anyway? I've never heard you speak publicly. You can barely express yourself at home in that tiny apartment. How will you fill a convention hall?"

"Look in the blue folder inside Zoe's backpack. Olivia gave me a list of bullet points, key words and phrases that will help me if I get stuck. They are more guidelines really. I can ad lib the rest. I did stand-up in college."

"You are not funny."

Maren alighted Zoe onto the king size bed, sliding a rattler into her jittery fingers to keep her occupied. The baby fat made them like miniature pigs-in-the-blanket, ready to nibble on. Exhausted from the three-hour drive, Maren rummaged through the baby kit, dropping diapers, baby wipes, various lotions and creams into a small pile on the far side of the bed, out of Zoe's reach. When Maren spotted the folder, she opened it like a precious watch with the gears exposed.

Light blue sheets of paper with the familiar flying saucer logo contained a list of all the different panels and workshops, as well as the speaking schedule: Equal Pay For Equal Work, Women in Hollywood, Raising A Feminist Man, Psychology of Feminism, Mary Wellington, CEO of Pink Elephant Feminine Products, How Not to Raise a Feminist, Politics and Women. Women's Reproductive Rights—Under Assault By the Right Wing. Congresswoman Deborah Miles, Radical Feminism, Corporate Raiders—Women On Top. After Olivia's bullet-point inserted flash cards saying "Lactation Story," "Mr. Mom" and "Appreciation of Women's Suffrage and Suffering," at the very bottom of the third blue sheet and surrounded by three asterisks on either side, it read: Calder Boyd, Keynote Speaker, 9 p.m. Grand Ballroom, Exhibit Hall A.

Zoe coughed again. After a quick feeding, the family fell into an easy sleep. As Calder faded on the lumpy mattress, a sense of doom washed over him.

Feb. 21
In Atlantic City
10:26-10:37 p.m. Bottle fed Zoe 125 ml of formula. Put her to sleep in her crib at 10:39 p.m. She woke up about 15 minutes later choking/coughing on phlegm. Maren cradled her back to sleep.

Two hours later, the fireworks erupted.
At 1:47 a.m. Maren's grumpiness flared. Calder

had forgotten Zoe's down jacket, and the room was frigid.

"You always forget something. It never fails. Where did you think we were going? Disneyworld?"

At 2:22, Maren became a detective.

"Who is Brook Holster?"

Calder's head exploded. Posterity was a pain in his ass. He ascertained he should have destroyed Brook's inappropriate letter along with all the rest. He didn't even try to defend himself. Exasperation, exhaustion and exacerbation swirled in the darkness of the night, all three claiming a piece of his soul.

Maren soon moved to another topic, a plethora of possibilities.

Feb. 22
2:15-2:24 a.m. Bottle fed Zoe 125 ml of pumped breast milk. My nipples hurt. Changed her diaper (pee). Put lotion on her torso and legs. Put her back to sleep in the bed between us at 2:32 a.m. Her breathing seems much better. Less coughing.

Another flare up happened at 3:23 a.m., when it took Calder an unusually long time to breastfeed Zoe, and she began coughing furiously. The biting tone chafed Calder's ears, but he grinned and imagined Iceland.

"She's sick. Changing her diaper isn't important. She needs milk."

If it's not one thing, it's another.

At 3:41 a.m. Maren could hold it back no longer.

His wife's dam broke and water flooded into the hotel room with the view of the broken down pier, a signpost in the chilling moonlight. It was bound to happen. Calder's health—and indirectly Maren's fit of food poisoning—shielded him for as long as it could, but no longer. Calder didn't blame her. He deserved it. Her timing, however, was lousy.

"I have to give a speech tomorrow," he pleaded.

No consolation. Maren gave her speech tonight.

"You can sleep when you die."

Maren threw Calder's oft-uttered phrase back at him. The hollow sound reverberated off the walls. She let him have it.

Hanging out with a porn star, hanging out with Astrid without her knowledge, being on the front page of the *Post* with his face in Essy's breasts, lying about being laid off, lying about his drinking, lying about his lactation ability, all points were in play, especially delaying treatment for the pituitary tumor.

"Go see a damn doctor," Maren implored as Zoe choked on sputum. The pinnacle of Maren's ire was reached, he hoped. Calder rushed to Zoe's aid. He picked her up and collected a milky white string of phlegm on the end of his right index finger. "Not being treated so you can lord over me like some sort of vigilante breastfeeding lunatic is ridiculous," Maren continued.

Calder conceded this point and many others. He just wanted to go to sleep.

"I'll go to the doctor first thing when we get back to the city. I promise."

"Your promises aren't worth anything," Maren

shot back. "You said you would work less at the theater and you haven't."

"I don't have a job, remember," he replied. "I need the money. I'm not going because I want to. I *need* to."

"I make enough money. You can be a stay-at-home dad."

"Are you really okay with that?"

Maren nodded in the affirmative. "We'll get to spend more time as a family."

The storm passed; Maren satiated, Calder expected to fall back to sleep. The gods laughed. At 4:14 a.m., all of Maren's old grievances reemerged: the lack of ambition, the lack of saved money, the lack of romance, the lack of cleaning up after himself, the lack of common sense. And then the old standard fired up on the jukebox: living in a tiny apartment. "This shitty hotel room is bigger," Maren crooned— one of the things Calder chose to remember the next day.

At 5:05 a.m. Maren mercifully ended her tirade and fell asleep. Zoe slept through it all. But as soon as Maren went to bed, a furious coughing jag began.

Zoe Boyd had a cold.

Maren blamed her husband. "You gave it to her. You don't sleep enough, you don't sleep with me and sleeping on the sofa—Sofa Island my ass—has weakened your immune system and made you susceptible to catching a cold and you passed it to Zoe. It's your fault. You take care of it."

Calder interpreted "it" as "her," as in Zoe.

He picked Zoe up, rubbing her back softly like a

warm teddy bear, and escaped into the bathroom. He turn on the shower as hot as it would go and steamed up the room. Calder held Zoe in his arms for 15 minutes and she fell into a cough-free slumber. Before he left, Calder traced his finger on the fogged mirror, three letters surrounded by small droplets of beaded water clinging to the glass like spiders: his daughter's name in steam.

Calder retreated into his imagination. The hotel room became a Magritte painting: the bed and curtains were a roiling ocean lapping at the shores of a fiery background, flashes jumping out of the picture blinding him. He got less than 30 minutes sleep before steam treatment Round 2 commenced.

It seemed like the longest night of his life, and certainly of Zoe's. Her irregular breathing and fits of coughing required attention every 45 minutes to an hour, sometimes every 15 minutes. If he didn't get some sleep, Calder would be in no shape to deliver a keynote address that night, approximately 15 hours into his future.

Maybe they should have convinced Joy to stay a little longer; she had left in a huff after a minor tiff with her daughter over her treatment of her husband. Joy's second departure and the lack of anyone they trusted to watch Zoe overnight necessitated the family trip. Maren's mother still sided with Calder, even if it wore thin. He needed to find joy within himself.

At 5:59 a.m., Zoe was asleep, Maren was asleep, and Calder, despite the fact he was exhausted, could not sleep. He stared at the shadow of the TV set, imagining all the shows he hadn't had time to catch up on, and all the sporting events he had missed. He put on a pair of jeans and his black blazer and gray porkpie hat and quietly headed to the casino floor.

Calder headed straight for the two-for-one buffet. He looked at his watch: 6:06 a.m. He thought they might be merciful if he told them his story and extend the deal by 10 minutes. Lolita was there. But in this instance, she had no name. She was a stranger. And a stranger was what Calder needed. He ordered a double order of scrambled eggs, toast and bacon, and added a mimosa to top it off. She listened to his predicament. The lack of money, the lack of romance, the egotistical tendencies that shot himself in the foot, she heard them all.

"You need to get laid, dude," she said when he had finished, and with that she left. The grease left over from his cleaned plates was the only thing keeping him company.

He had to pay double.

23

The next morning, Calder heard no cries or sounds and saw no light. When he woke up, Zoe and Maren were gone. Their bags, the stroller and his family were all missing. He did not even think to go looking for them. He intuited Maren had taken Zoe back to NYC and the warmth of the radiator blasting their one-bedroom apartment. He glanced at the digital alarm clock resting on the pedestrian nightstand, on top of a Gideon bible. 2:12 p.m. He wasn't sure when he had dozed off, but the instant he woke up felt like the same moment.

Maren asked about the bus schedule a day earlier, and Calder suspected she and Zoe motored up the New Jersey Turnpike with a coffee-deprived 60-something male driver at the controls. Busses are safer, he convinced himself. The pediatrician pamphlet given to him at Zoe's two-month well visit said so.

A piece of hotel stationary hung on the mirror over the dresser, where the TV rested like a statue, indicating the location of his ladies. Maren had complained to the front desk that their "Hawaiian suite" was too cold and the same assistant manager who worked the bad gig in the manager's place had moved them to another room, an L-shaped room just off the main heating shaft. Hot air glided through the room in such a way that it felt like the molecules in their bodies realigned.

Calder stayed in bed for another 45 minutes, staring at the ceiling and looking over his notes. Olivia's notes occupied several inches of the room's desk space. He wanted to give a good speech, but more sleep would do him well.

He decided, at last, that he had had enough, the dark room a microcosm of a marriage that might fray further if he did not join his wife and daughter as soon as possible. Calder could feel his moment in the spotlight coming to a close and he wanted to celebrate the awkward days, weeks and months he had lived in lactation. This waning moment in a second tier hotel and casino on a ravaged seaboard screamed of possibility.

Calder bounded out of bed in a fit of energy. He dressed himself in his black Public Enemy T-shirt, black leather jacket and a pair of faded black jeans. His makeshift rucksack contained nothing more than toiletries and comfortable shoes. His suit and tie hung in a garment bag in the closet. He retrieved the rest of his belongings, including his blue-sheeted notes, took one last look about the room and left in a cacophony of determination. He glided on a $5 pair of Times Square sunglasses. He definitely didn't want to be recognized here, what with the Purple

Peril and assorted allies wandering the corridors of feminist power.

He pressed the button on the elevator bank and when it arrived, cowered as a man wearing a Militant Men's Society T-shirt stepped aside to let him in. There was an awkward silence before the man spoke. "We have to stick together around here." There was no need for an explanation; they were behind enemy lines. Calder as the invited guest less so, but he grunted in agreement to keep the man happy and unobtrusive. He got off one floor below Calder.

Exiting on the 15th floor, Calder passed a gaggle of teenage girls accompanied by their group leader. Their nametags, adhesive white squares attached to their matching purple sweatshirts, revealed their identity: Young Female Politicians of the Future. The group leader asked for Calder's autograph, having recognized the Public Enemy disguise from a throwaway line in Thomas Spooner's expose—the flashpoint that led Calder to this very moment. The teens surrounded him in a spat of giggles and quizzical glances. They dissipated after a few social media pictures that Calder obliged albeit with an uneasy smirk. Olivia said he would definitely be earning his speaker's fee and now he realized what she meant.

The Boyd family's' new room was around the corner from the elevator bank, and he didn't have far to go. Half asleep, Maren opened the door to the their heated habitat, Room 1515; Zoe's smile greeted him. Maren announced she was going to the spa on the fifth floor, Calder's arrival giving her the break she needed.

Not content to be cooped up in the hotel, Calder breast-fed his daughter for 30 minutes, and then prepared for her debut amongst the exhibition halls on the basement level. More elevators and more supportive onlookers. In Calder's experience, babies have a strong tendency to draw them in.

Zoe would be too young to remember but as Calder explored the grand market—a UFO bazaar peddling everything from self-help books on navigating and defeating a "man's world" to no less than the antidote for a discriminating society—he discovered his own masked visage, complete with lactating breasts, standing guard. A gag gift written into the UFO rider, he knew, but had forgotten. He hadn't made any outlandish rock star-like requests, such as a bowl solely comprised of blue M&M's, yet seeing himself lampooned in such a way underscored the absurdity of it all.

Life is not a sitcom.

Calder's basking ended in the same instant, a Warholian moment of truth. He chose not to fight it. Earning his keep, he understood. He delved into his back pocket, pulled out his credit card and bought a likeness of himself. He tossed the $5 sunglasses into the nearest trash receptacle; he wasted 10 minutes searching for one in the expensive basement labyrinth of exhibition stands. The next two hours, he showed Zoe to a group of small-town female mayors from the Great Lakes States, and lastly Olivia Finebaum.

"Looking forward to your speech tonight," she said, echoing the sentiment of all his previous hall and elevator fans. Calder leaned in and confessed his innermost secret. "I really don't know what I'm doing here."

"Don't worry. You're amongst friends. I'll see you in...three hours."

Olivia was then pulled aside by her attaché, PR flack and overall assistant, Glenda, a striking woman with long jet-black hair, with an odd resemblance to Morticia Addams or Elvira.

"Security is setting up the main exhibition hall now. Which doors do you want to use as the V.I.P. entrance?"

Glenda, seeing Calder for the first time, noticed that he was watching and then pulled Olivia aside and whispered in her ear. Olivia looked concerned. She held up her finger to Calder, telegraphing the universal sign for wait a second. Glenda bent her ear for another three minutes before Olivia finally mouthed the word 'sorry' and waved as she scurried to some other pressing engagement. A cadre of security guards followed her. Calder waved back like a schoolboy saying goodbye to his favorite teacher at the end of the year.

The milkman of the hour returned to Room 1515. Maren unwound from her spa treatment on the sofa, looking out over the placid Atlantic with a blue hotel towel wrapped around her head. The waves lapped at the boardwalk.

Calder's gray suit, crisp white dress shirt and light blue tie with silver flecks was laid out on the bed where Maren had placed it.

"Knock 'em dead tonight." She laughed as the

words left her mouth. "Just tell them what they want to hear and you'll do fine."

Calder looked at the red digital alarm clock. 6:56 p.m. He had time to take a quick nap.

***

Pernille stood on the edge of the searing black asphalt, where a three-point line would have been if it hadn't been worn down. She called her shot.

"Off the top of the backboard, off the front of the rim and into the hole."

Thirty-year-old Calder watched from the free throw line and accepted the doom that awaited him. He already had H-O-R-S. If his mom made this shot, there was no way he could. It was her signature game of H-O-R-S-E closer; he'd seen her hustle playground kids on more than one occasion just to prove a point, never collecting on her bets. If she won, Calder would have to relinquish his old bedroom to be converted into her art studio.

The fading sunlight at the elementary school nestled in the shadows of the L.A. Memorial Coliseum became Calder's ally. The bent backboard and crooked rim also made gallant foot soldiers in his battle to retain the last claim to some piece of his childhood, as did the smell of ancient cigarette butts stinging the air.

Pernille and James Boyd used to cohabitate in a tiny apartment down the street before Calder was even an inkling in their minds. Back then, a few burned-out vestiges of the 1965 Watts Riots remained.

Calder was on the verge of asking his Norwegian girlfriend to marry him and he sought his mother's advice. She opted for a game of H-O-R-S-E in a secluded corner in the old neighborhood. Her true purpose was to check on the status of a mural she had painted on commission.

The mural glistened as the sun's long fingers of light hit the stunning work flush, creating a spectral explosion of yellows, oranges and a perspective placing streak of burnt umber. Two distant downtown skyscrapers stabbed the pink sky just above the massive tapestry of schoolchildren interlocking hands on a golden seashore. The neighborhood was predominately black but Pernille chose to portray a rainbow of all cultures: Japanese, Mexican, African, Scandinavian, Chinese, Indian, Middle Eastern and Native American.

She had the full support of the Los Angeles Unified School District, yet many in the neighborhood protested that there were not enough black faces. Some suggested they should all be black. In the ensuing controversy, the large piece was vandalized on more than one occasion, graffiti from the local gangs or a black face or African artifact randomly painted over one of the non-black children. Invariably, it was the Scandinavian one.

Today, as Pernille lined up her expert shot beneath the rim, the sun hit the Scandinavian girl— some thought a representation of the artist embedded in the work—illuminating her erased face. Her face had been altered into a black one and over time it had been replaced with graffiti and then white washed completely as if the girl never existed at all by an unseen protestor, only her two red shoes remained intact near the bottom of the mural.

Pernille executed her trick shot perfectly. It was her opponents' Everest. She collected the rolling basketball and passed it to her son. He knew if he hesitated, thought about the shot for long, he had no shot. So he lined it up and went on instinct.

"I met your father here you know," Pernille said.

After a noticeable hesitation, she continued: "There's something else you need to know before you marry this girl. Your father and I were never legally married."

It all came down to this.

At the start of the game, his mother issued a warning. Her dominant left arm—never recovered from the accident some 20 years earlier—hung slightly askew at the elbow, a jumble of permanent scar tissue and subsequent surgeries and dislocations. The dark discoloration marked her otherwise pale skin, a monument to a faraway winter's day. If an observer looked at the watchful mural closely, the lone black child wore a T-shirt bearing a solemn grove of birch trees standing guard.

Calder recognized it several years later when he was old enough to understand his mother's hidden symbolism. Now he just wanted his room kept intact, as if the prodigal son would return to live there and reclaim it at any instant. The block letters of his childhood bedroom were a beacon to a bucolic time, one that lacked responsibility.

Pernille saved her pearl for the moment her son

tried to duplicate her called shot. The revelation startled him just enough to distract his aim. The basketball soared upwards a black sphere against the sky's pastel warriors. Dusk also played her part.

Calder's shot clanked off the front of the distorted rim—neighborhood kids practiced dunks and suspended from it—and bounced straight down. He hadn't put enough English on the shot; he had taken it easy on her.

"In principle, I win," Pernille said. "But I take no joy in it." The basketball rolled to her feet and she stooped to pick it up.

"That accident was my fault. I've never admitted that to you and I've always wanted to."

"Stop it. Right now."

Pernille dribbled the ball around in circles with her right hand.

"It's true. I threw the book on the windshield, and when it slid over and popped up, it blocked your view. If you would have noticed the fog earlier, you could have braked in time. Your art career suffered. And I'm responsible. I just wanted to acknowledge it. It's eaten away a part of my heart all this time."

"Never second-guess yourself. You know you are marrying Maren. You are certain of it, correct?"

"Yes."

"If you second-guess the past, you'll be second-guessing your future at some point too. You are certain of your path with Maren today. Be certain tomorrow, and be certain thousands of tomorrows from now."

Pernille lined up a shot from the tip of the nonexistent key. "Double or nothing."

"I'm quitting while I'm ahead."

"I didn't raise a quitter."

"I know. You raised a very intelligent young man."

They both smiled.

There was about five minutes of available light remaining. Pernille stopped dribbling and tossed the basketball to Calder.

"I'm leaving the room as is," she said. "It's yours and always will be. I want you to always feel that no matter what happens in life, you always have a place to call home."

***

Calder stood before the throng of feminists and did not know where to begin. He felt disjointed and out of place. He glanced at Olivia's blue notes under the dais as he waited for his introduction to end. Her slogans rang hollow. They were not words he had prepared for a multi-million dollar ad campaign and therefore he felt out of sorts.

He *was* a feminist icon.

All eyes glued to him. He catalogued the faces staring back at him, surveying Exhibit Hall A from right to left. He almost choked when he saw familiar faces interspersed throughout the crowd.

Astrid and Varick held hands and Varick winked at him. He saw the two Columbia grad students, Rhea, with her red hair flowing over her white turtleneck—a UFO necklace bedazzling the top—and Susan, her dark hair blended into the UFO logo on her conventioneers' shirt. Were they tracking him that night at the bar? Stalking him now? In reality, they were nothing more than curious spectators. Calder swore he saw Essy in disguise in his peripheral vision, her own agent in the pro-sexual liberation faction of UFO. He did a double take but he lost the person in the crowd.

Straining his eyes, Calder glimpsed Maren against the far wall directly opposite from his position. Zoe's legs dangled from her ergonomic carrier. Maren dressed her in a UFO onesie with a small female alien emerging from the flying saucer. Calder knew where he should begin. But before he could, he noticed someone else.

This last person Calder saw unnerved him. The man on the elevator. His Militant Men's Society T-shirt gave way to a charcoal suit and black tie as not to look out of place. He could pass for a secret service agent. The man wafted through the crowd like a wisp of smoke, his eyes never leaving Calder's. He held up his right hand and Calder saw the tattoo; for a few seconds, he furtively contorted the hand into the shape of a pistol, firing an imagined bullet into his right temple. He was the man who wrote the threatening letter; he was sure of it now. Standing two feet to his left, Olivia noticed Calder's uneasiness as she continued to speak into the microphone.

"When I asked Calder Boyd to speak at our executive board meeting, I was met with skeptical looks and more than a few groans. But I think his story is unique and offers to pull the curtain back on gender roles. His unique gift can help illuminate and educate our society. And when I say society, I mean male society."

The room erupted into fits of laughter. But all Calder heard were a smattering of boos. He tensed and hoped sweat didn't put him underwater like a trapped fish at the aquarium in Bergen.

"Without further ado, I'd like to welcome Calder Boyd, known endearingly as The Milkman."

Olivia conceded the spotlight to the well-paid keynote orator. As Calder moved toward the microphone, the pit of his stomach sank and felt like he'd inhaled hundreds of Icelandic black sand beach pebbles.

"I am not a man. I am a hypocrite." The auspicious opening remarks of Calder's keynote address caused a woman in the front row to gasp. It occurred at the perfect moment of silence when the entire room was quiet, and the gasp echoed throughout Exhibit Hall A.

"I have been an active participant in the objectification of women. I have a confession to make. A couple months ago, I was feeling alienated. Losing my male identity due to my special gift. I attended a male empowerment seminar."

Somewhere in the rapt crowd, Varick turned to Astrid and whispered, "Say my name. Any publicity is good publicity. Good or bad."

Astrid looked perturbed. "Is it true?"

Echoes of disbelief filled the air. A cadre of Purple Peril onlookers shook their heads and then turned their backs on Calder in a silent, but highly visible, protest. The secret-service look alike muscled his toward the disturbance. Turns out, he was hired by UFO to watch the Purple Peril. He was no threat.

Unfazed, Calder continued his speech, feeling more comfortable the longer he spoke.

"Surprisingly, it was not entirely what it seemed. I did learn one thing that is especially relevant here today. Make every day with my wife and daughter like it's the first day I met them, to show how important they are, to ensure there is a bright future with them. Now I have not always been successful. But it made me realize and appreciate the fact that nobody, no human on Earth would exist without the struggle, the labor of a woman. When I began to lactate, I kept it secret from my wife. I wanted to use my new power to selfishly keep power over my individual freedom....."

Calder spoke for nearly 40 minutes, peeling back the onion layers on his life of lactation and at times, expounding on the same answers he had given on *The Andrea Peabody Show*.

"We are all feminists. In a nutshell, the only male empowerment worth its salt means empowering the two most important feminists in my life: my wife and daughter."

As he neared the end of his keynote address, Calder noticed a hooded figure in a UFO sweatshirt approach the dais. The figure was out of place among the mostly formal wear. Calder looked toward the back, beyond the approaching shape. Maren held up Zoe's right hand, helping her to wave. He put his arm up to wave back, and that's when it happened. "I love my family..."

The black handgun looked like a child's toy, but the bullets were real enough. The hooded figure exposed his identity—a different member of the Militant Men's Society, Jacob—and fired three quick blasts.

24

Snow and ice. Maren could not escape winter's minions. Outside, a Nor'easter attacked the southeast-facing wing of the Atlantic City hospital. From the 6th floor, the battered boardwalk looked like the carcass of a massive white whale heading into glacial oblivion. The howling winds rallied to a confluence just beyond the glass window of Room 67-B. At least it was a private room; paid for by hers truly.

Calder slept, oblivious to it all. One bullet rested in his left shoulder just above the collarbone. The other had grazed his right temple, and the third one left a small gash on the gaudy 1970s era wallpaper in Exhibit Hall A. As a result, the ballroom might get its overdue facelift.

Maren held her smartphone inches from her face with her right hand as she cradled Zoe with her left hand over her left shoulder, an infinitely better denizen than a bullet. The electric glow made Maren's flawless skin appear like that of an android. The glass of the hospital window silhouetted her body in the darkened room. The monitors and other medical equipment connected to the man in the bed, her husband, looked like a fallen constellation

The winter never ended even in cyberspace. The video was shot—an odd choice of words given her prone husband's wound—nearly two months earlier, and the landscape of endless white in Central Park fused into the raging whiteout. Her hands trembled as she steadied the smartphone. She peered into a miniature sea of pixels, noticing tiny grains of ice inside the edges of the frame. Winter gets everywhere. She wasn't sure how she had missed this email. Somehow it wound up in her spam, probably because of the size of Calder's video attachment. Maren was thankful she hadn't mistakenly erased it. Her habit of saving every email—it could be from or pertain to a client or a styling job query—proved intelligent. The only reason she found it today, of all days, was a keyword search for her husband's insurance information. He had sent it to her shortly after the first of the year because they had changed insurance carriers.

Calder's video testimonial to his wife would win no Oscars, but its dated effect illuminated a perfectly needed prescient present. The darkness of the room hid Maren's apprehensive gaze and the bouquets from hundreds of anonymous well wishers. She turned the sound down just enough that it didn't wake Calder and wasn't broadcast into the hallway, and conversely loud enough for her to hear above the blizzard. She hesitated, much like Calder had on the day he made the video, before pressing play.

Calder knelt down next to a snowy Central Park bench.

"I'm leaving this breast milk bottle in the hopes that it lasts the entire winter without being discovered. It's a video art project to see if anyone notices or cares what it means to be alive and a lactating male...." Calder paused, and his body lurched toward the mini-tripod. He hesitated, then retreated back toward the focal point, and continued:"....it's also because you know that I am not a vocal person. So I hope you understand. Maren, I have to tell you something."

The dawn light—"magic hour" in film parlance—bathed Calder in loving eminence. The black edges of the sky turned cerulean and the ice glowed in turn, imitating the heavens. Having mapped out the light on a previous Central Park morning excursion, Calder knew exactly where his best mark was. As the light grew in intensity and blue and white filled the sky above, and the snow below, he repeated a series of words over and over, a mantra for a new day.

"Maren, I want to have a better marriage, I want to have better tomorrows with you. I want to have thousands of tomorrows."

He stood still in the frame and Maren witnessed a surreal, two-minute time lapse. The morning gloss and reflected sunlight beaming upward from the snow combined to make Calder look like a living snow angel. And then the video ended and began again in a constant loop.

His wife's tears worked in Calder's favor. Thankful her husband was simply alive—a sad threshold to expect in her marriage—Maren's eyes welled up in tandem with Calder's personal confession. She thought he was depressed, and now there was little doubt, but not about the message he was conveying. He was in pain. As Maren watched the video, Calder involuntarily pressed the self-medication button like a hibernating bear.

Maren empathized with her husband. She felt cold and lonely, bristling at his numerous attempts to rekindle their initial spark, and this video art piece in the guise of a confessional opened her heart, if not her mind, to the greater need for solidarity amongst the parents. Zoe's warmth was their warmth. Zoe's heart was their heart. Zoe's hunger was theirs too. And the little angel's cries for her father's breast opened the floodgates. Maren cried and could not stop, the tears a cathartic baptism.

She watched the video again and again deep into the night, mesmerized until dawn overtook her and she joined her sleeping husband.

25

Dr. West's office looked nothing like it had only months earlier. The doctor's move into new digs transformed the drab early incarnation into a palace of waiting and examination room bliss.

A small rock garden and recycled water waterfall spirited through the reception area and a modernized sound system piped soothing Muzak through unseen but pitch perfect speakers. Each waiting room chair—Calder counted 10—was custom designed, and there were also two white Eames chairs. Silent television monitors lined the walls, displaying a rotating visual mural of exotic travel locales: Zanzibar, Tunisia, Easter Island, Egypt's White Desert, Greece, Mauritius, Iguaçu Falls, the Galápagos Islands, Antarctica, Namibia and one Calder recognized instantly, Iceland. He was mesmerized.

A sleek new magazine rack contained actual magazines and periodicals, current ones no less. *GQ. Esquire. Popular Mechanics. Essence. Time. People. Scientific American. The New England Journal of*

Medicine. Even the *Sports Illustrated* swimsuit issue.

There were two receptionists. Calder tried to ascertain which one was snarkier and which one he had interacted with in the office's former capacity as a masquerading facade.

The meeting with his multidisciplinary team took place in a secluded back room that overlooked the Rockefeller Center ice skating rink. Calder dreamt of a young couple meeting there right now amid the falling snow. An endocrinologist, Dr. Alston, and his colleagues, a neurosurgeon, an ear, nose and throat specialist, and though Calder's eyesight remained unaffected, an ophthalmologist, along with Dr. West, passed a medical folder back and forth and discussed terms such as endoscope, sphenoid sinus and transsphenoidal. The light monitor also displayed a virtual map showing the innards of Calder's skull.

It was determined that the tumor had not enlarged and endoscopic surgery should eliminate the tumor. The Band-Aid attached to the side of his right temple made Calder the epitome of a sixth grader. His striped black and white shirt and Converse sneakers pushed him over the top.

The neurosurgeon, Dr. Edgar Hopper, was his regular primary care physician's father. He would be the one performing the surgery. He showed Calder a series of diagrams outlining the procedure.

"Will I be awake?"

"No, don't worry. We'll knock you out. You won't feel a thing. Other than perhaps a slight itching sensation," the elder Dr. Hopper replied. "My daughter is still upset at you, you know. She didn't like being deceitful about the reason for your initial visit."

"Tell her I'm sorry. Add it to my apology tour."

Calder looked at his wife, sitting dutifully by his side. Maren caressed his right hand while her left arm draped across his shoulder. A date was set, St. Patrick's Day, three days hence.

Calder spent the interim at home nursing his head wound. He changed the dressing once a day and, at the behest of the doctor who treated him in the Atlantic City emergency room, applied cocoa butter to help prevent scarring. At his first opportunity, Calder even introduced himself to the new mailman. His name was Julius, a 59-year-old who had been born and raised in Harlem. As for Calder's former letter carrier, Varick and Astrid split two weeks after Atlantic City, and she returned to Stockholm without a television deal. Calder never heard from him again, though Julius let slip one day that he thought Varick had reconciled with his ex.

Maren worked less, taking jobs that paid her normal rate, or if they didn't, could lead to higher-paying jobs in the future. Calder and his wife made a point to have "date night" once a week with Zoe always in tow. *Family*.

***

The Rabbi resurfaced the day before the surgery. A blanket of snow still covered Central Park, and the temperature had only reached above freezing once to a balmy 35 degrees. Calder hadn't seen the ground in more than two months.

The Rabbi met Calder at the Whisper Bench, and metaphorically whispered in his ear. He said he knew a movie agent out in L.A. that would buy the movie rights to his life.

"What about the book rights? I'm almost done with the first draft of my memoirs. I've had some free time."

"Sure," the Rabbi responded, and touched Calder's shoulder. "Though we might need to hire a ghostwriter. Do you know Thomas Spooner?"

Calder said nothing.

The next day, St. Patrick's Day, it snowed, a light dusting enough to fog up the windows at Mount Sinai Roosevelt. The surgery took two hours. That night, the last drops of lactate emerged from Calder's nipples. He dreamed of Iceland, holding hands on the shore with a grown Zoe and his gray-haired wife. The present-day mother and daughter smiled as they watched him sleep.

26

Ninety-six elephants are killed every day in Africa.
Don't let elephants go extinct.

The electronic Times Square billboards flashed advertisements, promotions and occasionally stone-cold facts about the fragile world everyone lived in. Today, it was elephants. Writ large, it sounded even more shocking.

Calder wafted through the maddening throng. Seventh Avenue between 42nd and 47th Streets was a canyon of electricity. Thousands of lights and neon signs made it look like a vampire's bane, perennial daylight. There were at least 10 electronic billboards. He never counted, but tonight, given its nature, he hazarded a guess. He never understood the people who gawked up at the electronic billboard on the corner of 43rd and Broadway, waiting to see themselves on the large screen. Tourists lost their minds as if they were time-traveling Neanderthals suddenly plopped down in the 21st century, never having seen a television or even their reflection. They cheered and took photos of themselves taking a photo. The wormhole never ended.

There were six Elmos, three Mickey Mouses, two Minnies, two Spidermen, the Joker, three Cookie Monsters, two Iron Men and two pairs of topless women in bikini bottoms with body-painted breasts wandering through Times Square. Calder saw this panoply from the grand lobby of the theater every night he worked. Worse, four of the six Elmos congregated within 20 feet of each other, a strange version of St. Elmo's Fire. They accosted people, shaking them down for photographs and the expected tip money.

That night Calder relayed the alarming elephant fact to one of the other ushers, Nina, who replied: "That was some random ass shit." It was. Without context, it sounded obscure, if not a little bit crazy. Calder enjoyed messing with people's minds by using non sequiturs. Tonight, he actually responded to the mystified colleague, instead of walking away, leaving her confused, or frightened of him.

"No, getting shot is," he said. They talked for two hours, the entire running time of the performance, everything that they had always wanted to say but were too shy or guarded before the prospect of not being able to forever—death's reward—formed a deep and real stain in their minds. Getting shot will do that to you. Nina asked about the baby and they discussed the meaning of life and other weighty issues that seemed better suited to a PhD-level philosophy course. Calder steered the conversation in this direction because he savored this line of thinking.

Maren was incensed he still clung to the ushering gig. Time outdid money. Two weeks later, Calder's shoulder bore no evidence of its flesh being torn asunder. The bullet had passed just over the collarbone and done no life-threatening damage. He was tender, yes, but alive. There was one major announcement brewing in his head, something he didn't tell Maren when he left the apartment earlier that evening: This was his last shift as a Broadway usher. He didn't tell anyone except the head usher, Dolly, and he waited until the tragic grand finale when the magician saws his wife in two and discovers, to his horror, that he has actually sawed her in half.

27

The phone call came at 3:43 p.m. on March 20, the snowy first day of spring.

"If there's anything you want, come out and take it," his mother said. "I'm not keeping the World Book encyclopedias."

Not the encyclopedias. Calder read them from A to Z backwards and forwards as a six-year-old. Calder had to fly out. If he didn't, he would regret it the rest of his days. He had to take one last tour of his childhood home.

Pernille was packing the house her three boys had grown up in, where Calder learned to ride a bike in the backyard with his father and traded bouts of injuries that required numerous stitches amongst his brothers. She finally sold the house and was moving to Orlando. Many things would vanish: the room Alan saw "Santa Claus" in when he was five, the paint marks on the walls behind the dresser where Pernille charted her boys' growth, the entertainment center in the den, where he and his father watched the big games; it would be sold to whatever family moved in.

Calder prayed he would remember things just the way they were and not embellish them in his older years with false memories.

Negotiating a flight back to L.A. when his bank account contained a precious $1.42 was not easy. The rent took his entire bi-weekly severance paycheck and then some. Calder would still receive 35 more weeks of compensation, but he lived in the low margins near the first of the month under any scenario. Rent was deducted directly from his account. If he didn't keep the usher job, he would have zero disposable cash and they would have to rely solely on Maren's income.

Fortuitously, Calder had enough frequent flier miles and available credit on his maxed out Visa. But it had to be done, he told Maren, who said she understood. Calder contemplated bringing Zoe, but that defeated the purpose of helping his mom and brothers pack up the kitchen and the garage.

The garage hung in his heart like a friendly phantom. The last time he'd seen his father functional they were going through the family heirlooms. His father and mother saved untold totems from his childhood, stacked to the ceiling on makeshift wooden shelves that lined the entire garage.

The flight from JFK to LAX allegedly took nearly six hours. Calder slept for an eternity but when he awoke the plane cruised somewhere in the eastern Colorado airspace between Horse Creek and Big Sandy Creek, only 100 miles further along than his last check of the interactive map. The yellow flight path line aimed dead for the Apishapa River.

The snowcapped Rockies loomed on the horizon. A great schism of rock thrust into the sky millions of years ago, sending rivers east and west. The Grand Canyon owed them a debt. How Calder had managed to right his own marital schism, he was sure, lay in the mercy of his wife. She did not want to give up so easily. Her perfectionist streak refused to let her fail. There was also the matter of his latest scar, a dark circular patch just above his left collarbone.

Perspective.

Alone with his thoughts at 38,000 feet, Calder replayed his father's dying words like a child hitting the same musical button on a toy over and over. A screaming toddler wailed one row behind him. The other passengers groaned and one unnerved man three rows behind Calder, in the last row of the cabin, shouted out: "Feed that baby." Calder didn't mind the baby's cries. That's what babies did. The boy reminded him of Zoe—he appeared to be around the same age—though in her defense, she rarely cried. Calder and Maren had taken Zoe on her first flight together to Miami a month earlier while Maren worked another pageant. She slept through the entire flights coming and going. If only this mother could be so fortunate.

Minutes later, the cute little dictator's incessant cries became a symphony of saliva-inflected shrieks, coos and ear-piercing laughs, rudimentary attempts at speech. Calder kept his eyes peeled at the view out of the right side of the plane. The flight was full but he had lucked out and switched from a dreaded middle seat to his current window perch.

The sand dunes abutting Mount Blanca looked like churned butter at this altitude. Perhaps the baby boy wanted to tell his mother of his own rocky path through her birth canal into this plane of existence. He may have been babbling the meaning of life, or conversely telling Calder there was none except life itself. His cries triggered another baby to cry on the opposite side of the plane, a cacophony of slobber and sobs. Calder chuckled. All parents were part of a greater society, the bond of quieting the storm.

The white-tipped peaks nearly ended but not before Calder spotted the mountain town Durango below courtesy of the in-flight map. James Boyd had driven his family there and taken them on an authentic narrow gauge railroad. An indelible impression to a seven-year-old, it remained one of Calder's favorite childhood memories.

Calder dozed off again as the brown and white of the chocolate cake with vanilla frosting Rockies gave way to the rust-colored mesas and gullies of southern Utah and northern Arizona. Monument Valley and Four Corners National Monument peppered the terrain miles beneath him, and the drone of the jet's engines lulled him into an even deeper sleep. He dreamt of his own Monument Valley and the Four Corners of the family garage, arbiter of the past and future remembrances.

He missed a spectacular view of the Grand Canyon, the captain's intercom exhortation merely background noise in Calder's subconscious. "It's a better view than normal," a flight attendant said, before realizing Calder was asleep. He wouldn't wake up until the plane had already taxied to the gate.

***

Calder checked into a tiny room at the Ocean Breeze Motel on Whittier Blvd. The room was lousy with the stench of inferiority. Calder needed to pinch pennies and staying at home was too depressing. He dreamed of a poolside bungalow at the Chateau Marmont.

He plopped onto the tightly made bed and turned on the television—a new flat screen, the only thing sparkling in the unadorned room. It was the five o'clock news. He didn't recognize any of the newscasters.

It was of no consequence.

Nothing had changed in Southern California. Shootings, hit and runs, sunny and mild weather, the marine layer burns off by noon, a 1940s Hollywood starlet dies, traffic on the 405. Just another day in sunny L.A. He might as well have been watching the news in the late 1980s.

What's old is news again. What's new is old news.

The TV news circled the fantastical edges of seriousness. Surreal reports coming in by the minute. Hyper reality, better than reality.

ABC 7 Breaking News...Shooting Investigation, South Los Angeles.

Breaking News...Marijuana Bust, El Monte.

Breaking News...Big Tech Corporation Releases big new tech product: "The most personal device we have ever created. It's not with you. It's part of you."

What PR flack or copywriter wrote this? Calder

knew, someone from one of the big agencies, no doubt. It proffered an idea. Calder should apply at said Big Tech Company.

He was about to change the channel when he imagined the perfect slogan for the newscast:

Breaking News...There will be no more breaking news....

He turned off the TV. Calder had to escape. He could not take one more minute in the throes of grief, alone, in a heat-choked low-rent motel. His younger brothers, Alan and Brice, arrived later that night, but they had families of their own and would stay at the house. Calder liked to stay up late and wanted to be able to watch whatever he wanted. In reality, he didn't want to be around anyone who would bring up stories about his father; furthermore, he wanted to mourn the loss of his childhood home his own way—alone. The drive over to his father's office—he was expecting it to be empty on a Sunday—took only 35 minutes. There was little traffic on the 605 and the 210 backed up only around the Santa Anita racetrack exit.

When Calder opened the door to the small pest control business, his father's longtime business partner, Edward Maldonado, greeted him. He was a man of medium height in his early sixties with gentle eyes and a shock of white hair.

"Your dad had a big heart," said Edward, who in a previous life had been the Lakers' equipment manager.

They reminisced for an hour until Calder made an excuse to get back home. Instead, he went alone to catch the final post at Santa Anita racetrack. He and his father had gone countless times. He remembered playing in the infield when he wasn't old enough to see over the railing at the finish line. He put $20 across the board on a horse named Mother's Milk in the eighth race. It was money he really didn't have, but he had to. The 20-1 long shot won, and all was well. He collected $101.23.

Just as he pulled back into the Ocean Breeze Motel, his smartphone rang. Brice called and told him their mother was upset that they wouldn't spend their last two nights in the home together. He could take her room if he wanted to stay up later and watch TV or write. She just wanted him there. Selfish to the end, Calder corrected himself. He looked around at the take-out food, the Taco Bell he hadn't had the appetite to finish, and knew his brother was right.

He checked out, leaving a $20 tip for whoever serviced the room.

28

Thursday, May 13, 1976

Dearest Calder:

You are my son. You were born today at 4:06 p.m. at Cedars-Sinai Medical Center. That is a terrible opening. You know all of this from your birth certificate.

I apologize in advance. I am not a great writer. I hope you do not inherit my unfortunate grasp on the English language. I'm probably much more proficient at verbalizing my feelings than writing. These are some things I want you to know.

Priority one: I love you more than you know. If you get nothing else from this letter, know that. Spread love in this world and it will follow. When in doubt, always fall back on love.

Priority two: Never let the color of your skin define who you are as a person. You are a man of two worlds only in the eyes of the narrow-minded: black and white. Do not be categorized. First and foremost, you are a human being. Plain and simple. You bleed and you die. Same as everyone else.

Priority three: You are a citizen of the world. Learn from all cultures and learn from others, their successes and failures.

Priority four: Follow the golden rule. I'm sure you have learned it by now, but here's my version of it. Never ask anyone to do something that you are not willing to do yourself.

Remember these four things and you will go far in life.

By the way, I think some Hollywood celebrity is in the recovery room next door. At least, their alleged kid and said mother of the child are next door. That's what the nurses said. I don't know if they can be trusted. They handled you well enough though.

I want great things for you. And I want you to succeed in trying and in doing. Maybe you'll be the first black president. It will happen one day. But if it is you, tell them you don't want to be the first. You are a man, a man of color, and a man who happens to be president. You speak for all, and you speak for none because one and none are all together in the same field known as humanity. I am rambling; sometimes I lose focus. The doctors say you might have a similar tendency, I sincerely hope so. Dreamers are needed. Be a dreaming doer.

Enough with the posturing and lecturing. Let me come right out and say it, the two main reasons I am writing this letter.

First, I was wary when Pernille (your mother)

told me she was pregnant. I didn't know if the child was mine, a terrible thing to think, I know. If I haven't already told you this in person, face-to-face as a man, do not think poorly of your mother. We are all human. I was also unfaithful.

There is a safe deposit box and inside there will be a paternity test letter from an L.A. law firm by the name of Wilson, Lambert and Klein. I plan on destroying the results. I don't know if I am making the right choice by telling you any of this. My brother Davis is the only one who knows besides your mother. I don't want my legacy to you to be one of doubt or deception, hence the transparency. By the way, your Uncle Davis helped me with this letter. He is a much more eloquent writer and speaker than I am.

The paternity test was done to ensure you are, indeed, my son and not the product of an affair your mother had. I plan on destroying it, if I have the strength of will. But seeing you now, your golden blonde curls, high cheekbones, the tiny uplift on the right corner of your mouth, and the Boyd "nose," there is no question are my son. I love you.

Addendum: Feb. 2, 2013, notarized William Klein, Esquire

As you now know, I did not destroy the paternity letter. I never opened it. But thought it was a decision best left to you because it's your life. At your mother's bidding—God bless her soul—I gave you the key to the safe deposit box at the Grand Canyon.

I am gone now. Stomach cancer riddled my body and weakened my immune system. I didn't want you or your brothers to worry. There is one other thing I want you all to know, the real reason I quit the NBA in my prime:

Athletics is a game. It provided me with money that I parlayed into starting three businesses, two successfully. The games were beautiful. Basketball is and was a means to an end. I wanted to be a successful person, not a successful black person. I felt the weight of expectations on black people to be athletes or entertainers blinded us from becoming successful in other areas. That's not to say there aren't successful black people in every field of endeavor, today and throughout history. Thurgood Marshall, Benjamin Banneker, W.E.B. Du Bois, Frederick Douglass, Harriet Tubman, Martin Luther King, Jr. The list goes on (you were beaten to the punch at becoming the first black president). I wanted to show that the public reaction to my decision was misguided. I wanted to succeed where it wasn't expected. Everyone expects something. Buck expectation. Follow your own path. And love. I wanted to raise my family myself, and be there for you, not on the road at some arena in Milwaukee or Denver. There it is.

I hope you do the same for your family one day. I hope you buck expectations placed on you. I taught you to be able to blend in with any crowd, white, black, purple or green aliens from Mars. Do great things.

You are my first-born. I love you, your mother

and your brothers with all my soul.

Sincerely,
James Silas Boyd, Your Loving Father

29

Calder stood in a small room deep within the former First National Bank of Los Angeles. The depository had since been taken over by a bank "too big to fail." The claustrophobic walls were lime green, filled with safe deposit boxes on all sides that created the hypnotic effect of being underwater in a sea of kelp. He felt like he was inside a maze reserved for Poseidon. It was apropos in his mind. His father's memory deserved the mythology of a Greek god.

Calder inserted the bank's small duplicate key—his remained somewhere on the floor of the Grand Canyon—and turned. He opened the lime green facade and peered into the box, as if peering through a peephole back in time.

The contents of the box were simple, only one embossed letter inside a green Manila envelope and one gold bracelet. Calder immediately put the bracelet around his right wrist. It was his father's—his mother, Pernille, left it in the box two days after her husband's death for her son to discover—a symbol of the golden times they shared. If he looked at the bracelet, Calder looked back in time to the 1970s when his father bought it on the day he was born.

The bracelet hung loose on his wrist and he had to connect it two links up the chain to make it snug. Surprise heirloom in place, Calder turned his attention to the letter. The seal of a law firm emblazoned in red across the top of the green envelope: Wilson, Lambert & Klein. He could have tucked it under his arm, closed the safe deposit box and left, but curiosity got the better of him and he opened the letter inside Poseidon's lair.

Calder wept. His tears of relief stained the letter. He truly was underwater. He returned home for the last time and fell asleep on the sofa watching a documentary on the Discovery Channel about the Ring of Fire.

30

On Nov. 6, 1987, Calder purchased *The Running Man* novelization by Stephen King—writing as Richard Bachman—at the B. Dalton booksellers in Whittier, California. The receipt was still in the book, tucked into page 85.

He paid $4.21 for it, 21 cents tax.

Pernille left her eldest son in the garage to his own devices while Brice and Alan took their families to Disneyland. Their mother delineated separate times for the boys to rummage through the garage, allowing each the private commiseration of their lost youth.

The mass of keepsakes overwhelmed Calder. The previous worlds he had inhabited all laid bare before him across the uneven asphalt in front of the garage where his beloved pine tree once stood. Calder sat on a conveniently upturned chunk of asphalt. The tree's extensive root system still manipulated the ground, a personal memory that would exist as nothing more than an obtrusive lump for the next homeowner. He went through each box like an archaeologist hoping to find a long-lost totem or key to a long-lost civilization. His parents kept everything, and in the twilight of his childhood home, he was humbled and grateful.

His old Taco Bell nametag, including pay stubs—he made less than $1,000 in six months, a whopping $992.46 through Nov. 24—and all his SAT test results complete with their original envelopes were among the saved items. Nothing was detritus. Calder viewed it as a living connection to his father and when she passed—hopefully no time soon—his mother. The care, the joy, the love, it was all there.

A slogan book from an English composition class was the most telling, or damning depending on how the hilarious laughter was interpreted. Later that night, Alan, Brice and Calder would laugh for hours, their mother chiming in with an occasional, "You gotta keep that."

Letters from old girlfriends, he wondered if he wrote a letter now to the old address would they ever receive it.

You can't win if you don't play.

One never knows.

Truth is stranger than fiction.

The museum of Calder's life continued to unfurl beneath his glare. Shards of paper, that otherwise would mean nothing to anyone else outside of his parents and him, and other detritus of a personal history filled oodles of plastic containers and old cardboard file boxes. Miraculously, almost none of the papers succumbed to the erosion of time, or worse, bugs. Silverfish loved paper. A pest control man preserved the papers precisely, and the notion lifted another laugh deep from Calder's diaphragm.

In junior high, Calder and his best friend Mike Jones, who moved away to Big Bear in the summer before eighth grade, began writing a sequel to the original *Star Wars* trilogy, 30 years before Disney, after George Lucas's sale, made their clearly inferior version.

Class certificates went as far back as elementary school. Nothing was too small, nothing insignificant, a collection of non-description, items that when collected made a monument to memory and to life and love. His father reached from the beyond and Calder chuckled once again.

So enthralled with the travel through his childhood, Calder failed to hear his mother's approaching footsteps. She watched him for minute or two—reveling in his serene pleasure as he rediscovered his life—before he noticed her shadow on the dark asphalt. He could see she was holding something in her hand, something glass, rivulets of refracted light danced across his face. When he turned to face her, all he saw was a luminous halo outlining her body.

"We found this in the studs in the wall during the first addition to the house," she said. "When we added the family room and a new master bedroom. This was when you were 10 years old or so, before we added the second floor den. It was a long time ago. I think you should have it."

Pernille handed her son a 1950s-era Carnation milk bottle flush with red lettering, the word "Fresh" emblazoned in cursive on the center inside a red circle below the word "Carnation." A weathered piece of paper, a buffalo nickel and a simple wedding ring rested at the bottom of the lidless jar. Calder turned the bottle upside down and the contents fell lightly into the palm of his right hand.

"Go ahead. Read it."

In one delicate motion, to ensure no damage to the valuable contents, Calder opened the note and read seven short words:

Norma, will you marry me? Love, Thatcher.

"Your grandfather met your grandmother when he was a milkman delivering bottles to her family home to supplement his income," Pernille continued. "He delivered this particular bottle the first time he met her and later used it for a surprise proposal. The house was built in 1955. They dated for two years and when your paternal great-grandparents died, they moved here from Pasadena."

Calder returned the note and buffalo nickel to their sacred resting place; however, he kept the wedding ring between his right index finger and thumb. He held it up until it framed the sun.

"I'll leave you to it," she said, then made her way back toward the house.

"Mom, wait."

Calder rose like an ebullient giant and embraced his mother. Neither wanted to let go. "Thank you. I never knew you saved all of this stuff."

And both of them recalled James Boyd's final intelligible words: "Look in the garage."

Calder was home and forever would be.

That evening, he stood in the driveway in front of the house one last time as an official resident, staring at the chimney and the blue awnings that looked black as dusk reigned and the night took over. His eyes rose into the rising darkness as the stars became pinpricks of light that looked like Lite Brite pegs.

The constellation Orion dovetailed above the edge of the roof. Orion the Hunter—the constellation his parents used for his middle name and taught him how to find in the Mojave Desert long ago—peered down on Calder, letting him know everything was well in the universe. Calder was no longer searching. The stars were Zoe's, the stars were Maren's, and the stars were his. He couldn't wait to go home to his family.

The following day, at 38,000 feet, he would see the blue strip of the mighty Mississippi River disappear into the orange haze of sunset in the distance under a canopy of pink cirrus clouds. He was more than halfway home.

And his hunch had been right: his wife was sleeping with the milkman. Calder gave himself a high five, then thought of a new slogan. He would make it the first line of his latest memoir about his time in the advertising trenches.

War with pussy is for suckas.

***

Calder landed at JFK and made one important—yet completely out of the way—sojourn before going home. After he dropped his passenger off at the corner of Fifth Avenue and 79th Street in a spring blizzard, the taxi driver looked incredulously as the strange man trudged into Central Park. It was April Fool's Day.

When Calder arrived at their new two-bedroom apartment in Brooklyn at 10:27 p.m., Maren greeted him with a silent embrace. She handed Zoe into his eager arms and the little angel and the big angel both smiled. Maren leaned in close and whispered in Calder's ear. "I'm pregnant." The words lit up the dark. One more emitted a neon wave.

"Da-da." Zoe's first word soared. She drooled all over his arm, and it was supreme.

Later that night, he took a swig from the Central Park milk bottle and placed it in the refrigerator, an heirloom to show Zoe one day, to say, yes, it really happened. It had remained untouched all winter, right where he had left it.

ACKNOWLEDGEMENTS

There are so many people I want (and need) to thank that I don't know where to begin. These acknowledgements could be a novel in and of themselves. And please forgive me if I accidentally leave anyone (*you*) out. It wasn't intentional. First and foremost, I'd like to thank mom and dad, who went to the baby store, looked into my big brown eyes, and took me home. I am forever your son and forever grateful. To my wife, thank you for everything—your love, support, generosity, humor and numerous other one-in-a-million qualities—and for pushing me to finish this book. To our daughter, thank you for the amount of love, laughter and joy you bring into our lives on a daily basis. Words don't even describe how blessed I am to have you and your mother in my life. Family is the most important thing. To my brothers Brian and Chris, and their families, thank you for your love and support. To my late grandparents, Dr. and Mrs. Raymond J. Pitts, who taught me to work hard and Dream Big. Thank you to the Bias, Pitts and Smith Families. To my family in Japan and Thailand, thank you for welcoming me with open arms.

To my New York City friends, thank you for your immeasurable help over the years: Robson Garcia (and family in Brazil), Chilembwe Mason; Jimmy Chan, Hiromi Saeki, Chi Mac, Faisal Azam, Erica Velis, John Plenge, Paul Gutierrez, Karen Lee, Ancel Bowlin, Scott Hevesy, Jaramay Aref, Gene Menez, Tracy Mothershed, Karen Strauss, Karen Meneghin. Everyone at *Sports Illustrated* (cktk only everyone), especially Katherine Pradt, who parsed my often convoluted words, and Gabe Miller, who has listened to my ideas—baked, half-baked and unbaked—for two decades (And yes, I'm still planning on Zigzagging), as well as librarians, Joy Birdsong, Natasha Simon and Susan Szeliga. The SI library on the 18th floor of the Time & Life Building is no more, but the conversations that took place there exist eternally. To my Norwegian friends Anne Vallersnes and Linda Bukasen, any Norwegian mistakes are mine and mine alone. Dimitry Leger, thank you for your friendship, suggestions, and paving the way with *God Loves Haiti*; Brian Jaramillo, who gave me my first journalism job at the *Arizona Daily Wildcat*; Everyone at the Minskoff; my friends and former colleagues at *The Dallas Morning News*; Alexei Barrionuevo; Mrs. Pell, wherever you are, thank you for typing the stunted beginnings of my (still unpublished) first novel attempt, *The Sword & Shield of Coromir*, a blatant J.R.R. Tolkien ripoff; Jackie Bergman, thank you to Marina and Jason Anderson of Polgarus Studio for formatting

Milkman, Everyone at St. Matthias, The Cervantes Family; Sigur Family and Everyone on Light Street; Willie Joe Philbin and The Philbin Family, my friends, fraternity brothers and football teammates at the University of Arizona, my professors and classmates at NYU. Thank you, the reader. And to all writers and fellow dreamers, keep writing and keep dreaming. Everyone has helped me on my journey as a writer, artist and human being. Thank you.

Kelvin C. Bias, New York City, May 2016

ABOUT THE AUTHOR

Kelvin C. Bias is a journalist, filmmaker and raconteur. However, his most important title is father. He is definitely *not* the Lord of East 81st Street, and unfortunately, he is not lactating. He lives in New York City with his wife and daughter. *Milkman* is his first novel. Connect with Kelvin. Instagram & Twitter: @archivezero.